Four Summers Waiting

Four Summers Waiting

Mary Fremont Schoenecker

Five Star • Waterville, Maine

First Edition
Second Printing: January 2007

Published in 2006 in conjunction with Tekno Books.

Set in 11 pt. Plantin by Al Chase.

Printed in the United States on permanent paper.

Library of Congress Cataloging-in-Publication Data

Schoenecker, Mary Fremont.
    Four summers waiting / Mary Fremont Schoenecker.—1st ed.
      p. cm.
    ISBN 1-59414-475-3 (hc : alk. paper)
    1. Abolitionists—Fiction. 2. Physicians—Fiction. 3. United States—Civil War, 1861–1865—Fiction. I. Title: 4 summers waiting. II. Title.
    PS3619.C4493F68 2006
    813'.6—dc22   2005036149

To my writer friends, Ginny, Gwyn, Maddy and Marge,
for their help and encouragement,
and to Chuck for listening, reading and advising.
To my devoted husband Tom,
blessings for his dedication to me and my Simms children,
Monica, Michael, Timothy and Philip,
without whom this tale would not have been told.

Chapter One

Evergreen Park, Long Island, New York
22 July 1860
"There's too much to do for the little ones, and too little time for beaus." So said Sarah today. Heaven knows there has *been little time, and little chance for anything out of the ordinary since our year of mourning ended. I do wish Sarah* wanted *a beau in her life. She is the eldest, after all, yet she shows little interest in the gentlemen who have begun to call. She caters to Father's moods and acts like a mother hen. Mothering, smothering . . . her own hopes and mine too! She would never approve of my decision to go down to the city with Carolyn, and heaven knows what Father would do if he knew the* real *reason for this trip. He would definitely raise Cain. Oh, to be like Carolyn. She follows her heart and nothing seems to get in the way.*
Maria O.

Maria Onderdonk stared at the inkpot in the flickering light of the oil lamp, deep in the web of her thoughts. Writing in her diary usually gave her words to frame the feelings that tossed in her mind. But not this time. She pressed fingers to her mouth, shaking her head slowly. *I sorely miss Mother at times like this. She would be good counsel in affairs of the heart.* Maria rested her pen in its brass stand, blotted the page, and closed the small book.

She tiptoed away from the writing table in her room, into the hall and past the closed bedroom doors. Rumbling thunder sent her hurrying downstairs. She stood close to the windows in the back parlor, trying to read a small gold timepiece pinned to her bodice. The rain made long runnels down the pane and a sudden crash of thunder sent lightning dancing across the window. Maria jumped back, her brow knitted in a frown, her thoughts all jumbled. *If only I hadn't agreed to go with Carolyn today.*

The Honorable Horatio Onderdonk had not encouraged Maria's friendship with Carolyn Grisham once he learned that the young Miss Grisham was a budding abolitionist. Maria understood her friend's activities were not the things a proper young lady would do, but Maria was less inclined than her older sister, Sarah, to do the things expected of her.

Standing on tiptoe, she gazed at her reflection in the mirror over the fireplace. Loose wisps of auburn hair curled at her temples. She reached behind to secure a pin in thick braids wound in a figure eight at the nape of her neck. Her dark brown eyes snapped at the reflection of her father's portrait hanging on the opposite wall. She turned away from his luminous eyes, the mirror image of her own.

Loud knocking at the back door was followed by the sound of their housekeeper Bridget's heavy footsteps plodding down the hall. Maria peeked around the parlor archway as Bridget smoothed her apron and opened the back door.

The Grishams' carriage driver towered over Bridget, standing in the doorway. He was a giant of a man with wooly hair and skin almost as white as Bridget's. Rain dripped from the wide brim of Big John's hat when he removed it, and the housekeeper stepped back with a scowl. "Saints preserve us, Big John!" she scolded.

"Beggin' yer pardon, Ma'am. Miss Carolyn be in a hurry

to get to the ferry, and she say to come right to your door so Miss Maria not get too wet."

"Never mind, Bridget," Maria called from the parlor. "I'm ready and waiting." She tied the strings of her bonnet, fastened a cape under her chin and hurried to the door. "Tell Sarah not to worry," she said as she swished past the house-keeper and stepped out to the edge of the back porch.

Big John was by Maria's side in one long stride. He splashed down the steps behind her, holding a black um-brella over her head until she climbed into the carriage. Big John closed the umbrella and climbed aboard the driver's box.

Maria had hardly settled herself on the seat when the horses broke into a trot and the carriage lumbered away, taking the road toward Brooklyn. She greeted her friend with a nervous smile. "I didn't think you would come in this storm, Carolyn. I've had second thoughts about this trip since dawn."

"Well, it's too late for any second thoughts on my part. I have something to confess." Carolyn clutched Maria's hand. "You know how I've been helping the Anti-Slavery Society by my donations?"

Maria nodded solemnly.

"This time I've agreed to much more. I'm taking a special journey today, and you will be the only person to know, be-sides Big John."

Carolyn pointed to the seat opposite them and Maria gaped at a large valise. "That is filled with clothing for a twelve-year-old boy—a mulatto boy with very light skin like Big John's." Carolyn spoke rapidly, tucking in fiery red curls that popped out of her bonnet as the carriage bounced over the rutted road.

"I must ask you to keep my secret, Maria. I'm going to be a

9

conductor for the Underground Railroad today, and Big John is going to help me."

A loud clap of thunder punctuated Carolyn's words. The horses shied and the carriage pitched wildly. Maria drew in her breath and grasped the edge of the seat, but it was not the jolting of the fast-moving carriage that frightened her. She felt the blood pound in her temples as she stared, wordlessly, at Carolyn.

"Do you understand what I'm saying, Maria? I'm going to escort a young fugitive slave on his way to freedom. I must have your promise to tell no one, unless . . . unless something happens to us and then—"

"Us! But . . . I . . . you . . . you said that the Society was collecting clothes and funds for fugitive slaves. I thought we were going to a meeting where you give donations. I cannot—"

"We *are* going to the meeting, but Big John will drive me away from the meeting in a carriage supplied by the Committee in New York. There's nothing unusual about that. Big John has been driving me since my papa freed him back on our plantation, long before we moved to New York."

"I can understand Big John's need to help, and I do want to learn about the cause, but you, Carolyn? A conductor?"

Carolyn straightened her shoulders and pursed her lips. "I was a logical choice because I can still speak with a Southern drawl, when I wish. I can assume the role of governess of the young mistress of a plantation."

"I don't understand. You spoke of a runaway boy, not a young mistress. If you drive away with Big John, what will I do? Oh, Carolyn, when I made up the story of a shopping trip to my father I thought we were just donating—"

"The clothing donation is true, and it is *part* of what I will be doing today. This is a runaway boy, but inside the valise are a long-sleeved dress, bonnet, gloves and shoes for a well-

10

dressed young girl. Hopefully the clothing will disguise him."

Maria pressed trembling fingers to her lips and swallowed hard. "Where is he?"

"He is carefully hidden in a house on Queen Street in New York City, the same house where the Anti-Slavery Society meets. The pretense is, the child and I will be traveling to visit relatives in Albany."

Carolyn flashed a confident smile Maria's way, but Maria was frowning, staring straight ahead, her hand to her cheek. Slaves hiding, pretenses and the Underground Railroad! It was hard to believe the trip to New York was unfolding this way.

"It's all planned, Maria. Big John will leave you at the Metropolitan Hotel while I am conducting my pupil to a farmhouse along the northern outskirts of the city. It's a safe house where he'll be hidden until river transportation to Albany can be arranged. Once we have the boy there, I will return to the city to meet you at the hotel. No one will dream that you and I have not spent the entire day shopping."

Maria looked out the carriage window, wishing desperately that something would happen to stop Carolyn's plan. *Getting away from Evergreen Park, especially with someone as daring as Carolyn, was what I wished for. A little adventure, yes, but this was not what I expected.* Her thoughts clashed like swords. *I do want to help the slaves, despite Papa's feelings, but this goes too far. It's against the law!*

The rain showed little sign of stopping. Moments later, Maria's wishes proved worthless when the brick ferry house loomed into view. The carriage rolled to a stop at the Brooklyn dock.

Big John gave the reins to a stable boy at the ferry house and helped the girls down the ramp to the waiting boat. The only other passenger was a farmer carrying two crates of chickens. The farmer moved to the stern of the boat with Big John.

Carolyn was silent while the ferry crossed the East River to New York. She struggled to hold the big umbrella over their heads, while her valise rested at their feet. Maria's head reeled with the pitch and toss of the boat on the storm-whipped river waves. When the ferry reached its slip in Manhattan, a queasy stomach added to her discomfort.

Big John carried the valise, helping Carolyn down the ramp first. Tight-lipped, Maria followed, clutching Carolyn's arm. They walked along the landing through a long line of waiting carriages.

Carolyn stopped suddenly. She nodded to a man in a broad black hat and plain clothes, standing half-hidden among the carriages. The man helped the girls inside his one-horse shay, its small canopy offering little protection from rain that had changed to drizzle. Big John climbed up to sit beside the driver on the box.

The rain had stopped by the time they reached 11 Queen Street. The house was set back from the street, folded into rain-glistened greenery that shimmered in the sudden sun-light.

Carolyn looked up with a smile as Big John helped her down from the carriage. She reached for Maria's hand, and drew a deep breath. "The rain-freshened air smells sweet, Maria. Thank the good Lord for sunshine," she said.

Maria could not even force a smile. The sun did nothing to brighten her spirits.

Once inside the house, Carolyn was careful to bolt the door. The parlor shutters were drawn. The only light came from oil lamps around a room to their right where men and women sat talking in low voices.

Carolyn hung their soggy cloaks and hats on a hall tree.

12

She took Maria's hand and tugged her along to the front of the parlor. Wedging her way past two well-dressed Negro men, Carolyn pushed Maria gently into an empty chair and bent to whisper in her ear.

"Big John and I will be gone for a few minutes to prepare the boy for his journey. You have no one to fear in this room, Maria. The director for today is a new man who has been helping in Philadelphia. He will be in shortly, and I'll be back as soon as I can."

Maria looked wide-eyed around the room. A woman dressed in the somber clothing of a Quaker sat on a bench to Maria's left. Minutes after Maria was seated, the carriage driver appeared and took a seat on the bench beside the lady. The Negro men at her right sat on a horsehair sofa, talking quietly.

No sooner had Carolyn left the parlor than the director entered it. Maria was surprised to see a young white gentleman striding to the front of the room. He carried himself with an easy confidence that seemed to have a relaxing effect on the people seated around her. They smiled and nodded.

Maria stared at the sleek fit of his black frockcoat across broad shoulders. Black hair curled at his white shirt collar. She studied his features. He had a handsome cleft chin and dimples that broadened to side-whiskers as he smoothed his mustache.

His eyes glinted and darted around the room. He threaded his fingers through thick, wavy hair, but it was his eyes that Maria found disarming. They were wide-set, intensely sea-green, and incredibly long-lashed for a man.

When his eyes rested on her she could feel the deep scrutiny of his gaze. She drew in her breath. Startled by the intensity of her emotions, she forced herself to look away.

"We are here today for Daniel," the director began in a

13

voice that was rich and cultured and had just a hint of a southern drawl. "Two weeks ago Luke and Daniel left a Maryland plantation with Daniel's father and an older cousin. The group walked all night to get to the first safe house."

"Amen," one of the men on her right called out. Maria started, but the director gave no pause. He walked back and forth before the group, his hands clasped behind his back.

Maria found she could not look away from him. It was as though her eyes had a mind of their own.

"After three days of walking, the group waited to cross the Susquehanna River. When the boat didn't appear, Daniel's father and the older cousin left the two younger boys hidden near the river bank."

A low murmur came from the back of the room. The director's eyes snapped a gray-green warning. "Yes, that was a mistake," he said, pausing to nod his head in grim silence. "The group had been instructed to stay together. They didn't. The two that went foraging for food were caught."

He paused to drink from a water glass and Maria licked her own dry lips. She could not tear her eyes away, but neither could she tell if the uneasiness she felt was fear or fascination.

"At dawn, Daniel and Luke went on alone. They walked upstream until they found a shallow place to ford the river. Once across, the boys hid by day and ran by night." The director paused to smile and nod his head. "They remembered to watch for the star in the night sky that leads to freedom—"

"Praise the Lord. Thank you, Jesus," cried a voice behind Maria.

This time the director pointed his finger toward the voice, nodded his head to acknowledge the speaker. "Indeed, we all need faith on the freedom road. Faith in Him who makes it

14

possible. It is a long and perilous journey. During the day these boys were hidden in Quaker homes in Philadelphia. I helped the last stationmaster hide Luke and Daniel aboard a freight train headed to New York."

He paused to clear his throat and Maria's fingers brushed at her neck. She could feel a lump rising in her throat, and there was a curious feeling in her chest.

"Today, Luke leaves on a steamship sailing for England, but we have other plans for Daniel. Being small and fair-skinned, Daniel will continue his journey to freedom in disguise as 'Mistress Sally.' *Mistress Sally* will be traveling with Miss Carolyn today."

Maria drew in a deep breath at Carolyn's name and instinctively her hand flew back to her throat. The room seemed suddenly warm. Her pulse throbbed beneath her fingers.

The director's eyes met hers once more. This time the sheer force of his gaze was almost palpable. Maria found she could not look away. She felt a growing sensation of fear mingled with fascination. He was standing so close. Could he see her racing heart?

"Conductors on this road to freedom are people of conscience and courage—" He stopped mid-sentence. Carolyn and Big John emerged from the hall with a child whose gloved hand was lost in the big, brown hand of John. The child's downcast face was hidden under a poke bonnet, eyes fixed on shiny shoes barely visible under a swishing, full skirt.

"Daniel be ready, suh," Big John said.

The director grimaced. "That will never do! White folks rarely take the hands of their servants. You should know better, John."

Maria felt the flush flee from her cheeks. Her stomach tightened when she looked from Carolyn to the director.

His deep, resonant voice took on a stern tone. "And you, Mistress Sally, will not hear the name *Daniel* again until you are safe in Albany." He gave Carolyn a meaningful look, punctuated by a long moment of silence.

Carolyn's blue eyes blazed. Her chin pushed up, pressing her lips into a thin line. Big John broke the silence. "I was only trying to calm the boy by taking his hand, suh."

Tension filled the room. The director did not acknowledge Big John's plea, but as quickly as his voice had risen in judgment, he gentled it and patiently began to explain directions for the journey.

"Those who came in support of Daniel may give your contributions to Reverend Mr. Emmet, here," the director said, gesturing with his outstretched hand to a Negro clergyman seated at his right. "And, remember to leave by the back entry. A few at a time, please."

As soon as the directions were given, people rose and started to leave the room.

A riot of emotions filled Maria's mind and heart as she, too, rose to leave. She sought Carolyn's eyes. Carolyn merely motioned toward the door. "We will meet you at the front gate," she said, before disappearing down the hall with Daniel and Big John.

Maria had knotted two gold coins in a handkerchief. She pulled it from her reticule, twisting the handkerchief in her hand. She followed behind the Quaker couple, then placed her coins in the Reverend's basket. Only a few steps into the hall she heard the director's voice behind her.

"Begging your pardon, Miss, may I have a word, please?" Maria stood stock-still at the coat rack before turning stiffly. She clutched her cloak and opened her mouth as if to speak, then closed it again.

"I couldn't help but notice that you . . . well, you seemed

to be upset. I wish to reassure you about the protection of your friend, Miss Carolyn. I'm told Big John is most reliable, and Miss Carolyn has been well trained for her journey. It *is* your friend, Miss Carolyn, who is escorting the boy on his journey?"

Maria blinked and nodded as she tied sodden bonnet strings under her chin. Caught up in emotions she had never before experienced, she was entranced by the director's manner, yet frightened to think of his dangerous involvement with the Underground Railroad. Three years of studying at Miss Adrian's Seminary hadn't prepared her for anything like this.

His gaze softened as his eyes met hers. He offered his arm. "My name is Henry Simms. May I escort you to the gate to wait for Miss Carolyn?"

Maria sensed a calm and silent strength in this man. She wanted to gather that strength to shore up her own depleted resources. Tucking her hand into the crook of his arm, she said, "Please do, sir," in a voice just above a whisper.

As soon as they were outside, her steps and her spirit faltered. The Queen Street sign at the hitching post was a stark reminder of where she was. *Papa is only blocks away in his office.* Her father's image rose before her, his stern disapproval of Carolyn chafed at her mind. *How can I ever explain what is about to happen?*

The carriage clattered around the side of the house. Tears burned her eyes. She moved away from Henry's side, dipping her head to hide her tears. Maria squeezed her eyes shut, trying desperately to keep a tight rein on conflicting emotions. She grasped the ring on the hitching post and stared up at the street sign.

No sooner had Big John reined in the horse than Maria suddenly felt strong hands spread around her waist, lifting her into the carriage. She turned startled eyes on the director. His touch had sent tingling charges up her spine. Her breath quickened and her lips parted, but her words drifted into silence.

Henry Simms couldn't seem to focus on anything except the feel of Maria's slim waist under his fingers and her deep brown eyes brimming with tears. He had an unexplainable yearning to enfold her in his arms and kiss away those tears, but Big John was already snapping the reins. The carriage rumbled away.

Maria hung on to the carriage seat, watching from the window until Henry Simms and 11 Queen Street were out of sight. She realized with regret that she had hardly spoken a word to this man who had set her senses reeling.

Her thoughts were in such turmoil that, once she turned to Carolyn, anguish gave way. Tears flowed. Words tumbled out. "Carolyn. I am so sorry. I wanted to explain to the director, but I couldn't, and now it's even harder to tell you."

"Tell me what?"

"I'm afraid to be involved in this. I cannot go to the hotel!"

Big John's hands tightened on the reins. "Mistress Sally" fidgeted and tugged on Carolyn's sleeve.

"But Maria," Carolyn wailed. "All you have to do is wait for me."

"I cannot do this, Carolyn. I cannot. Part of it has to do with my father. I must ask you to take me to Papa's office on Nassau Street. I'll pretend to be feeling ill. That won't be far from the truth, but I promise not to reveal anything confidential about today."

"I know I should have forewarned you. I thought you and I were of the same sentiment. I believed I could trust you."

"I know you did. I'm sorry. Please do trust me still, Carolyn, but I must ask you to take me to my father's office. I'll tell my father we were on our way to meet your aunt for shopping when I began feeling unwell. I cannot go to the hotel to wait for you. I just cannot."

"Then how will you know if my journey is successful? What if something goes wrong and I'm unable to return to the hotel?"

Maria shuddered. "I will find out somehow. I'll send word to your parents if anything does go wrong. Please, please try to understand."

Without another word, Carolyn called out to Big John. "Turn, John. We must go first to Nassau Street."

Chapter Two

Annie Onderdonk hurried out of the house as soon as she saw Maria being helped down from the carriage. She took her sister's hand and tugged her toward the veranda steps.

Jo stood in the doorway, arms opened wide to hug Maria. "We have been worried about you. I so wished you were home this afternoon," she said. "Sarah went off to visit Reverend Cox and, wouldn't you know, Cousin Andrew came to tea right after she left."

Annie clung to Maria's arm. "Bridget made do, but it wasn't the same without you, Maria."

Maria slowly released Annie's grip to untie the strings of her bonnet. She squeezed her eyes shut. Her head was aching. *Sarah would never have deceived everyone as I did.* She let the soggy hat strings dangle from her fingers as she walked between her sisters the length of the long center hall.

Jo peeked over her shoulder just as their father came in the front door. She urged Maria toward the coat rack, Annie trudging close behind. Standing on tiptoe, Annie managed to reach around Maria's shoulders to pull off her damp cloak.

Covering the side of her mouth with her hand, Jo spoke softly, close to Maria's ear. "Andrew told us he had a special invitation for you and Sarah—"

"But he wanted to talk to Papa about it first," Annie whispered.

"Hold on now, girls," Horatio called, hurrying toward

them. "Maria is feeling unwell. That's why she came home with me." Setting his carpetbag down, he put a hand under Maria's elbow, drawing her into the back parlor.

"Rest easy for a while, my dear," he said, patting her shoulder as Maria settled into a chair. "I'll call down to the kitchen to see that Bridget brings you tea. I'm going out to the office to finish some work for the post"—raising an eyebrow he nodded toward Jo and Annie with a meaningful look— "and I expect your sisters to see to your needs."

Maria glanced from her father to Annie and Jo. Tears burned her eyes. Deception was not part of her nature. Her heart twisted with anguish as the lies spun in her mind.

Annie came to sit on the ottoman at Maria's feet. "Didn't you get to do any shopping?" she asked.

Maria bit her lip and grasped Annie's hand. "But if I had, my first purchase would have been the ribbons I promised to get for you, Miss Anna." Her lips curved in a weak smile as she leaned forward to brush Annie's hair away from her eyes.

"I bet it was that nasty ferry ride that made you sick. Sarah was surprised you went out in such a storm. She said the river was bound to be rough." Annie's brow puckered in a frown. "Why did you go, Maria?"

Maria gulped. Her heart lurched when she looked into Annie's eyes. To keep up this ruse was more hurtful than her aching head.

"I don't think Maria is up to any more questions," Jo said. "I think she needs to lay her head down for a while. When Bridget brings your tea, I'll bring it upstairs to you, all right?"

Maria nodded, rising wearily from the chair.

Sarah's questions about the failed shopping excursion only added to Maria's misery when the family gathered at the dining table that evening. She picked at her food, asking to be excused early.

The kitchen was downstairs, below where they sat. Maria went down and spoke quietly to Bridget so no one would hear her abovestairs.

"I'd like to take some warm milk up to my room, Bridget. Would you please wake me at daybreak? I will need Martin to harness Molly first thing in the morning. Don't mention it to anyone unless they ask my whereabouts. If they inquire, just say that I've gone to visit Cousin Andrew."

"Yes, Miss Maria," Bridget said, patting her hand. "Your cousin Andrew is a fine young man. That he is. An' 'tis sure he'll have some fancy plans for you soon. Now, what else can I do for your comfort?"

"Nothing more, Bridget, thank you," she said with a sharpness in her tone. She picked up the tray and steadied her gaze on the milk as she climbed two sets of stairs. *Nothing remains private around here.*

She set the cup on the bedside table. Taking her diary from the writing table drawer, she turned its pages to her last entry.

My feelings written yesterday about Sarah seem petty when I compare them to what happened today. Maria stared at the page before picking up her pen.

> *23 July*
> *I went to an Anti-Slavery Society meeting with Carolyn today. Papa will never understand about slaves wanting freedom, or my wanting to help them. . . . and surely not about a man with strong arms and beguiling sea-green eyes whom I cannot seem to forget. Jo would understand, but I'm too ashamed to tell her about deceiving Papa. Nor should Annie know. She has such a trusting heart. Oh, how I miss you, Mother. I think you would understand. Maria O.*

The sun dipped below the stable roof as she stared out the window. That was as good a reason as any to undress for bed. Maria hung her clothes carefully in the clothes press before pulling a long cotton nightgown over her head. She knelt beside her bed.

"Dear Lord, bless all my loved ones and have mercy on Carolyn, Big John and Daniel. Keep them safe and, please, Father, grant me the courage to bear whatever tomorrow brings. I am truly sorry for having deceived Papa."

She climbed into bed and gazed at a sickle moon rising sharp and white in the black sky framed by her window. Weak, silvery light disappeared as the moon was wrapped in clouds. Maria shuddered and snuggled under the counterpane. Squeezing her eyes shut did not stop the shadowy figures of Big John, Carolyn and "Mistress Sally" that loomed before her.

She tried to push frightening thoughts out of her mind by thinking about the puzzling invitation Cousin Andrew brought. The scene at the house on Queen Street kept running before her eyes, the words of the director repeating in her mind. "Conductors who help on this road to freedom are people of conscience and courage."

In her mind, Henry Simms's sea-green eyes snapped and sparkled. His strong arms lifted her into a carriage. Once again, Maria felt that shocking, sweet thrill—so real that she clutched her pillow to her breast.

When sleep finally came, Carolyn's journey twisted and tangled in Maria's dreams. Small arms clothed in a long-sleeved dress reached up to her. Dark arms, long and muscled, broken and bleeding, waved at her. The arms were blurred by Carolyn's terrified face.

The strong presence of Carolyn and John rendered the dream so real Maria wanted to cry out. She covered her mouth with her hand. Someone gave her shoulder a light shake and she bolted straight up with a muffled scream.

"Shhh, lass. It's morning, Miss Maria," Bridget whispered. Bridget pointed at Sara asleep beside Maria in the rumpled bed. She put a finger to her lips. "I've set a pot of good strong tea and biscuits in the dining room for you."

Maria sat on the edge of the bed, rubbing the sleep from her eyes. "Thank you, Bridget," she mumbled.

"I'll be goin' to your father's office to tidy up if you need me," the housekeeper whispered before taking last night's tray from the marble-topped bedside table.

Maria splashed water on her face from a bowl on the commode and dressed quickly. She slipped from her room and tiptoed down the stairs.

Stopping in the dining room she took a sip of tea. *Bridget does have a good heart, but she is always snooping. There's no telling when she's listening.*

Across the carriage drive, Martin opened the stable doors. He scowled and shook his head as he helped his mistress into Molly's saddle and handed over the reins.

"Ah, Miss Maria, I don't know what your father would say about his daughter ridin' out unescorted before the cock crows."

She rubbed the neck of the little sorrel mare. "There's no need to worry, Martin. I'm only riding to Cousin Andrew's. I'm sure to be back before anyone misses me."

Maria snapped Molly's reins and was off. She scarcely noticed the horses at the stage stop or the pastures of the neighboring farm on the short ride to Uncle James's house. Worry lay heavy on her mind. *Cousin Andrew is the one person with whom I can share about yesterday and trust that he will help me find out what happened.*

She could see Andrew inside the barn, checking the bridle

on his horse. Dropping Molly's reins, she slid to the ground quickly and entered the barn.

"Ah, Maria, you're out early this morning. I was about to leave for the stage stop. I have business in town today."

"I was hoping to catch you. That's why I'm here so early. I've something important to ask of you, if you've time."

Andrew led her to a bench just inside the barn. "Yes, of course, what is it?"

He listened to her recount the events of yesterday's trip with Carolyn. Without hesitation, he assured her he would inquire at the Metropolitan Hotel, and at 11 Queen Street. Withdrawing a notebook from his coat pocket, he wrote down a description of the location of the house, just in case it was needed.

"Promise you will come to me directly with the news, whatever it is?" She looked away for a moment and swallowed hard. "But, please tell no one, especially if you're speaking with my father. I gave my word to Carolyn."

"Of course, I'll do whatever's necessary. I have to admire your loyalty to your friend, but I certainly doubt her judgment. She shouldn't have involved you in a scheme far too risky and unseemly for you or for her."

Tears filled Maria's eyes. She couldn't tell Andrew how much she had truly wanted to help Carolyn and young Daniel. Nor, for certain, could she mention the director. She was sure he wouldn't approve.

"Tears soften our sorrows, Maria, but of all of Uncle's daughters, you've always been the strong-hearted and forthright one. I have every confidence that you did the right thing yesterday."

"Oh, Andrew, I'm not sure I deserve your confidence. I felt so wretched about leaving Carolyn that I've come to you for help when I probably should have gone straight to Sarah.

25

It's just that I dare not confide in her. She would never understand my having deceived Papa." Maria hung her head. "I feel so ashamed and helpless."

"Helpless, you're not, else you wouldn't have come here in the first place." He raised her chin with one finger. "Maria, if you really want me to find out about your friend, you must leave this in my hands." He looked at his pocket watch. "I have to hurry to catch the early stage. Come, I'll ride back with you as far as the stage stop. I want you to stop fretting, go home and wait for me to bring word to you."

Andrew took Maria's hand in his as they walked his horse outside. "No more thoughts about it now, hear? I want to see that pretty smile again and I'm sure I will, once I've spoken to your father about a special occasion that's coming up."

Maria forced a weak smile. "Jo told me you came to see us yesterday with an invitation. Does it have anything to do with the trip that's planned?"

"No, but I will be seeing your father in the city today, and more I cannot say just yet. You will know all the details soon enough, and you and Cousin Sarah will both be smiling. I promise."

The registrar at the Metropolitan Hotel told Andrew that a reservation for a Miss C. Grisham had been canceled the previous night. The house on Queen Street was not difficult to find, but Andrew found only two people there. Both were Negroes. One was clothed in the uniform of a maid and the other wore the collar of a preacher. At first they denied knowing anything, but after Andrew described Maria in detail, the preacher clearly remembered that she had attended the meeting with Carolyn the previous day.

Andrew told the preacher Maria's promise to help Miss Carolyn in the case of any emergency. He pleaded for information.

While the preacher was hesitant at first, after more prodding he began to tell what happened.

"Miss Carolyn and Big John conducted young Daniel to the farm jus' fine, you see, sir, but on their return at dusk, the carriage was stopped by a gang of toughs. Big John was bigger than most of the rowdies, but there was too many of 'em." The minister paused. He shook his head, looking away. "John fought hard, but—"

"Reverend, I only want to help Miss Carolyn on behalf of her friend. Be assured no harm will come to the Society," Andrew said quietly.

The preacher studied Andrew for a long moment, then nodded his head and cleared his throat. "John was knifed in the back when he tried to protect Miss Carolyn from the thieves."

"But what of Miss Carolyn?"

"They fled with her jewelry and an empty valise. John was hurt bad, sir, and the young miss had no choice but to drive the carriage carryin' him back to this house."

"Are they here now, Reverend?"

"Big John is upstairs, but he is failin' fast. I do believe that our merciful Lord will soon relieve him of his sufferin'."

"And Miss Carolyn? Is she all right? Is she upstairs too?"

"No, sir. A Quaker gentleman and his lady took Miss Carolyn to the ferry this mornin'. She's all right, but she was mighty sad to go home without Big John."

Andrew thanked the preacher and left the house. It would not be an easy task to break this news to Maria without shattering her spirit.

When Andrew arrived back at Evergreen Park late in the afternoon he was able to talk with Maria in private. The rest of the family had gone with Sarah to hear a lecture at Dutch

Church. He was not first with the disastrous news, however.

As they walked outside near the pine grove, Maria took a crumpled, tear-stained note from her pocket and handed it to Andrew. "This was delivered by a Grisham servant just before noon."

> *Dearest Maria,*
>
> *Something terrible happened after we left Daniel at the farm. Our carriage was attacked by rowdies, and now John lies near death at the Queen Street house. I do not know how I shall go on without him. My father will go to him today. Please remain my friend and keep this from your father. I cannot tell more at this time.*
>
> *Carolyn*

Andrew returned Carolyn's note and repeated the details told him by the Negro minister in New York. Maria stared at the note in her hand, and shook her head.

"I feel her pain in my heart, Andrew." She bit her lip and turned away from him, her back straight.

His hands were gentle on her shoulders as he turned her to face him. "What is it?"

Color rose in her cheeks as she met his gaze. "There is something about this that I don't understand." She pointed to a line on Carolyn's note. "Didn't you think anything curious about these words she wrote about Big John?"

Andrew's eyes did not reveal his feelings when he glanced at the words Maria pointed to. *I do not know how I shall go on without him.* He closed his eyes for a second and cleared his throat. "I'm sure you will hear more from Carolyn about that. Time will heal, Maria."

"But I've sworn secrecy to her, and it is so hard to keep silent."

"Some things are better left unsaid, Maria. You can share Carolyn's grief by being her friend, but remember that this was not your plan and none of your fault. You must stop brooding about it and begin to concentrate on other things."

"I know. You are right. We leave with Father for New England in five more days and I should be helping Jo get our clothes ready for packing. I do thank you, Andrew, for all that you've done."

"No thanks are necessary, but I do have something to tell you that should definitely cheer you up. Your father has given his consent for me to escort you and Sarah to a ball in New York this very weekend."

"Oh, Andrew! Father agreed to a dance? I can scarcely believe it. Does Sarah know?"

"Not yet, but you can be the bearer of good news. It's to be a midsummer supper party at the St. Nicholas Hotel, followed by dancing. It promises to be a grand affair and you can tell Sarah to count on that."

Later that evening, Maria sat at the writing table in her room, her eyes fixed on the blank page of her diary. She usually found it a relief to pour her heart out on the pages, writing things she dared not say aloud. Her mind whirled from Carolyn and Big John, to Andrew's invitation. She thrust her pen into a small brass inkwell.

24 July 1860

I pray for answers, dear Lord. My heart weeps for Carolyn, yet I scarcely know how to comfort her. You kept me from harm while Carolyn and Big John were in harm's way. She says she doesn't know how to go on without Big John. I'm not sure what that means. Could it be about her involvement with the Anti-Slavery Association? I wish I

could go to her. I feel so guilty keeping everything inside, yet I dare not chance losing Father's trust in me were I to tell him the truth. Andrew says time heals. Bless Andrew. Marvel of marvels; he has Papa's permission to take us to a ball!
Maria O.

Chapter Three

Soon after their arrival in New York, Andrew escorted Maria and Sarah to the registration desk at the Metropolitan Hotel. While a porter took their valise, the desk clerk suggested the ladies might like to visit the Sky Parlor before going to their rooms. They said their farewell to Andrew, promising to be ready by six.

The Metropolitan's Sky Parlor was an elegantly furnished room on the hotel's top floor, where ladies could sit in the open air and look down on the fashionable bustle of Broadway. Tradesmen plying their wares in carts of every description moved alongside stylish ladies and gentlemen promenading the avenue. Minutes before, when Maria and Sarah strolled with Cousin Andrew, they were part of the scene they now gazed down upon.

"Sarah, look at that lady in the green velvet gown. I wish my dress for tonight were that color. Although I wouldn't want to be in velvet, I do like that color."

"You will be lovely in your blue silk. Just be thankful you are not with the gentleman escorting the lady in green. He looks like a plum pudding waddling beside her. At least we know Cousin Andrew will be dashing, and I'm sure he will be an excellent dance partner for both of us."

Maria drew her shawl closer as a cool breeze blew through the parlor. "Not quite so, Sarah. You must not have heard Andrew when we boarded the ferry. He told Papa about a *friend* he expects to come to the party."

Sarah shrugged. "Hmm . . . I must have missed that conversation. I didn't know anyone else was expected."

"Andrew's friend is completing his studies at a college in Philadelphia." Maria's eyebrows arched and her eyes brightened. "So, we won't have to share Andrew for all the dances."

Sarah tossed her head from side to side. "Andrew, Andrew. To think he has friends from as far away as Philadelphia."

"I wonder what his friend is like? Aren't you curious?" Maria prodded. "Do you suppose Cousin Andrew's playing cupid for you?"

"Oh, fiddle. I wouldn't suspect Cousin Andrew of *that*," she said, drawing the word out. "I would think anyone he brings along would be a . . . a gentleman. You know what I mean, someone Father would approve of."

"Yes, I know exactly what you mean. I'm sure Andrew must have convinced Papa about the integrity of his friend. Else surely, Papa would have planned an appearance at the ball to see for himself."

"I suppose you are right. It's rare enough just to attend an evening affair in New York. But even if I were interested in gentlemen callers, it would surprise me if anyone could meet Father's standards."

Maria rolled her eyes. "I know Papa booked these rooms so we would be near his office on Nassau Street, and he only agreed we could come to New York provided we all traveled together on the afternoon ferry."

"What's more surprising is he told Andrew to order a hackney at six to take us to the supper without him! Father expects us to be returned to our hotel at a proper hour, which means early"—Sarah rose and drew her arm through Maria's—"so we'd best go to our room now to get ready."

Cousin Andrew stood at the side of the barouche, helping the driver hand the girls down to the street. He ushered them around the dung heaps and past the carriages lined up in front of the elegant marble entry of the St. Nicholas Hotel.

Andrew sensed a big difference in his cousins, and it wasn't just their looks. They both wore their hair in the same coronet of braids, but their appearance was strikingly different. *Maria could be a match,* he mused. Her blue silk gown was closely fitted to her softly rounded body. Its low neckline discreetly covered her ample bosom with a lace bertha. A gold locket hung from a chain around her neck, and earbobs sparkled on her ears . . . *She's certainly beguiling . . . strong in spirit, but tender in heart . . . a delightful combination of quick wit and sensitivity.*

He glanced at Sarah. *Maria is petite and buxom, while Sarah is tall and slender, almost regal in appearance.* She wore a high-necked dress of gray crepe, only a shade away from the black mourning dresses he'd seen her wear all year. Other than a bit of lace at the neck, her only adornment was a string of pearls. *Definitely calm and collected, very intelligent and impeccably loyal. Sarah is much to be admired for her porcelain-like beauty. I think I know which one my friend will favor.*

Heads turned as Andrew ushered the sisters to seats in the crowded dining room. "I'm feeling mighty proud to have two such lovely ladies with me this evening."

"And you, sir, are a handsome escort," Maria said.

She was too excited to eat much of her supper, but her eyebrows rose when the waiter served wine. An impish smile lighting her features, she raised her glass. "To Andrew, for bringing us." Her eyes snapped over the rim of the glass. "And to Father, for allowing it." With a slight shake of her head, Sarah closed her eyes and heaved a sigh.

Andrew watched them both with an amused grin.

The first strains of music came from the ballroom as they finished pineapple trifle for dessert. "Will your friend be here for the dancing?" Maria asked.

"I thought he would be here long before the dancing began. If you will excuse me, I'd like to check the lobby. I'll be back here within ten minutes to take you into the ballroom, with or without him."

"As long as you are going in search of your friend, would you take us to the ladies' parlor first?" Sarah asked.

"Of course," Andrew replied, escorting them from the dining room.

When Maria and Sarah exited the ladies' parlor ten minutes later they found Andrew standing near the door, talking eagerly to a man whose back was to them.

As soon as he saw them, Andrew took his guest's elbow and wheeled him around to face Maria and Sarah. "Here are my lovely cousins, Miss Sarah and Maria Onderdonk. Meet my friend, and soon to be *Doctor*, Henry Simms."

Maria's mouth dropped open. Her dark eyes widened, darting from Andrew back to the young man. Sarah extended her hand and nudged Maria to do the same. Henry made a slight bow and kissed the hands offered to him, first Sarah's and then Maria's. When she met his gaze, her quick intake of breath brought an easy smile to Henry's lips, but no acknowledgment in his eyes.

"It's a pleasure to make your acquaintance, ladies." His gaze lingered on Maria. "And I'm sorry to have missed any part of this evening. The train from Philadelphia was very late."

A shiver of excitement raced up her spine. Flushed and flustered, Maria shook her head, trying to drive off unsettling thoughts. She did the opposite of what she would have liked

34

to do. She seized Andrew's arm and left Sarah to be escorted into the ballroom by Mr. Henry Simms.

Maria's frustration was not lost on Andrew. "My friend seems to have made quite an impression on you. His good looks, no doubt," Andrew said, cocking an eyebrow at her, "but I think you will find him to be more than just a handsome young man. He is very bright and has strong convictions about most things—almost as courageous in spirit as you."

She bit her lip, giving no response. The orchestra was playing a polka and Andrew lost no time in drawing Maria onto the floor. "This dance will give your cheeks more color," he teased as he whirled her around to the music. Maria could only breathlessly nod, for her head was filled with questions. *But where to begin and how?*

She tried to smile her pleasure when Andrew bowed to her at the final *oom-pa-pa* of the polka, but her face betrayed her fearful emotion.

"He's a nice young man, Maria. I'm surprised you are acting so shy. Give him a chance, won't you?" he said, leading her back to Henry and Sarah.

"Would you like to give this waltz a try?" Henry asked. "I haven't learned the new polka you just danced, but I do think I can manage this one, Miss Maria."

Henry fixed his gaze on her. Amber light from the chandelier played on his face. His steady sea-green eyes held such honest emotion.

"But of course, er . . . Mr. Simms," she said.

Henry took her hand to lead her onto the dance floor. Excitement prickled her skin. Her fingers twitched and tingled. No sooner had they reached the dancers, than Maria looked warily at him and spoke in a strained voice. "Whatever are you doing here?"

"I'm dancing with a lovely young lady," he replied, taking her into his arms and guiding her masterfully around the ballroom.

"But . . . but, Andrew said you are in medical school and . . . I . . . you . . ." she whispered, "I remember you from Queen Street!"

His hand pressed firmly on her back, drawing her a little closer while his eyes sparked a warning. "Andrew knows nothing about my activities on Queen Street."

Her heart skipped a beat. "But Cousin Andrew *does* know that my friend, Carolyn, brought me there," she said.

His pursed lips deepened the cleft in his chin. Maria heard his swift intake of breath over the lilting music that swept dancers around the room.

He lowered his head close to her ear, close enough for her to feel his warm breath on her neck. "We shall have to keep it our secret then, won't we?"

The masculine scent of him dizzied her. She tried to concentrate on keeping step to the music, but her mind was whirling. *Does he know that I didn't go along with Carolyn's plan? Does he know what happened to Big John?*

Henry's steps never wavered as they glided across the floor. Maria moved as in a dream, the scenes from Queen Street crowding her mind. She remembered his strong hands lifting her into the carriage, the kindness in his eyes when she turned toward him. Those unsettling green eyes had the same effect today.

Henry squeezed her hand gently and bowed graciously when the waltz ended.

There was little chance for any questions or answers in the dances that followed. All four joined in a quadrille, after which Andrew claimed Maria for a sprightly gavotte, the last dance before intermission.

As they sipped punch, Henry gazed from Maria to Sarah. "Andrew tells me your families are neighbors, Miss Sarah. Evergreen Park, isn't it?"

"Evergreen Park is just the name of our land," Sarah said, "and our home where we all grew up. Andrew's farm is close by. All the land used to be called Cow Neck when our grandfather farmed there."

Henry's eyes shifted to Maria. "It must take some getting used to, traveling by boat to come to New York, or to most anywhere, for that matter."

Feeling a swift frisson of alarm, Maria forced herself to look away from his winsome eyes, afraid her own would reveal too much of what she was thinking.

"As to traveling, we don't travel into the city often, except for Father, of course," Sarah said. "He has an office on our property at home and one in New York City."

"But some of us are not content to always stay at home and—" The words flew out before she thought to stop them. Maria bit her lip without finishing. *Why ever did I say such a thing?*

Andrew cleared his throat. "I'm afraid Long Island is less exciting than growing up in our nation's capitol. Tell us about Washington City, Henry."

"Well, I grew up in a big family, three brothers and four sisters. So ours was a busy household and Washington City has sort of grown up with us." He gave a soft chuckle. "You might say the city is still growing."

"My father says they are working on the dome of the capitol. Have you seen it recently, Dr. Simms?" Sarah asked.

Henry's dimpled cheeks spread in a grin. "Yes, indeed. I live very near the capitol, Miss Sarah. Actually, our home on Third and C Street is just around the corner from Pennsylvania Avenue where my father's business is located. We can see the capitol from there."

He turned to face Andrew. "Speaking of business, the next time your uncle Horatio travels to Washington City, I would like to arrange for him to meet my father. I think the gentlemen may have some mutual interests."

Maria's eyes widened as she looked from Andrew to Sarah. *What if Papa were to accept the doctor's invitation? It's just like him to want to know all about his daughter's acquaintances.* Her stomach clenched.

Andrew checked his pocket watch. "We have time for one last dance if I'm to keep my promise to the judge and return you to your hotel on time." Andrew guided Sarah to the dance floor, leaving Maria at Henry's side.

Henry placed a hand at the small of her back, guiding her to the dance floor. There had been precious little experience being close to a man this past year, much less in one's arms. Yet, her arms flew up like puppet strings to his shoulder and hand.

The orchestra played a pavane, a soft, dreamy melody, dissolving the ballroom into something distant and unreal. Her feet glided effortlessly this time, and she dared to look into Henry's eyes. His body heat rushed over her as his arms pulled her close. Henry's eyes hardly left hers until the music stopped.

No one had ever looked at her quite the way he did, and under his constant gaze she found no relief from the unnerving emotions that rushed their way into her mind.

Henry made sure it was Maria he escorted to the carriage. As they walked away from the hotel, he lowered his head and whispered in her ear, "I don't know which is more beguiling, your candor or your beauty."

Her heart drummed and words stuck in her throat.

When they reached the carriage, Henry raised her hand to

his lips, caressing the inside of her wrist. She felt color rise in her cheeks.

He tilted his head, his eyes shining and gentle. "With your consent, Miss Maria, I would like to write to you. I have much to tell you."

She pressed a hand to her fast-tripping heart and found her voice. "I would like that, Dr. Simms."

Chapter Four

Hugging her favorite yellow silk dress to her breast, Jo Onderdonk raised one arm up to an imaginary dance partner and waltzed around the steamer trunk. She stopped at Maria's feet when her sister abruptly stood.

"I hope you get to wear that pretty dress," Maria said. "Papa has plans for almost every day of our trip, and we will be in the mountains the whole first week, you know."

She took the dress from Jo's hands, folded it over Sarah's day dress and closed the lid of the trunk.

Jo sighed dreamily, "I still can't believe Father let Andrew take you two to a ball. I wish I had been there. Papa said Andrew invited a nice young gent to the ball. This trip may be the only chance for *my* turn to do some dancing. Don't you yearn for a handsome dance partner, Sarah?"

Sarah lowered her eyes to the book she held. She traced her fingers over the smooth leather cover of Maria's old diary, ignoring the question. "You are only fifteen, Josephine, and you will have many opportunities for dancing."

Sarah tossed the diary on the chair and stepped to the dresser to peer at her image in the oval mirror that hung behind it. "Besides, as I've said before, there's too much to do at home since Mama's passing, and I'll probably not find a suitor Father totally approves of, even if I wished for one."

Maria sighed. "I know Papa expects us all to be courted

one day, but he keeps such a tight rein on the three of us, how can anything happen?"

She went to her sister's side so that Sarah could not escape her reflection in the mirror.

"I truly hope you don't lose hope for finding a beau, despite Papa, and despite Annie, Libby, and Andrew. You are the eldest after all, and . . . and you cannot really be expected to shepherd the family forever."

Sarah whirled to face her. "First daughter—first to marry doesn't always happen, you know," she snapped.

Maria stepped back and sat down on the steamer trunk, her eyelashes fluttering. She clutched her hands together and stared at Sarah for a long moment.

"But you and I know that's probably just what Father *wants* to happen, Sarah." *There. I've said it. Words not to be taken back.*

Sarah bristled. "Father has been generous with us. He wants nothing but the best for each of us, and from us. Why, every detail of this trip was planned to provide the finest cultural experiences for the three of us. I think he is really trying now that mourning is over. Let's not forget that."

She did it again. Turned the focus away from herself and back to Papa . . . just as though I hadn't said a word about her. Maria pursed her lips and shook her head. Turning her back to Sarah, she opened her hands with a shrug of her shoulders, darting a glance at Jo.

Jo jumped and retrieved Maria's diary. "We still haven't read some of the funny things that happened last year," she said. "Remember the names we gave to fellow passengers on the steamboat, Maria?"

Jo boosted herself up on the big four-poster bed and leafed quickly through Maria's journal. Hugging a feather pillow, she rolled her eyes and pointed to a line. "Heavens, how could we forget 'University Gent'? He was so shy it's a miracle he finally found courage to speak to us at the St. John landing. If it wasn't for him, we never would have known about—"

"McCalifornia!" Maria said, nodding to Jo with the start of a smile. "The crippled gold miner who rescued the lady that walked overboard at the landing." Maria came to Jo's side, laughing now as she leaned over to find the place in her diary.

The tension had broken. Maria read aloud "University Gent's" description of "McCalifornia" leading the lady out of the muddy river. Jo's giggle was contagious and Maria's words were caught up in laughter. Although Sarah kept her back to them, fussing with things on the dresser, she, too, was smiling.

Their laughter muffled the sounds of hurried footsteps on the stairs. Maria and Sarah spun around as their younger sister Annie burst into the room spouting a stream of questions.

"Whatever is taking so long up here? Bridget sent me to see if your trunk is ready."

Without a pause, Annie turned to Maria. "Will you be stopping at Saratoga this trip? You did promise to tell me about the Indian spring and the round railroad at Saratoga. Remember?"

"Slow down, Annie. One question at a time," she replied, slipping her arm around her little sister's waist. "No, we are not going to Saratoga, but the spring there is called a mineral spring. There just happens to be an Indian legend about it, and grown-ups call the round rail a circular railroad. Father will be impressed if you speak of all these things correctly. Impressed enough to maybe take you along next year."

Annie's brows shot up and her eyes brightened. "Do you really think so?"

Maria nodded and gave Annie a hug of encouragement. She nudged her into the bedside chair and handed her the small leather diary. "If you wish, you may read aloud about what we did in Saratoga on our trip last year. Then you'll be better prepared to convince Father you are ready to travel with him next time."

"I'll go down to Bridget about the trunk," Sarah said.

Annie leaned back, turned to the ribbon-marked page and began to read.

12 August 1859
We reached Albany at 5:30 o'clock, took a small boat to Troy, and then cars to Saratoga, arriving at 7:45 p.m. Took an omnibus to Union Hall, the United States Hotel being already full. We had a great time dressing for supper. After supper we walked about the parlors, then took a walk to Congress Spring. There was a crowd there and it took two boys to hand the water fast enough for them to drink. Some drank it as if it were actually good! I don't know what I would have done if the taste had not left my mouth immediately. It tasted just like salts with gas, vinegar and all unpleasant things mixed with it.
We next went 'round the park and saw the Circular Railroad. Two persons get on a kind of buggy-wagon and turn a crank fast or slow, as they wish to go—two shillings to go a mile around. We walked through the village. I shall never forget how beautiful the stores looked. There were gas lamps all around.

Maria went to Annie's side, turned several pages in the diary and marked a page with ribbon. "Now you know all about the Circular Railroad, Annie. You read that beautifully. I've marked the part about the spring with the Indian

43

legend, and you may borrow my diary to read it to yourself later. Mind that you return it tonight, so I can pack it in my reticule. I'll put in a good word for you about traveling with Papa next summer."

Annie clutched at Maria's arm. "But you didn't tell me about your journey that begins tomorrow!"

"Now, hear this," Maria said, cupping her hands around her mouth as though she were speaking into a megaphone: "New York to Troy, by steamer. On by cars to Boston. Last stop, Maine and New Hampshire's White Mountains." She patted Annie's head. "There's your ticket, Annie."

"Oh, Maria, please, pretty please, promise to tell me about the mountains when you come back. I'm going right out to Father's office to see if I can trace your route on his big map." Annie hurried out of the bedroom, clutching Maria's diary to her breast.

Not long after sunrise the next morning, Horatio crossed the east lawn. He entered a white one-room building that duplicated the design of his stately mansion, wide Greek columns and all. The park-like estate that the Onderdonk home and office were built upon was a small section of a large tract of farmland Horatio's father had farmed.

Shafts of sunlight spilled through the tall windows to light the one large room. Horatio sat at a broad wooden desk. There were papers to be signed before he could start on this summer excursion with his daughters.

His eyes misted as he ran his hands over the black walnut desktop. Shaking his head to clear his mind, he scrawled his signature on documents for the post, placing them in his portmanteau.

Opening a small drawer, he carefully withdrew a packet of his father's old letters. A faded scrap of folded red ribbon fell from the fold of the topmost letter. He held it gently between his fingers. How well he knew the story of his father's red cockade. Since childhood, Horatio had listened to stories about the colonies' struggle for freedom, about Cow Neck where they lived, and patriots like his grandfather and uncle. He knew the contents of many of these letters by heart.

A boy's voice called through the open window. "It's time. It's time, Papa. The girls are in the carriage and Bridget says it's time for you to leave if you mean to catch the ferry."

Horatio replaced the emblem in the packet of letters, closed them into the drawer then hurried out to the carriage lane.

His bright-eyed, youngest daughter, Libby, left Bridget's side and raised her arms to him. Horatio stooped to hug her, then placed a hasty kiss on the foreheads of Andrew and Annie.

"Mind your manners and your elders, children. I want to hear good reports from Bridget and your aunt Jane when we return," he said. The judge climbed into the carriage, signaling Martin to start. Maria, Sarah and Jo waved as the coachman drove briskly down the lane.

The steady pace of the team put the miles to the ferry behind them before the sun had climbed very high into a blue summer sky.

Martin reined in the team at the Brooklyn boat landing, tethered the horses and shouldered the steamer trunk to secure it aboard the boat. Horatio carried his portmanteau and hurried his daughters up the ramp.

Maria's heart raced as the ferry began to churn across the short stretch of river. Remembering the ill-fated ferry ride with Carolyn, she shuddered, shaking anxious thoughts from her mind.

This sunny morning the ferry settled gently into a slip at

the eastside dock. The sisters quickly gathered their belongings and waited with their trunk while Horatio searched for a hackney to take them across town. Maria watched closely until he signaled to them from the last hack in a row. The driver came forward to fetch the trunk and Sarah led the way.

Horatio checked his pocket watch. He handed Sarah, then Jo and Maria, into the gig, climbing in beside them. "Well, my dears, one more ride and we shall be boarding the steamer."

It seemed to Maria it was taking forever to reach the Hudson River piers on the west side of the city. The docks were a clamor of activity. The driver threaded his way past carts and carriages unloading people and goods. He reined in at the *Bay State*'s dock just as the boat's bell clanged. The girls lifted their long skirts and hurried up the boarding ramp of the crowded steamer while Horatio directed a porter with the baggage.

As soon as they were aboard, the *Bay State* blasted its signal. The crew secured the ramp and the steamer eased out into the river.

Chapter Five

After Horatio secured the baggage in their rooms he retired to the lounge. Maria suggested they go to the promenade deck to watch the sunset on the water.

Rugged cliffs rose up on the west side of the river. Horsetail clouds lay close to cliffs, the horizon streaked with crimson and violet. Wooded land, looking north, rose up to rocky ledges. "How beautiful," Jo said.

"God's painting a magnificent mural this evening, wouldn't you say?" An older woman spoke. She sat alone in the middle of a row of deck chairs. She introduced herself as Mrs. True, from Ohio. "I'm traveling alone to Boston, and I would be grateful for company, ladies."

The sisters eagerly joined her and they talked together with Mrs. True for a time. At Sarah's suggestion, Jo and Maria began singing a folk song to entertain the widow. Jo had a sweet soprano voice and Maria loved to sing harmony with her. Everyone looked up in surprise when a gentleman at the rail joined in singing the song, "Nellie Bly."

When the song ended Maria boldly asked, "Do you know any other verses, sir?"

"Louis Beauregard Dubigny, Madame, Mademoiselles," the young man said as he made a flourishing bow. "Pleased to make your acquaintance, but I regret I don't know any more verses."

He moved from the rail to stand beside the empty chair

next to Sarah. More than a little flustered, Sarah turned to Maria with a disapproving look. Mrs. True came to the rescue by introducing herself to the young man. Then, with a protective gesture, she presented "the Onderdonk sisters from Long Island."

"Do I detect a French or Southern accent, sir?" Maria asked as the young man took the seat next to Sarah without asking.

"Indeed, a little of both, Mademoiselle. My family came from France seven years ago. We've lived at Poplar Bluff, our plantation in Louisiana, and it has taken most of that time to learn to speak your Anglaise."

He then proceeded in a lengthy conversation with Mrs. True about the beauty of languages. She thought Spanish the sweetest, but Mr. Dubigny countered with, "I prefer French myself. You can converse for hours with a lady in French and talk about nothing, so many little words and so nice for chit-chat."

"*Au contraire,* Mr. Dubigny," Maria piped in, "English is my preference for social conversation."

His expression suddenly became intense, and he turned to Maria. "Perhaps you will favor me with discourse that is a little more serious, miss? I travel north every summer, and am quite familiar with New York and New England, but I know very little about the true sentiments of Northern people regarding the slavery issue."

Sarah drew in her breath and scowled at Maria. Such a direct statement from a stranger surprised all of them. Topics such as this were not discussed in mixed company, and Maria had all but invited it.

Jo looked anxiously at her sisters. "I wish Father were here. He could give a learned point of view about the Fugitive Slave Law," she said.

What kind of a man would ask such questions? Certainly not a gentleman, Maria thought. The slavery issue and Big John's death still harrowed her mind. She carried the memory in her heart like a wound that would not heal. Mindful of Sarah's shock and Jo's anxiety, Maria mentally resolved to give this man a comeuppance.

She raised her chin, tilting her head toward Mr. Dubigny. "I have a friend who attends meetings of the Friends Society. Are you familiar with the Quakers?" Maria gave no pause for his answer. "Are you aware, sir, that they were among the originators of the Underground Railway? A devout Quaker lady, named Lucretia Mott, has spoken at the Friends Meeting House near our home. She speaks about that system that *helps* runaway slaves."

Sarah's and Jo's eyes grew round. Mr. Dubigny's eyes narrowed. His eyebrows knit in a scowl. "I've never heard of your Mrs. Mott, but I've read some of the outrageous accounts in your Northern papers about how we Southerners treat Nigras. They print abolitionist lies!"

An image of Dr. Simms's face rose before Maria, the sound of his voice, and his flashing eyes, as vivid as if he were here beside her. *There had been no abolitionist lies at 11 Queen Street.* Her face flushed when she borrowed from Henry's words.

"Abolitionists who work for the Underground Railroad are people of conscience and courage, *not liars,* sir!"

Sarah stood, her lips drawn in a thin line. She glared at Maria with disbelieving eyes. "Time to retire." she said, barely nodding her head toward Mr. Dubigny with an icy stare. Sarah sputtered, "Sir."

Bending to Mrs. True she asked, "Coming, dear lady?" Without waiting for an answer, Sarah pulled the little woman up and away from the deck chair. Maria and Jo were quick to follow Sarah's hasty departure down the promenade deck, away from Mr. Dubigny.

After a leave-taking of the elderly widow, the sisters settled into their stateroom for the night. Hardly a word was spoken as they undressed for bed.

Jo whispered to Maria as she climbed into her bunk, "What do you think Father would say about that gentleman we chanced to meet?"

Maria cast a glance at Sarah's back. "That man was not a gentleman. Don't give him another thought, Jo. I plan to tell father all about Mr. Dubigny at breakfast."

The slavery debate touched much too close to the events of the previous week, and the impertinent slaveholder brought it all back to Maria's mind. The next morning, she told her father just enough details of last evening's conversation to earn Horatio's disapproval of the man's behavior without disclosing her own sentiments, *or* Sarah's reaction.

Maria was thankful for her father's presence in the dining room at midday, when Mr. Dubigny entered. The disreputable young man was quarrelling with the waiter about not being called to dine on time, and having to eat at the second table. Suddenly Dubigny jumped up from his seat, red-faced and seemingly angry because the waiter spilled a little tea. Maria cringed as she watched him strike the Negro's legs with his cane, again and again.

The thugs who had beaten Big John to death sprang vividly to her mind. She closed her eyes, trying to will her thoughts away.

Declining his usual second cup of coffee, Horatio provided a solution to the uncomfortable situation by hurrying his daughters out of the dining room.

Maria left her sisters on deck, gathered her writing materials and found a quiet place in the salon to calm herself. It was time to write an overdue letter to Carolyn.

Aboard Bay State, *August*
Dearest friend,
There hasn't been one day since Queen Street that you have been out of my thoughts. Neither was there an opportunity for me to come to you before departing on this trip. My father planned this excursion weeks ago and Sarah says our holiday is Papa's way of trying to brighten our spirits since the long time of mourning ended.

These first two days aboard the Bay State *have been a bit distressing. We chanced to meet a Southern slaveholder who posed rude questions about slavery. Mr. Dubigny's (the slaveholder) words earned him little respect in our eyes.*

I tried to tell him about the Quakers' work with the Underground Railroad, but I couldn't say much in Sarah's presence. Oh, how I wish you were here with me, Carolyn. I wished I could tell that callow man about Daniel and Big John, but of course, as you wished, no one knows about it except my cousin Andrew.

You will hardly believe what I must tell you now. Before we left on this trip, my father gave permission for us to go to a ball in New York with our cousin Andrew. A friend of Andrew's from Philadelphia met us at the ball. Lo and behold, it was the director from Queen Street, Mr. Henry Simms! My cousin knew nothing about Mr. Simms's connection to Queen Street, but Andrew did help me find out about Big John. Someday soon, dear Carolyn, we must talk about it. My heart still grieves over that terrible day, and there is much more about Mr. Henry Simms that I must confide to you.

As to the slaveholder I mentioned earlier, Papa has assured us we will disembark in Troy without crossing his path again.

My heart was set on hoping that Sara would meet some dashing young gentleman on this trip, but not someone who insults our thoughts and sensibilities!

Please know that your true friend sends loving wishes that I would see you soon after our return. Ever your confidante,
Maria

The next days were filled with seeing the wonders of Boston, making new acquaintances at seaside hotels and stopping places along the rocky seacoast of Maine. Their second week began with exciting excursions into the White Mountains of New Hampshire. Horatio had spared no expense to ensure a memorable vacation trip, just as Sarah had said.

On their last night aboard a steamer bound for home, Jo fell asleep almost as soon as she laid her head down.

Maria whispered to Sarah, "Did you have a favorite fellow passenger this time?"

Sarah stifled a yawn. "I would have to say Captain Armstrong was the most gentlemanly at the last hotel. He certainly made us laugh a lot, but I'm not sure that's what you are asking."

"Mercy sakes, Sarah Onderdonk, you know perfectly well what I'm asking," she said in a less-than-quiet voice. "We don't have to guard our every thought for Father's sake, do we? Surely there was someone among the gentlemen we've met whom you would choose to consider as more than just a mere acquaintance?"

The only response was Sarah's slow, measured breathing, and the whiffle of a snore.

"Fiddlesticks," muttered Maria. She sat on the edge of her bunk and opened her journal. Her thoughts raced over the last week. *Captain Armstrong was funny, and he did try to make*

Sarah laugh. He probably thought she was dull as a doorstop, and he wouldn't be far from wrong.

"Oh, Sarah, Sarah. I can't write hateful words about you . . ." she muttered to herself. "God knows you probably won't change." She dutifully wrote some lines about their adventures in the mountains of New Hampshire . . . for her sister, Annie.

Wednesday morning at nine, the ladies in our group started for Mt. Washington. We rode part of the way in carriages and the other part on horseback—on little sure-footed Canadian ponies. We soon started for the "Notch." There we saw many wonderful things (the celebrated Notch mentioned in our school books, but of which it is difficult to form an idea without having seen). Imagine two, or perhaps one mountain split in the center to a wonderful depth and a carriage track made, with difficulty, through the rocks! We saw the "Old Man of the Mountain," which appears to be a piece of rock, which has become, by some means, the exact profile of a face! We viewed many other rock formations and the Silver Cascade (a stream tumbling from the height of the mountain to its base).

Thursday morning after breakfast, we had a right happy dance, the Virginia reel. Capt. Armstrong played on the Jews' harp until both breath and strength failed.

Maria O.

Maria closed the diary and tucked it safely in her reticule. She pulled the thin blanket snugly around her on the narrow bunk and tried to concentrate on prayer.

"Bless Papa and all my family. Guide us, especially Sarah, with your grace, and please, Heavenly Father, grant me a sweeter spirit. Amen."

Sleep finally came. In a dream she rode a little pony up a mountain trail, danced the quadrille, and suddenly a young man, waving his cane, was chasing her down the gangplank. "No!" she shouted, jarring herself awake.

She opened her eyes to gray dawn filtering through the transom. The cabin was still. The only sound was the ship's engine, idling, as the riverboat eased into a berth at the New York docks.

Chapter Six

10 September 1860
A letter came in the post from Dr. Simms. Written
shortly after the St. Nicholas dance. The letter waited at
Evergreen Park for our return. I know Sarah saw it on the
hall table but, thankfully, she did not inquire about it. My
heart still flutters at the opening line, "Because you remain
happily in my thoughts."
At times like this, I long for Mother's counsel. I do feel
sad for Sarah, yet I cannot bring myself to share with her
the joy and hope this letter brought to me. Sarah seems to
have no dreams like mine.
Maria O.

Horatio was away. With no word about when he would return
from a business trip to Washington City, Maria escaped the
house to sit in his office and compose a reply to Henry's letter.

A crowd of pleasant fancies pressed on her mind. She
propped her chin on one hand and stared at a sheet of blank
paper. *Should I address him as Doctor? I did so at the party and I
think it pleased him. Since he is almost finished with his medical
studies, my guess is, it would be proper.* Her heart beat fast as she
reread his letter one last time.

Jefferson Medical College
Philadelphia, Pennsylvania
August 30
Dear Miss Maria,

Because you remain happily in my thoughts since that evening at the St. Nicholas, it has been difficult to concentrate on my thesis. The most gratifying evidence of my state of mind is that, with your consent, I am writing to you. In a letter to my father, I enquired if he had made the acquaintance of Judge Onderdonk, but I have not had a reply. From what Andrew has told me about your father's business interests in Washington, I feel certain that my father's government connections would be of interest to him.

I am presently trying to decide where to begin practicing medicine when I finish my studies here next spring. I feel a certain loyalty to my father's wishes for me to practice in Washington City, but a friend at college has been urging me to locate in New York.

This decision proves to be a difficult one, particularly since I now have the desire to see much more of New York than the island of Manhattan. Perhaps my desire will be understood if you return to the first sentence of this letter. Please do not think me presumptuous, but there is much more I feel compelled to tell you. I look forward to a reply.

Very sincerely yours,
Henry C. Simms

Maria did not think Dr. Simms presumptuous at all. Rather, she was, as Jo quipped, "smitten with a mysterious stranger." Before she could raise a pen to begin, the door flew open and Annie rushed into the office.

"Maria, I've been looking everywhere for you. Papa is home and he has gifts for everyone. Bridget says to come to the parlor right now."

When Annie turned to leave, Maria stuffed Dr. Simms's letter into the long sleeve of her dress. She hurried out after Annie, following her across the lawn and up the steps of the wide, columned porch.

Bridget opened the front door. "There you are, Miss Maria. Leave it to Annie to find you. Your father wants all the girls in the parlor with Andrew Joseph right away."

Horatio was talking to Sarah when Maria and Annie entered the room. "I've just returned from some successful negotiations for the WC&R Railroad and I'm eager to tell you all about meeting the Edward Simms family in Washington City."

He looked from Sarah to Maria. "I found Mr. Edward Simms to be a very successful businessman and banker in the city. I was impressed with his strong connections with the government, but I'm afraid our politics widely differ. First off, we disagreed about Lincoln to be the man to lead our nation."

Maria blinked in surprise. "But Father, surely you agreed that the Union should be preserved."

"Yes, of course, to arguments for our Union, but no to Mr. Simms's belief that there could be no real peace as long as slavery exists. I learned that the Simmses' house servants are freed people of color, and I sensed that Edward Simms has strong sentiments on the slavery issue."

Maria's face blanched. She looked away, brushing her fingers across her forehead. *Truth be known, he's not alone,* she thought.

"However, politics aside, the Simms family showed me true Southern hospitality," Horatio said. "I had the pleasure of meeting Mr. Simms's wife, Catherine, three of their daughters and their youngest son, Philip. Now I understand why the young doctor boasted about his family to Andrew. Edward Simms seemed very proud that his son will open a medical practice this summer."

Horatio gazed directly at Maria. "Sarah tells me you've had a letter from the young man. Did he write about his plans after graduation?"

The question was unexpected. Maria stole a glance at Sarah, but her sister's face revealed no emotion. Maria folded her arms, gripping her right sleeve tightly. She wanted desperately to be honest with her father. Her prior deception still weighed heavily on her conscience.

"Yes, he did write about trying to choose where he might open a medical practice," she said, hesitantly.

Sarah finally spoke up. "When we met him at the ball with Andrew, he did ask questions about Long Island."

"Hmm, sounds like he is thinking carefully before making decisions, and . . . uh, moving in the right direction." Judge Onderdonk cleared his throat and cocked his head in Sarah's direction. "Henry strikes me as a young man much to be admired. Perhaps we should invite him to Evergreen Park some weekend. Would you agree, Sarah?"

Sarah's composure gave no hint about her feelings. She stared at Maria. Maria struggled with her emotions. *Papa is obviously emphasizing Sarah's wishes in the matter, and she doesn't seem to give a fig about it.* "Father, I'm sure Sarah, and . . . and . . . well, everyone would like that," she said. "I could send a reply to his letter and tell him that you suggested a visit."

"I suppose that will do, but I would think your sister—"

Annie suddenly brought quick relief to Maria's discomfort by whispering loudly in her father's ear, "Can't we please have our gifts now, Father?"

Horatio harrumphed, sitting back in his chair. "Yes, of course, Miss Anna, my impatient one. You shall pass them 'round for me. First to Sarah," Horatio said, drawing a small jeweler's box from his carpetbag.

A gold seal atop the box was lettered "Gaults, Washington City." Annie took it to Sarah and waited while she opened it. Nestled in the velvet folds, a glittering brooch of jeweled blossoms spread from a delicate filigree of gold stems.

"Oh, Sarah, it's beautiful," Annie said.

Next, Horatio passed on an identical box for Jo. Annie and Jo exclaimed over a monogrammed breast pin. The golden letters "J.O." shone brightly as she held it up.

Father whispered to Annie to carry the carpetbag to Libby and help her draw out a box tied with ribbon. Libby tore off the ribbon and squealed with delight. She ran to Andrew and her sisters to show them a beautiful porcelain-faced baby doll.

Annie dashed back to her father. A large square box sat at his feet. Her name was scrawled on top. She tore at the strings and drew in her breath at a small desk globe on a wooden stand. "Oh, Papa," she cried, "now I can find all the places in the world we can travel to!"

Horatio laughed heartily as he passed the carpetbag to Maria. She reached in for the last gift and unwrapped a polished rosewood box. An intricately carved "M.O." was painted in gold leaf at the center of the lid. It was fastened with brass hinges and a tiny hasp that opened the velvet-lined box. Horatio had left a note inside: "for your keepsakes."

Maria was so charmed with the gift and the message that tears filled her eyes. "Oh, Papa, I'll treasure it always," she said.

While everyone examined each other's gifts, Andrew peeked into the carpetbag and looked up from its emptiness with sad eyes. "Nothing for me, Papa?"

"I've saved the best for last, son." Horatio drew an oddly shaped parcel from behind his chair and presented it to

Andrew. One look inside and Andrew's eyes grew wide. He lifted a beautifully carved wooden schooner from its wrappings. He whooped with joy.

"Look, everyone, a ship for my collection! Isn't she a beauty?"

He paraded around the parlor, first to Sarah, and then to each of his sisters, pointing out his discovery of every small detail of the sailing ship. At last he came to Maria. "Wouldn't you like to sail away aboard a ship like this, sister?"

She was deep in thought about Henry's letter tucked inside her sleeve, thinking about how it would fit nicely in her new treasure box.

"Sail away, Maria, in a ship like this?" Andrew repeated, thrusting the ship model close to her face.

Maria looked up from her gift and tweaked her brother's chin. She nodded. "I am ready for a new adventure, Andrew, if you will be my captain."

Chapter Seven

"Papa always says we can pray as effectively in one house of God as another," Maria said. "Our family attends devotions and services at Dutch Church, but at several other churches nearby, too. He could hardly deny our attending the Friends Meeting House today." Maria squeezed Carolyn's hand. "Besides, I've been *so* anxious to talk with you."

"And I with you. I'm glad I read the notice about the lecture. It was the perfect chance for us to get together. I know your papa is against the war, same as the Quakers, so I prayed he wouldn't object."

Maria and Carolyn walked hand in hand across the brown meadow grass of an ancient cow path beyond the barns. The meeting house stood at the far edge of the Onderdonk estate, a short distance from Dutch Church.

Elders welcomed the girls inside the sparse white building. The girls took their places with other ladies on wooden benches lining the side of the room. Men and boys sat opposite them.

The visiting speaker was a spokeswoman for doctors from the New York Infirmary for Women and Children in New York City. She described the misery and hopelessness of sick and abandoned women and children who came through the clinic's doors.

Maria and Carolyn were surprised to learn that two women doctors staffed the clinic. The lecture ended with a plea for volunteers, funds, supplies and clothing for mothers and children in her care.

"Now that sounds like something we could do," Carolyn whispered. "Collect supplies, that is. Surely your father wouldn't object to a merciful cause such as this."

Maria nodded hesitantly, clasping her hands tightly together. She was trying to model the silent prayer that seemed to conclude the meeting. It was their first time together since that dreadful event in New York, and Maria wanted desperately for things to be smooth between them. She sighed with relief when people rose one by one to leave the meeting room.

A gust of wind sent leaves flying over the meeting house yard. Maria pulled the hood of her dark blue cloak over her head, bending into the wind on the path back to Evergreen Park.

"Other than our getting together at last, was there another reason you were anxious to come to this lecture, Carolyn? Are you thinking of joining the Friends Society?"

"No, no. I do admire the Quakers, and certainly the work that they do. My father is as much against slavery and the war as they are, but he wouldn't approve of my leaving our church to join the Society of Friends."

"You're so lucky that your papa feels the same as you do."

"Yes, I know. Papa might even consider my volunteering at that infirmary. I wanted to hear the lecture, but I was really hoping to get involved with a charity that has to do with helping Negroes. I'm not sure if that clinic serves colored families.

Maria turned her head to look into Carolyn's face. "Are you ready to go back to Queen Street, then?"

Carolyn shivered and clutched Maria's arm tightly.

"No. We need to talk about that, Maria. That's the real reason for my coming here today. When we have some privacy, maybe I can answer that question."

"It wouldn't do to look for any privacy at my house today. Everyone is at home except my father, and we would definitely not be able to talk freely in the parlor."

The cold wind blew leaves in a swirl, twisting the folds of their skirts. Maria shivered and quickened her steps. "I have an idea that might work," she said. "We could go in and have tea to warm up, and afterward I'll ask Martin to drive you home in the barouche. No one will think a thing about my going along with you for company. As I told you in my letter from New England, we have lots of catching up to do."

"Tea sounds nice, and I'd much rather ride in your carriage than take the stage home."

They sat close together, spreading carriage robes over their knees, as Martin climbed to the high box and took the reins in hand.

"I miss our talks, Carolyn, but you know how my father feels about abolitionists. There's no middle road with him and I feel as if I'm caught at the crossing."

"I try to understand. In a way, it's like the conflict at my home. That's one of the things I wanted to tell you about. My mama is a true Southern belle, you know. She still has family in Maryland. I have second cousins living at Fairleigh Oaks with Aunt Persephone. Papa sold our plantation to them, you see. Mama's thoughts lately are always there in the South."

"Do your parents disagree about secession?"

"Very strongly disagree. Mama has been unhappy ever since secession talks started."

"Oh, Carolyn. I'm so sorry. I had no idea—"

"I speak to you in confidence, Maria. You have to know about this in order to understand how I feel about Big John. You see, when my grandmother Fairleigh died, Mama was only twelve. My grandfather was the master at Fairleigh Plantation, and my mama was raised by a house slave, named Sally."

"When you first came here, Carolyn, I thought you told me that your mother was raised by your aunt?"

"That's true. My great-aunt Persephone who came to live with Grandpa. But Sally was more like a mother to my mama than Aunt Pers ever was. Big John was Sally's grandson. When John was but a baby, my grandfather sold his mama away." Carolyn's lip trembled. She sniffed and covered her mouth with her hand.

"Is that where you first knew Big John—at your grandfather's plantation?"

"Well, yes, but I haven't got to *me* yet. Not long after Mama and Papa were married, my grandfather died. He had no sons, so Mama inherited everything."

"Did that include Big John and all the slaves?"

"Yes, of course. You see, my father was a lawyer in the Alexandria law office that settled the Fairleigh estate. My mama fell in love with him and when they married and moved to Fairleigh Oaks, Papa became an instant planter. First thing he did was free all the house slaves. Sally and Big John were some of the few who stayed on. John was about five when I was born."

"I'm beginning to understand now why your father doesn't object to your helping the Anti-Slavery Society."

"Papa was never meant to be a Southern planter, Maria. He hated plantation life and because of that, or in spite of it, there was always trouble. Either trouble with the overseer, or the field hands. My father wanted nothing more than to be a lawyer. He stayed because Mama loved it so."

Carolyn began to twist a handkerchief in her hands. "Big John and I grew up at Fairleigh Oaks. He always looked out

64

for me. We played together. I taught him to read, though Mama didn't know. After we were older, John and I shared a secret . . ." Her lips began to tremble and of a sudden, tears coursed down Carolyn's cheeks. She took a deep breath. "We believed we had the same grandfather," she blurted out, burying her face in a lace-edged handkerchief.

Maria put her arm around Carolyn, squeezing her shoulder. "I think I understand now about Big John, but let's speak no more of it for now. It's too hurtful for you, and for me too. I still feel ashamed that I wasn't there for you in New York, when you needed me."

Carolyn wiped her eyes and blew her nose. "Believe me, Maria, it's best that you weren't. I never expected Daniel's journey to end in violence. I selfishly involved you without telling you first, and—"

"But something good came of my being there. Truly it did. That is what I have to tell you about. It's confidential, too, Carolyn." Maria held Carolyn's hand and drew a long steadying breath. "Mr. Henry Simms, the director for the day at Queen Street, has written a letter to me since we met at the supper dance in New York."

"A letter? Does your father know?"

"Well, yes, he knows about the letter, and he knows Mr. Simms is studying to be a doctor. But I've only told Father that Henry Simms is thinking about opening a medical office somewhere in New York. No one knows about the rest of the letter."

"Mercy sakes, tell me quick."

Maria blushed. "Well, he said that he was so happy to be writing to me, that *I* remained happily in his thoughts, and there was much he wanted to tell me. He wants us to correspond."

"It sounds as though you must have made quite an impression on Henry Simms. How do *you* feel about *him?*"

"I was shocked to meet him at the dance with Cousin Andrew, and at first it was hard to tell if I was afraid of or fascinated by him. Since then, I've had time to sort out my feelings, and I'm sure it's more than fascination."

Maria paused as color crept up her cheeks. "Honestly, I get all fluttery inside when I think of him. He has the most beautiful green eyes, and such a gentle manner, but he's strong. It's hard to explain, Carolyn, but there is such a manly strength about him, I feel I can trust him with my life."

"Was he at the dance with your cousin Andrew as result of the Anti-Slavery Society?"

"Oh, mercy, no. Andrew knows nothing about that. Dr. Simms is simply a friend my cousin met in Philadelphia. Andrew admires him, but I truly believe my cousin suspects Dr. Simms would like to be more than a friend to me."

Carolyn clasped both of Maria's hands in hers. "Do you think you will see him again?"

"Yes, because, best of all, when my father learned about the letter he said we should invite Dr. Simms to visit Evergreen Park!"

Evergreen Park
Sunday morning
Starting with Doctor's arrival on Friday's noon stage, Papa planned almost every hour of his visit. Dr. Simms has a tender gallantry that endeared him to everyone. To all appearances so far, though, he paid no more attention to one of us than the other. Even Jo's eyes were twinkling at him. I am rather puzzled, but maybe he's just being a gentleman.

Today may be different. Sarah doesn't feel well this morning, so Papa, Dr. Simms and I will attend the little

*church at Flower Hill. We've been invited to stop and visit
at Cousin Andrew's after the service!*
Maria O.

"I'm thankful your cousin suggested a walk on the ceme-
tery path," Henry said as he walked with Maria up a slope of
brown grass toward the burial grounds. "I was afraid there
wouldn't be a moment alone to speak to you, Miss Maria."

"Cousin Andrew is very perceptive," Maria said. A shy
smile curved Maria's lips and softened her eyes.

"I can't tell you how much pleasure your letter gave me,"
Henry said.

They were approaching her grandfather's grave and Maria
sent him a sidelong glance as they skirted a sectioned-off
burial plot. *What would be an appropriate reply? It wouldn't do
to tell him that the pleasure was shared. Not just yet.*

Maria pressed her hands against her grandfather's granite
headstone, letting out her breath in a long sigh. "My grandfather Joseph was a much more ardent correspondent than I
am, Mr. Simms. If only you could have known him. He was a
strong, proud man who could surprise you with gentleness.
Few people would suspect he was a rebel during the War for
Independence."

"It seems our forbears were patriots alike, then. My grandfather marched with the Maryland militia during the war."

Henry paused, then reached out to take her hand in his.
"Ever since I saw you at Queen Street I've wanted to explain
my sentiments to you and, more importantly, I've wanted to
know yours. Forgive the question, for I know ladies of pro-
priety don't usually discuss such matters, but there is much
about you that I'd like to know. Do you ever think about your
own place in history, Miss Maria? Where you stand on important issues facing our Union?"

The hand holding hers felt firm and strong. Maria drew a long, steadying breath. "I know women aren't supposed to have opinions on such things. Father thinks women should lead by example of their virtue and sweet temper, but I think I have inherited some of my grandfather Joseph's spirit in things that matter. I make up my own mind about . . ."

She stopped abruptly, looking down at the polished stone. The faces of Carolyn, Daniel and Big John flashed before her eyes. She traced her finger absently over the inscription on the tombstone, staring intently at it, searching for the right words.

"Well, I find it hard to act on my conscience as some people do. I believe that slaves should be free . . . but I went against my father's wishes when I went with Carolyn Grisham to Queen Street. Everything went wrong, and Big John—" Maria bit her lip, and looked away.

Henry reached out, hesitantly, to cup her chin and turn her face gently to him. She looked into his eyes and sensed his understanding before his words reassured her. "I know, Maria. I know all about it. It was a tragedy, but things will be better soon and hearts will mend."

She nodded, but words wouldn't come.

"I have to be honest with you. I help the Anti-Slavery Society because I believe so strongly in their cause, but very few people know what I do. My involvement started with a Quaker friend at my college in Philadelphia. Your friendship with Carolyn brought you to Queen Street, I hope, for the same reasons. That's what I admire about you. You are forthright, caring, and courageous."

"Oh, I wish I were courageous. My friend Carolyn opened my eyes to the terrible cruelty of slavery, but when she called upon me to help, I couldn't. I didn't have the courage to go against my father's wishes . . . or the law." She pulled a handkerchief from her pocket, twisting it in her hands, unable to meet his eyes. "I've not been able to talk about it with anyone except Cousin Andrew. Andrew interceded for me and found out what happened to Big John."

"I think you were right to follow your conscience, and I'm glad you inherited your grandfather's spirit in things that matter." Henry looked down at the gravestone. "I'd like to hear more about your grandfather. You said he was a rebel. Did he fight with the Continentals?"

"No, he was too young." Her eyes gleamed and her lips curved in a smile. "He was a spirited rebel, though. He did a good bit of spying on the British, and he rescued his dearest friend who escaped from a prison ship!"

Henry's eyebrows raised in surprise. "I'll say he had spirit. Was his friend a captured soldier?"

"Yes. His name was Martin Freer. Grandfather eventually helped him return to his regiment. Martin Freer became my grandfather's lifelong correspondent thereafter. That's what I meant about my grandfather's correspondence. I learned all this from reading Grandfather Joseph's letters. Sometimes they were more interesting than my history lessons at Miss Adrian's Seminary."

"I've traced my family ancestry recently, too. My grandfather Simms was a militiaman, but I don't think he saw much action outside Maryland."

"Well, Grandfather Joseph had some amazing adventures. He met another escapee after the war ended, a friend to Martin Freer from that same prison ship. Grandpa Joseph corresponded with him too. I remember that Martin's friend was a Southern sea captain from Maryland. Jenkins, I think, was his name, but it's been a long time since I looked at Grandfather's old letters, and I could be mistaken."

"If you're not mistaken about the sea captain, it would be intriguing to find out about him. My father and all his ancestors were from Maryland, and that name sounds awfully familiar. Perhaps our forbears have a greater part in our destiny than we know."

Henry took her hands from the stone and twined his fingers through hers. Maria felt a tingle of excitement as their hands held fast. There was an eager light in his eyes and it set her pulse racing.

"I think you and I are much alike, Miss Maria. Kindred spirits, I'd say." His eyes sought hers and held her gaze without wavering. "Kindred spirits belong together."

Her heart drummed at the thought. Kindred spirits. Heat raced up her neck. She freed one hand and tried to raise it to her flaming cheeks, but Henry caught it and brought it to his lips, caressing the inside of her wrist. His long dark lashes swept her skin.

"Somehow I get the sense that your heart carries the same sentiment. Is that true?" he asked.

For a moment, she couldn't answer. She stared at the hand that clasped hers and raised her head to meet the searching look in Henry's eyes. Words caught in her throat.

"I . . . I think we are of one mind, Dr. Simms, but I really can't speak about my sentiments . . ."

Henry raised one finger to her lips. "Until you can tell me plainly what is in your heart, that is all I shall hope for. Please say that I may keep hope alive?"

Maria looked away with a confusion of emotions. She struggled with a compelling desire to be enfolded in his arms. Drawing a deep breath, she tried to steady her whirling thoughts. *Sarah doesn't even have a suitor yet, and I haven't reached my eighteenth year.*

After a long moment, she met his gaze. "Yes, I hope that

70

you will," she whispered, tucking her hand inside the crook of his arm.

Henry smiled, brushing a thumb along her cheek. He covered her hand with his and led her gently down the grassy slope, away from the gravestone of Joseph Onderdonk.

November, 1860

I scarcely knew what to say or do when we left Andrew's house yesterday. Dr. Simms's words still thunder in my ears. "We are kindred spirits. Kindred spirits belong together!" My legs trembled like a newborn calf and my heart thumped in my chest when he asked about my sentiments. I couldn't dare to answer him. Not yet. But I know. Oh yes, I know.

Maria O.

Chapter Eight

The envelope that came by post from 390 C Street, Washington City, was addressed to the Honorable H. G. Onderdonk. Maria looked at the familiar handwriting and turned the letter over. Sealing wax imprinted the initials H.C.S. on the back.

I've had two letters from him this month, but this one is posted to Father. I wonder what Dr. Simms could be writing about? Placing the envelope back on the silver tray, she hoped her father would share its contents.

True to her wishes, after Bridget cleared the dinner dishes from the dining table that evening, Horatio made an announcement. "A letter of invitation has come from Washington City which concerns . . . ahem . . . all of us." He hooked his reading glasses over his ears. Looking over them at Sarah and Maria, he pulled the letter from his coat pocket. "Best I should read it aloud."

10 December 1860
Washington City
Honorable Judge Onderdonk,
My father told us you should be in Washington early in January to attend some festivities for President Buchanan. It is with haste that I convey my mother's wishes that you, and any of your family who might accompany you to Washington City, would favor us with your presence at a dinner party that same week. A small celebration is planned on the occasion of my fa-

ther's birthday, January 13.

My hope is that your daughters will be in your company. My mother and sisters are looking forward to meeting your family. Since we are trying to keep the dinner party a surprise, I ask that you send a reply to my sister, Sienna, in New York City. I know that my father spoke to you about Sienna and my brother-in-law, the Honorable Judge Smith. If you will respond to my sister, she will bring your reply to us when she comes for a Christmas visit. In that manner, we will be able to keep the gathering a surprise.

Until we meet, I send best wishes to you and your family for good health in the New Year.

Respectfully yours,

H. C. Simms

"Well, girls, I'm surprised to be invited to a Simms *family* party, but I rather suspect the invitation is the idea of young Henry." He looked at Maria, then at Sarah. "How do you think I should respond?"

Maria shot a glance at Sarah. As eldest, she would be expected to reply.

"It is a surprising, but generous, invitation," Sarah said, pausing. "But you know how I feel about traveling in the wintertime, and of course, someone should be here with Bridget to see that the children attend to their studies. Perhaps it would be best, Papa, if you traveled with Jo and Maria. I know they would be honored to attend the president's party as well as Mr. Simms's birthday dinner."

Hardly able to contain her excitement, Jo squeezed Maria's hand under the table.

Horatio looked thoughtfully at Sarah. "I'm sorry you do not wish to go, my dear. Are you sure you won't change your mind?"

73

"No, Father. Libby would be happy to go off to Aunt Jane's anytime, but Andrew and Annie really need my help with their lessons."

"Well, I'm certainly appreciative of your concern for the children, but I'm sure you will be missed," he said, sending a curious look in Jo's and Maria's direction. Neither of them blinked an eye. "I must conclude it is decided then. I'll notify Judge Smith immediately."

January held a whirlwind of festivities for Washingtonians. Maria and Jo were awed by the splendor and gaiety of the social scene, but less than happy with their surroundings in Washington City.

10 January 1861

It's hard to believe that this dirty city is our capitol. Most of the streets are unpaved, and carriages sink up to their axles in mud. Papa had to buy us high, cloth-topped boots to navigate the muddy streets. Horses clop by pulling peddlers' wagons, and pigs and geese roam around with hapless pedestrians like us.

Yesterday we happened upon a drover herding cows along in front of the president's house! Today was threatening snow, so Papa sent us in a hack to drive around the city while he conducted business. We went to C Street to see where the Simms family lives.

Dr. Simms's home is a handsome brick house with wooden sidewalks lining the street all the way to Washington Circle. The cab driver told us that a statue of General Washington is to be unveiled by President Buchanan next month at Washington Circle. I wish we could see it, but I am counting time until Mr. Simms's birthday party. Last night Father took us to a hop at the Willard (where we

are registered). Jo really enjoyed it, but I can hardly wait for January 13.
Maria O.

When the day came for the grand levee given for outgoing President Buchanan, Judge Onderdonk proudly escorted his daughters to the president's house.

Upon entering the reception room, a daughter on each arm, Horatio paused amidst a throng of people. "I'm told that fifteen hundred were invited to this party, so stay close, my dears. I'm going to try to move on into the East Room."

Jo clutched her father's arm tightly. "I think all the invited guests must be in this hall right now, Papa. I can barely put one foot in front of the other."

The East Room was aglow with light. Maria moved forward on her father's arm, unconcerned about the press of military officers, foreign ministers, handsome gentlemen and elegantly dressed ladies.

"There's such a sea of heads bobbing up and down, I'm not sure what the music is I'm hearing," Maria said.

"Is it a dance, Papa?" asked Jo.

"It's an Austrian quadrille, my dear, and you are right, it is much too crowded to observe anything from here. Let's go below to the supper tables. I'm sure it will be the finest spread you'll ever see."

When they reached the tables, they gazed in wonder at stuffed squab, oyster pie, baked ham, roast beef, and all manner of hot and cold side dishes. In the center was a large illuminated confection that was hard to identify. "My goodness, Papa, there's a bouquet of real flowers on top of that dessert," Jo said.

Miss Harriet Lane moved through the crowd, smiling and speaking to the guests. "Is that young woman always hostess for the president?" Jo whispered.

"Mostly yes, I'd say. She is his niece. But today, rumor has it that President Buchanan will be escorting Mrs. Madison down to supper. We shall see soon enough."

Maria feigned interest in what her father was saying, but she was really sorting through her whirling thoughts about a very different dinner party, wondering what January thirteenth would bring.

Edward Simms's birthday dinner was a complete surprise to him. Fine damask, silver, china and crystal adorned the table. Mary Catherine sat at her husband's left, and Judge Onderdonk on Edward's right. To Henry's dismay, he was seated between his mother and Maria's sister, Jo.

Across the wide table, Maria sat between Henry's sisters, Georgiana and Virginia. The youngest Simms siblings, Edwina and Philip, sat at the lower end of the table.

Distance did not stop Philip from posing endless questions to Maria about Long Island and New York City. Henry's sisters talked easily with her, too. Maria's face glowed with pleasure.

Henry caught her eye a few times. Her smile was infectious, but what he loved most about her was her guileless manner. Yes, she had strong convictions about things that mattered, but seldom did she stray from the vision of the sensitive person that she was.

After the sumptuous meal, an iced cake was served, and the cook's son, Massie, came to the dining room to play the fiddle for Mr. Edward.

Afterward, the family gathered around Edwina, playing her father's favorites on the pianoforte in the parlor. When Jo added her sweet voice to the singing, Henry took the opportunity to quietly draw Maria out to the settee in the hall for some precious minutes alone.

He looked back at the open parlor door, pulled at his mustache, and turned his eyes to Maria. Clasping her hand in his he touched his lips gently to her fingers. "I've tried to read an answer between the lines of your letters, but I did not find one. I want to hear it from your lips, Maria. Can you tell me yet if your heart carries the same sentiments as mine?"

She placed her hands lightly on his chest and drew a long steadying breath. Timidly she said his given name. "Henry . . ." Long seconds passed. "I can truly answer yes, but . . . my father . . . well, you see, Sarah is eldest and . . . and, I'm afraid we must wait—"

Henry touched her lips lightly with one fingertip. "Yes is all I need to know for now." He drew her close, brushed his lips against her cheek, then lowered his mouth to hers. His lips were soft and gentle, and though the kiss lasted no more than a few seconds, Maria came away with her pulse pounding in her ears. She met his gaze with eyes as innocent as starlight.

Maria's lips and the wonder he beheld in her eyes held Henry's thoughts as he settled into his seat in the passenger car. He closed his eyes and tried to shut out the rumble of the train by savoring the memory of that kiss. It seemed like yesterday, but three months had passed since he had seen Maria.

There had been no time for any trips to 11 Queen Street for Henry in these months. His medical thesis and then graduation left him little time for anything except letters. Letters went back and forth from Thomas Jefferson University to Evergreen Park, Long Island. Henry held on to the hope that he could speak to Maria's father before the summer ended.

A fellow passenger's voice brought him out of his reverie. "What's troubling you, Henry?" Dr. May asked. "You picked at your breakfast in Philadelphia and you've hardly talked since we changed cars in Baltimore." Dr. John May did not wait for Henry's reply. "Don't tell me it's that fracas at the graduation celebration?"

A long pause and a sigh followed as Henry placed one hand on his furrowed brow. *What's bothering me will be difficult to put into words for my father, much less for a long-time friend of his.*

"No, certainly not, Dr. May. I did avoid getting involved in the melee, probably because I didn't drink as much as most of the fellows," Henry replied in a half-hearted attempt to make light of the question. "But then, you left the tavern before the group became rowdy. Johnson and I took the brunt of the anger, solely because we were the two Southerners in our class."

"Surely they didn't blame you for the slave states' point of view? This turmoil over secession certainly won't be resolved by a handful of medical school graduates."

"It's my guess they didn't think much about where *our* sympathies lie. They just lumped the two of us together because my roommate, Dr. Johnson, is from Georgia, and from time to time, I've boasted about my Maryland Simms ancestors. None of the fellows knew that Will Johnson's father is a cotton planter who actually granted his slaves freedom."

He continued without pause. "Will's father says the North, through its control of trade and manufacturing, gets forty cents of each cotton dollar. Did you know that, sir?"

"I know the South is in a bad way economically, and the tariffs do seem unfair, but I'm a strong believer that the Union must be preserved, Henry."

"I agree, sir, but the slavery issue—well, that's why things got out of hand at the party. Will Johnson and I think alike on most things, only this time, Will's quick temper got the better of him. I was thankful he didn't challenge one of the New Englanders to a duel!"

"But, surely, Henry, these young men must realize we've got to find a way to equalize injustice and remain a united nation. They could have demonstrated more gentlemanly conduct, given the fine reputation of the university, and the grand occasion of graduation."

"It didn't really mar the glory of the occasion, sir. For my part, I had already developed strong feelings about slavery during my previous year at Berkshire Medical College. This last year at Jefferson actually strengthened my point of view. Trouble was, most of the partygoers didn't know I was on their side." Henry drew in a breath. *Nor did anyone know I've been helping slaves escape to freedom,* he thought, looking guardedly at his seatmate.

Dr. May smoothed his beard and looked off in the distance. "Aha, I see. Well I'm glad to know you are strongly for the Union, son."

Henry lowered his eyes and fidgeted in his seat. "Truth be known, sir, that controversy is not what I've been brooding about. When I get home, I must speak to my father about a personal decision about my future . . . that is, where I'll be practicing medicine." Henry nervously smoothed his side-whiskers, sending Dr. May a sidelong glance. "You will undoubtedly hear about it soon enough."

John Frederick May had been Henry's preceptor at college, and he was also a family friend and neighbor in Washington City. Being certain he would hear about it in due time, he rode the train in silence for the last few miles to Washington City.

When the train pulled into the station, the bustle of people preparing to leave the cars spared Henry any further conversation. Darkening clouds were gathering as they stepped out on the crowded platform.

"My son, William, should be waiting with my gig. Since your father doesn't know of your arrival today, will you ride with me to C Street?"

"I'd be grateful, sir," Henry replied.

Dr. May spied his son in the line of waiting carriages and hailed him. Thunder rumbled and a gusty wind blew as they hoisted the valises and Henry's portmanteau up to the driver's seat. The men hastily boarded the carriage in a sudden slash of rain.

More than Henry's spirit was dampened minutes later when they arrived in a downpour at his C Street home.

Chapter Nine

Male voices intermingled with the sound of logs snapping in the parlor fireplace. Ordinarily, Henry would have gone directly to his father to give the warm greeting Edward Simms always looked for. Today he put his hat and gloves on the console table, took off his wet coat and paused in the hall to listen.

His father was entertaining a small gathering of men and there was no mistaking one of the voices. Henry recognized the deep bass voice of Mr. Madison White, a member of the Associated Soldiers of the War of 1812. Edward Simms had been a member of that militia group for as long as Henry could remember, and Madison was his old friend.

The cook's son, Massie, came down the hall smiling his welcome. Henry put a finger to his lips to silence him. He quietly asked him to bring his belongings upstairs to his room.

As he was about to go into the kitchen, Henry recognized the story his father was telling. Edward Simms was a wonderful orator, much revered by his acquaintances. They, too, had heard the story before, but they knew it was a true one and they relished hearing it as much as Edward did the telling of it.

Henry smiled. It was a pleasant diversion from the heavy thoughts that worried him, so he sat on the hall settee to listen to his father's story drifting in from the open parlor door.

"I remember catching my first glimpse of Pennsylvania Avenue when I came here as a young boy of twelve. I was riding on a wagon that creaked and swayed under a high mound of oats it carried down Frederick Road to Washington City. I hung on to the wooden seat and lurched into the Negro driver, Luke, as the wheels pitched in and out of clay ruts.

" 'Hold on, Mistuh Edward,' old Luke said, 'we gwine to make it across de bridge and into Washton City with these oats befo' Mistuh Presdent's hosses knows dey hungry.'

"A twist of wind whirled away the early morning fog, and stretched out before us was a raised road with footpaths on either side of a long row of poplars leading to the president's house.

" 'Is that where President Jefferson lives, Luke? Is that where we're going? To that grand big house?' I asked.

" 'Yes an' no,' old Luke said, smiling. 'Presdent do live hyere, but we is goin' to his stables.' "

Henry's sister, Eddie, hurried down the long stairway as fast as her hoops would allow. Henry reached the bottom stair just as she did. He caught her by the shoulders and whispered, "Father doesn't know I'm here, and I've decided to wait until he finishes his story." He gestured toward the parlor, and taking his sister's hand, drew her to the settee. "Where are Mother and the girls?" he asked in a low voice.

Eddie whispered back, "They've gone to a church sewing circle. We thought you might come home tomorrow. Oh, Henry, I am so happy you're here. Let's—"

Henry shushed her as their father's voice continued. "Wait, Eddie, this is the best part."

"I stared at the imposing figure of the president's coachman. He was dressed in livery—knee britches and a blue coat with crimson and lace trimming. I was so impressed I took no notice of the tall man walking away from the horse stalls. Luke gave me a hand to jump down from the wagon, and whispered to me, 'Look sharp, Mistuh Edward. Never you mind Mr. Dougherty. He only de coachman. Presdent Jefson comin roun' de wagon.'

"I had never seen a liveried coachman, much less a president, and when President Jefferson greeted me with the question, 'How did you get here, my boy?' my awestruck reply was, 'I came with the oats, sir.' "

Hearty laughter punctuated the end of his father's story. Henry and Eddie grinned at one another. "It's best I go in now and make my appearance on a happy note," he said to Eddie.

Eddie went to the kitchen to tell Elizabeth to expect one more for dinner. Henry entered the parlor as the men were rising to take their leave.

Edward Simms rose from his chair with a startled look, which quickly changed to a broad smile. "Gentlemen. You remember my son, Henry Constantine. Well, I'm proud to reintroduce him now as Dr. Simms," he said, putting an arm around Henry's shoulders.

Congratulations were given all around before the gentlemen left. As Edward returned from seeing his guests to the door, he could see Henry restlessly pacing back and forth in front of the fire.

"Well, son, you seem in poor spirits. Is something wrong?"

"No, no, Father. Nothing is wrong. I . . . I have something to tell you that might be upsetting to you, even though I've hoped in my heart that it would not be."

"Your spirits do not usually sink under difficulty, Henry. Has all this rumble about secession gotten to you, or have I been so stern a father that you fear confiding in me?"

Henry nervously smoothed his mustache. "Oh, no sir, it's nothing like that. You see, it's just that you've denied me nothing through all my studies to become a doctor, with the hopes, I'm sure, that I would open a practice here in town. But, I've made a decision to locate elsewhere."

He paused to look into his father's troubled eyes. "In Brooklyn, New York. And I know that must be disappointing to you and Mother, but I hoped that the reason for my decision might soften the news."

He had hardly finished his sentence when Edward's troubled frown changed to a smile.

"Brooklyn!" He grasped Henry's arm, his dark eyes gleaming. "If the reason has to do with Maria Onderdonk, all of our wishes for your practicing medicine here can fly with the wind. That young lady has endeared herself to all of us. Nothing could make us happier, Henry, than to have you say that she will someday be one of us."

With a great sigh of relief, Henry's face beamed. "Our love is mutual, but there are no definite plans yet, Father. We've spoken to no one about a betrothal. We're waiting for the right time, you see."

The Simmses' cook, Elizabeth, entered the parlor with a full tea tray. Eddie paused behind her at the parlor entry long enough to hear Henry's announcement. At the same time, the front door suddenly opened to Mary Catherine Simms and her elder daughters. Hesitating only long enough to call a greeting over her shoulder, Eddie shouted, "Come quickly into the parlor, everyone. Henry's home with wonderful news!"

Washington City, 16 April 1861
My Dearest Maria,
   It is with a heavy heart I write to you of a delay in my plan to come speak to your father. After a week at home, I came to Brooklyn to open my new office, but I had scarcely been there a

few days when I received a telegram from my father. I had to leave in haste to come back home. Washington City is in chaos. The capitol has been hastily fortified, and regiments from New England crowd the streets. Lincoln's call for troops roused the South as well as the North, but not in the way he intended. Across the Potomac, General McDowell is drawing up war plans in the mansion that General Robert E. Lee abandoned!

Father has asked my help to conduct some business for him. A cousin of ours (my brother's namesake), Mister Philip Simms of New Orleans, has a wholesale dry goods firm called Peet and Simms. Cloth for Army uniforms is much in demand and Father is hoping Cousin Philip will give him a contract. He tried to telegraph our cousin but the lines have been impossible. I have agreed to go to New Orleans with my brother Philip. I don't think my father expects any trouble for us southwest of Washington, but I am less than sure about that.

Because he is a loyal Unionist, my father commands respect in Lincoln's administration. He wants to continue his good relationship with the War Department, although many of our relatives are not loyal to the Union. We have family in Maryland who have joined the Secesh side! Now that Louisiana has seceded, Father is hoping his nephew, Philip, is still a Unionist.

Negotiating is not what I wish to do, Maria, but Father feels that my brother Philip is too inexperienced to take on this task alone. We leave early tomorrow by train for Tennessee. Whether by train or steamboat, from there, we are headed for New Orleans.

Washington is a frightening place to be as the month of May approaches. It should be filled with birdsong and blossoms, and I long to be showing you the cherry trees in bloom. I want the Union of all the states preserved as much as my father does, but I also want our betrothal to be announced. I have a strong foreboding, though, about leaving a fiancée should we go to war.

I must put those thoughts aside for now and be thankful for our love. Please believe that my thankful heart will remain a strong one. It may be many weeks before we return. Give my kind remembrances to your family and please write to me at the C Street address.

 Yours devotedly,
 Henry C. Simms

Chapter Ten

Maria's hands trembled as she opened the envelope Jo handed her. She read the single page, tears flooding her eyes. "I'll read this to you, Jo," she said in a quavering voice, "but you must promise not to speak to Father or Sarah about it."

Washington City, 20 April 1861
My Dear Maria,

Our city has become a frightening place. Army wagons and artillery are continually rumbling through the streets. We cannot walk about the city safely. Edwina's intended, Willie Warren, has joined the Union Army, and she is heartsick with worry. I know now, dear Maria, that you must be worried about our brother at this time, too.

Henry told our father that when he returns from New Orleans, he would ask for your hand as soon as he arrives back in Brooklyn. Although he told us any plans for marriage must wait, our family is so very happy! We are all praying that your father will not discourage Henry. Georgiana, Edwina and I look forward to someday calling you "sister." We hope the war will end quickly, so we will soon have that pleasure. Our mother expresses her wishes for you to come visit us while Henry is away. Mother would dearly like to spend time with you. With kind regards to your family, I remain

Yours Sincerely,
Virginia Simms

Soon after the letter was received, Cousin Andrew brought a beautiful bouquet of spring flowers to the Onderdonk house.

"A late Easter season token for the ladies in the house," he said cheerfully to Maria.

"Well, Jo and I are the only ones at home just now, Andrew, but we can all use a bit of cheering up, what with the dreadful news about war. I just had a letter from Dr. Simms's sister, Virginia."

"Did she give you any news about Henry?"

"Virginia wrote about how frightening Washington City is," Maria said, pausing to catch herself before saying anything about her betrothal, "and a little bit about Henry."

"Well," Andrew said, drawing out the word, "as you may know, Henry's good friend, Dr. Cochran, has been helping to set up an office for him in Brooklyn. Henry wrote me briefly, asking for my help with some legal details. He also described the difficulties he and Philip were experiencing on the train trip through Virginia and Tennessee. The rest of his letter had a lot to do with . . . uh . . . his plans *after* New Orleans. Surely you've heard from him?"

"Yes, I did receive one letter, and I've been praying for his safety. Please don't tell me something bad has happened."

"Nothing bad, but as you can well imagine, life at his father's home in Washington City has been complicated by the start of this conflict. Henry is trying to hold things together for his father's sake."

"But that's what this trip is all about, isn't it?"

"Yes, of course, but Henry still plans to ask your father for your hand in marriage." Andrew paused when he noticed Maria's quick intake of breath and raised eyebrows.

"I know all about it, Maria. Henry shared his feelings about a month ago. He is not too hopeful, though. You see, he thinks your father will not consider a betrothal, at least not until this conflict between the states gets resolved."

He clasped her hand. "I do know that Henry wants very much for you to wait for him. He said as much, but the war—"

"Of course I mean to wait for him. We discussed secession and the survival of the Union, and I thought I understood his feelings about . . . the war." She bit her lip and looked searchingly into Andrew's eyes.

"I didn't expect him to . . . When you say he wants me to wait for him, are you trying to tell me that he wants to serve in the war?" She raised a hand to her lips.

"Perhaps, in the future, if it becomes necessary, yes. I think that is what Henry intends."

"I probably should have expected it. Dr. Simms feels so strongly about the Union." She clutched a gold cross hanging from a lavaliere around her neck.

"Everything will work out, Maria. You both have such strength of spirit. I am sure your faith in God will strengthen you for any separation that may come. Let's just hope none of it will be necessary."

Chapter Eleven

With bells clanging, a mule-drawn car of the street railway blocked their passage along Pennsylvania Avenue. Henry and Philip made their way carefully along the dung-strewn street, heading toward Willard's Hotel. They passed haberdashers, shops and saloons. People milled about in small groups, talking about secession and the threat of war.

At the National Hotel on Sixth Street Philip paused, put his hands behind his back, and mimicked President Lincoln's high pitched, much-imitated voice. " 'In your hands, my dissatisfied countrymen, and not in mine, is the momentous issue of civil war.' "

"I've heard Father quote that part of Lincoln's inaugural address time after time to folks coming into the store and into the bank," Philip said. "No one argues with him because he's so respected, but sometimes it seems like he's trying to convince everyone in the city that Lincoln's words are gospel truth."

Henry was amused and embarrassed by Philip's mimicry. He shook his head, suppressing a grin by covering his mouth with his hand. "Better tone it down, Philip. We'll be at the Willard in a minute."

Philip squeezed his nose to escape the foul odor drifting from the city canal across the avenue. "None too soon to be away from that stinking canal."

As he hurried Philip across the hotel lobby to the entrance

of the dining room, Henry noticed a well-dressed, portly gentleman seated alone at a table just inside the door.

He whispered in Philip's ear, "I believe that's one of our cousins on Father's side, one of old Raphael Semmes's sons from Georgetown. We shouldn't ignore him, Philip. We'd never hear the end of it from Father if we failed at least to say hello. Besides, I've something I've been meaning to find out about their side of the family, and he might have the answer."

Henry walked into the dining room, ignoring a waiter motioning him to a different table, and approached the gentleman. "Good day to you, Thomas. I've not seen you for a very long time. Actually since I went away to medical school. I'm Edward's son, Henry."

As the gentleman turned toward them, Henry gestured toward Philip. "You may not remember my younger brother, Philip." The man rose, extended his hand and smiled in one swift movement.

"Of course. Henry Constantine, isn't it? I'm not that much older than you, Henry, but it has been a while. Good to see you, young man," he said as he shook Philip's hand. "I'm Thomas Semmes, in case you don't remember. Won't you join me?"

Philip looked hesitantly at Henry, and Henry politely nodded and pulled out a chair. "It's been a long while since I've had the company of any of Cousin Edward's family," Thomas said. "How is your father?"

"Father is very well. His duties at the savings bank keep him busy, but he still keeps a strong hand in Upperman & Co.," Henry said.

"In fact, he's servicing government contracts that we—" A kick under the table from Henry brought a swift end to Philip's words.

"—that we . . . we recently learned of," Henry finished.

"Ah, yes, your father's mercantile," Thomas said, smoothing his mustache and giving Philip a wily look.

"But, speaking about family, Thomas, I have just learned that the Jenkins side of your family may have had a close connection to my fiancée's ancestor. Do you recall any stories passed down about Captain Thomas Jenkins?"

A look of surprise came over Thomas's face. "Why, Henry, when you inquire about Captain Jenkins, you speak of my grandfather! My mother was Captain Thomas Jenkins's youngest child, and I am his namesake. Yes, of course, I remember countless tales my mother told about Grandfather's seafaring days during the War for Independence. What is this tie that you speak of?"

"Well, it's a long story, but my fiancée's grandfather rescued a friend from a prison ship in New York, and Captain Jenkins was a prisoner on that very ship. The captain and my fiancée's grandfather became correspondents after the war."

"Well, well. Our history is intriguing, isn't it?" said Thomas. He cocked his head and gazed warily at the two younger men. "Loyalties and causes. Have they changed so in eighty-five years?"

Wary about the direction the conversation was taking, Henry raised his eyebrows and took in a deep breath. "Well, yes, Thomas, I suppose they have."

Thomas calmly stroked his mustache. "What do you think of this impending conflict? Most of my associates think it will be over quickly once all of our Southern states have seceded."

Henry shifted uneasily in his chair and nervously cleared his throat. "I don't have the answers, but I'm sure *you* can bring us up to date on the latest news. The last I heard, you were District Attorney for Louisiana. What brings you to Washington City?"

"I've come mainly to check on my mother's house in

92

Georgetown. Mother is presently in Virginia. There have been many changes in our lives since I resigned service with the U.S. government," he said with a deliberate pause, all the while watching Henry's face.

Philip shot an anxious glance at Henry, but Henry's eyes never left their cousin's face.

"I am presently serving in the *Confederate* Senate. You may have heard of my part in drafting the ordinance of secession at our Louisiana convention." He spoke rather smugly, cocking his head and raising an eyebrow at his cousins.

Henry's back stiffened. He pushed straight back in his chair, managing only to shake his head when words stuck in his throat. Philip looked nervously around to see if other diners were listening to the startling disclosure.

Thomas paused briefly, sipping from a glass of port. He noted their reaction with cold eyes, and continued confidently with even more surprising news.

"My mother just wrote from Virginia about our cousin Raphael's first high seas Navy command on the C.S.S. *Sumter*. I wouldn't be surprised if we hear great things about him one day."

This disclosure about both Semmes men was a double shock. Henry was suddenly glad he had not let Philip mention their travel plans. His eyebrows knit into a frown and he nervously ran his fingers through his hair.

Philip fidgeted with his ascot and looked again at Henry. There was a long, heavy silence broken by a waiter who came asking for their order.

"We will not be ordering lunch right now," Henry said brusquely. Rising from the table, he dismissed the waiter with a smile to conceal his agitation. He turned to Thomas Semmes. "Philip and I were supposed to meet our sister's fiancé here at the hotel, and since he doesn't appear to be in the dining room, I think we shall look for him in the lobby."

Casting a hasty glance at Philip, Henry thrust his hand out to his cousin. "Good to see you again. Enjoy your visit, Thomas."

Flustered and confused, Philip bowed. "Good day, er, uh . . . Senator. I'll tell Father you asked for him." He turned quickly to follow Henry out of the dining room.

As soon as they neared the lobby door, he wiped his forehead with a handkerchief. "Phew, Henry. I didn't know what to say in there after you cut me short about our trip to New Orleans. That was quick thinking to use Willie Warren as an excuse. Do you think Father knows about all this?"

Henry shook his head. "Well, he probably would not be as surprised as I was. At least, not about Thomas. Father may have heard about his resignation from someone in the government. It certainly shocked me, especially Raphael serving in the Confederate Navy! That branch of Father's family was always a mite confusing, and I don't mean just the way they spell their name."

"Just so, Henry. When I was younger, I didn't know we were related to them until Mother told me we just spell our name differently. There's a bunch more difference now. The Secesh side—wheweee! If Maria's grandfather *was* Thomas Jenkins's friend, it looks like our families have mighty different loyalties this time around."

Showers of sparks blew past the first passenger car where Henry and Philip rode. Burning chips were scattered in the wind, blown by the wood fire that powered the engine. Though the train rattled and shook, it was the news of the bombardment of Fort Sumter that rocked the passengers aboard the Orange and Alexandria cars leaving Fredericksburg the next day.

"I'll be thankful for a car at the back of the train when we change for the Virginia and Tennessee line," Philip said. "Father told me the train bowls along at thirty miles an hour. I feel so hot and dirty already, no telling what shape I'll be in when we reach Lynchburg. Do you think we'll get better seats, Henry?"

"You better be prepared for more of the same. It will be at least two days before we reach Tennessee and start the westward trek to Memphis. I worry more about the Southern attack on Fort Sumter and the stops we have to make in Virginia than I do about where our seats will be. No telling what this attack will provoke."

"By the looks of the station at Fredericksburg, it seems half of the Army of the South were headed for Washington City. I feel as if we are in enemy territory. Do you think Father knows about all this?"

"I'm sure he didn't anticipate these difficulties. The bombardment of Fort Sumter happened just as we arrived in Fredericksburg, but I doubt that news shattered him as much as the secession fever that is raging through the South. He is probably praying that his native Maryland doesn't join the Confederacy."

Henry was becoming more and more concerned about the danger that lay ahead on this journey. That night they stayed in a small hotel near the station. He managed to write a short letter to Maria.

Fredericksburg, Virginia
Dearest Maria,
Arriving here late tonight, we heard about the attack on Fort Sumter. There have been such wild crowds at the rail stations; I began to wish we were boarding a car to go back to Washington. Soldiers clamored to board the northbound

95

trains. Many had menservants carrying dress suits for them. They acted as excited as if they were going to a party. With four more stops in Virginia, the situation may get more hectic. I do not wish to alarm you, but I may not have the opportunity to write again. I ask that you pray for a safe journey for us. I will try to let you know when we arrive in New Orleans. My love and prayers attend you always.

Henry C. Simms

"Ro-a-noke, station is Roanoke," the conductor called as he moved through the cars. Henry prodded Philip to gather his belongings.

"We change lines in Bristol for Knoxville, so we better use this hour to find a place to eat a hearty meal, Philip. My stomach is grumbling fiercely."

They left the passenger car and attempted to move through the crowded station. Women and children surrounded them, moving across the platform toward a band playing "Dixie's Land" while a battery of soldiers boarded the cars of a northbound train.

Philip's head was turning in all directions as they tried to thread their way through the crowd. "Most of these fellas look like farm boys, Henry. No older than me, I'd wager. Where do you think they're headed?"

"Don't know," Henry said. "Looks like Confederate volunteers, eager for war, and anxious to be the first ones on the scene, wherever that may be."

As Philip looked back over his shoulder, he accidentally jostled a young girl carrying a basket of fruit toward the cars. Her straw hat fell off, and as she stooped to retrieve it, some of the fruit tumbled to the ground.

She apparently heard Henry's answer to Philip's question because she hollered at them in dismay. "Those soldiers are the best of the South, sir! And my brother is one of them, going to Harper's Ferry."

"I'm so sorry," Philip stammered as he stooped to pick up the fruit. When he placed it in her basket, the young woman rudely pushed him aside and moved off into the crowd.

Henry sensed his brother's embarrassment and placed a hand on Philip's shoulder. "Looks like everyone in town is out here, giving the boys a send-off," he said, steering his brother toward the edge of the platform. "This way, Philip. We just might get a seat in that tavern across the way."

The scene was the same from Bristol to Chattanooga. Weary of body and mind by the time they reached Memphis, Henry decided they would go no farther by train. He hired a hack to take them to the steamboat landing.

Chapter Twelve

Pastor Vanwerken scheduled a candlelight prayer service at Dutch Church. Maria walked with Jo down the center aisle following closely behind Sarah and their father. The Onderdonk box pew was third from the front on the left. It was near dusk and dim light filtered through the west stained-glass windows, enough for Maria to see Carolyn Grisham's rose-bedecked straw bonnet.

The Grisham family were seated across the aisle, not their usual place, but the church was crowded with parishioners come to hear the pastor pray for peace.

Maria had wanted to talk to Carolyn about the war, but her courage flagged every time she approached her father with a request to visit the Grishams. When Carolyn turned to pass candles to those behind her, she met Maria's eyes across the aisle. Maria cast her a furtive glance and Carolyn returned it with a smile and a nod.

Reverend Vanwerken began to preach about Christ's disciples. "The apostles' choice to follow Jesus is similar to our young men of today whose choice is to leave their homes and families to fight for a cause they believe in. Let us pray that our Father's boundless love and the grace of Christ will go with them."

Maria reached for Jo's hand and held tight.

The organist played "Blessed Assurance" as young boys moved along the aisle with tapers, lighting the candles of those persons sitting at the end of each pew. That person in turn lit the candle of the one next to him. Maria passed her flame to Jo's candle.

"Tonight, brothers and sisters, I ask you to reflect for a moment about peace. Peace in Hebrew does not mean merely freedom from trouble. It means all that makes for man's highest good. I would ask you to unite in prayer for God's peace, which passeth all understanding. Pray with me that the light of these candles will illuminate our hearts and minds."

Maria stared at her candle flame. The last words in Henry's letter played over and over in her mind: "My love and prayers attend you always." *'Tis I should be praying for you, dear Henry. Heavenly Father, please keep him in your loving hands.*

Jo nudged Maria to her feet. She was so deep in thought she was not aware the hymn had been announced. Jo's sweet soprano rang out. "Oh God, our help in ages past . . ."

Well into the second verse she heard her father's deep baritone, "Sufficient is your arm alone, and our defense is sure . . ." She caught her breath.

Pastor Vanwerken extended his hands in supplication. "Let us embrace hope, brothers and sisters, with our honest prayer for peace. Lord above, You kindle the stars. Let our candles be a symbol of your everlasting light to those gathered here in Christ's name. Bring light to their hearts. Praise and glory to you, our Lord and Savior. Amen."

The organist played a sending-forth hymn, and from the front, the congregation left their pews in groups of threes and fours. Candles flickered as families walked the long dim aisle. Father and Sarah walked beside Mr. and Mrs. Grisham, leaving Maria and Jo to link arms with Carolyn. As they extinguished the candles in the vestibule, Maria whispered to Carolyn, "We need to talk."

Maria could see her father speaking with Mr. Grisham in the twilight glow of the churchyard. She tugged Carolyn aside. "Papa can hardly say no to me in front of your parents if I invite you for supper, Carolyn. I have so much to tell you. Please say you will come!"

Chapter Thirteen

Carts, wagons, buggies and carriages vied for position to unload goods and passengers at the wharf. Young boys with pushcarts piled high with trunks and valises pushed their way through the crowds. Up and down the gangplanks, Negroes sang as they heaved heavy cargo from freight wagons onto the boats in Memphis Harbor.

Black smoke poured from the smokestacks of the largest paddleboat ready to depart for New Orleans. Henry and Philip hurried across the gangplank to board the *Memphis Queen* while a calliope played a jolly tune and flags fluttered from the masts of the magnificent steamer.

"I sure wish we had traveled all the way from Virginia aboard a boat like this," Philip said. "I'd be happy if I never rode another train in my lifetime."

"We may have to return by a steamship if the war situation worsens. Hopefully, Cousin Philip will know how to advise us when we get to New Orleans."

They walked up the stairway to the boiler deck and entered the main saloon. It was a long room that ran all the way to the stern of the boat. Crystal chandeliers glittered from high curved ceilings. Velvet draperies and gilded mirrors hung on the walls.

Henry and Philip gazed at a row of staterooms that ran along each side of the saloon. "I'm sure this will be set up for dining later on," Henry said. "Let's explore the rest of the boat before we find our stateroom. The gallery outside probably runs all around this deck."

Once outside, they looked upward at the third deck to see a short row of cabins with a pilothouse on top. A blast from the whistle drew their attention to the wharf. Roustabouts had just finished loading and stacking chunks of wood near the boilers when an order was called to cast off the mooring lines. Bells sounded in the engine room and the steamboat eased out into the river.

"Father was urging me to go abroad before this threat of war started, and now that I've seen the likes of this riverboat, I'm going to look into booking passage on a steamship to England as soon as we get back to Washington City," Philip said.

"First things first, Philip. Let's see how well you fare on this trip to New Orleans. The ticket clerk told me our first stop should be Vicksburg. We might just reach there by tomorrow at this time, unless this big old river has some other things in store for us before then."

On the hurricane deck later that day, they overheard the pilot talking to his apprentice.

"Water's riding high and deep this month. Not as much danger from reefs and sandbars except for the channels between the islands. Tonight's watch promises moonlight, so we're in luck."

Watching the river action by day made the next two days go quickly. There were two stops after Vicksburg, one at a wood yard and another at a small farm to take on crates of chickens.

Bells clanged for the river port, Natchez. Henry and Philip watched as boxes, barrels, and bales of cotton came aboard the *Queen* just before sunset.

Clouds formed into domes and banners of color blazing

across the sky, reflecting on the river's face. Henry's thoughts turned to Maria. There had been no opportunity to post a letter in Tennessee, but he planned to do that as soon as they arrived in New Orleans.

The riverboat made its last stop at Baton Rouge. Philip watched as a pretty young lady boarded on the arm of an elderly gentleman. "Look there, Henry. What a pretty one she is. I wonder where she is going in New Orleans."

"Yes, I see her, Philip, but, speaking of New Orleans, we should get back to our stateroom to gather our belongings. We have to look smart and be ready for the big city bright and early."

The levee at New Orleans swarmed with steamboats and ocean-going ships, busier and bigger by far than Memphis. The hum of labor as cargo was discharged and loaded, was like nothing Henry and Philip had ever heard or seen. Passengers threaded their way through a crowd of hawkers, food vendors and beggars toward a line of carriages.

Henry searched until he found an empty buggy for hire. He gave the driver a half-dollar to take them directly to the St. Louis Hotel. The driver's eyes grew round at the sight of the silver coin; it was only a short drive in Le Vieux Carre to Royal Street. The driver quickly piled their luggage in while Henry and Philip climbed into his open carriage.

Fascinated by the tangle of traffic and crowds of people, Philip's head swiveled from side to side along the busy street. "Henry, I just saw a sign for Chartres Street. Isn't that where our cousin lives?"

"Yes, but Cousin Philip's letter indicated there was a reason for our registering at the St. Louis."

The carriage pulled up to the entrance of a stately hotel. Tuscan columns and the simple, dignified front of the block-long hotel belied the grand appointments of its interior.

"Father says it's called the Exchange by people in New Orleans because the hotel has a magnificent rotunda which accommodates auctions of all sorts of property."

A porter gathered their baggage as Henry lowered his voice. "Our cousin may be conducting some business here for us, so we shouldn't have trouble getting a room. At any rate, we are very near Cousin Philip's home."

They were given a comfortable room on the second floor. Once inside, Henry pulled the bell cord for a maid. What they needed most was a bath and their clothes to be brushed and sponged.

"Bonjour, messieurs. Je suis Julie," said the maid upon entering the room. Henry gave a directive about their clothes while Philip's eyes followed the young woman moving gracefully about the room. Her head was wrapped in a bright red tignon, a striking contrast to her light brown skin and starched white apron. She filled a basin with warm water, placed linen towels and soap on the dresser, and curtsied at the door.

"I shall return quickly with your clothing, *messieurs.*"

Philip stared at the door as she closed it. "She definitely looks and sounds different from our Elizabeth back home," he said, shaking his head. "Did you notice she speaks two languages almost as well as I do one?"

"She's probably a free woman of color, maybe part Creole. You will probably see many differences in this city, and hear a lot more French spoken. Right now, I wish you would go ahead and bathe before she returns with our clothes. I need to do the same and I want to start a letter to Maria before we go to Cousin Philip."

Brick houses and shops enhanced with delicate wrought-iron grillwork lined the narrow street. Cousin Philip's home was a combined commercial and residential building. An iron-laced balcony skirted the second-floor rooms above a pilastered entry to the business at street level. At a side courtyard, a walled gate opened to a stairway curving up to the second floor. Henry pulled the cord on a small brass bell at the gate.

A servant opened the door as the brothers reached the top of the stairs. With a few words of introduction from Henry, the servant ushered them into a modest parlor.

"Well, let me look at you, young man," Cousin Philip said, holding his namesake at arm's length. "You have the Simms good looks all right," he said. "I'll wager you're a winner with the ladies."

He turned to Henry and thumped his shoulder, "Congratulations are in order, I hear, *Dr.* Simms." Henry's face beamed. "I'm eager to hear all the details of your journey."

"The steamboat down the Mississippi was the best part of the trip, sir," Philip said.

"I've no doubt of that. The rail lines have been terrible, but I don't imagine your father anticipated that, Henry."

"No, I'm sure not. Of course you've probably heard the news about Virginia being the eighth state to secede from the Union," Henry said. "It happened after we left Washington but it certainly complicated the first part of our trip."

"Yes, unfortunately the news spread quickly. You will soon see that Louisiana has war fever too, with companies drilling and preparing for the impending struggle. I should tell you right away, however, I am not one who favors being part of a Confederacy."

"You can't know how relieved we are to hear that," Henry said, unable to hide a smile of relief. "As Father no doubt wrote to you, his hopes are pinned on your ability to fill his government orders for woolen goods. The question is, are we going to be able to transport anything back to Washington?"

"I'm sure Edward couldn't foresee the difficulties you would encounter on the railroad, nor the problems we face here in our port, Henry. A steamship line from London brought our last shipment of wool earlier this month. If it were cotton you were seeking, I could be far more accommodating. We've been cut off from ocean trade by the blockading of the mouth of the river by a Federal ship."

"Father mentioned the auctions at the Exchange. Will we have any luck there?" Henry asked.

"I have managed to store a sizable quantity of wool in our warehouse, but whether we can find any more at the exchange is anyone's guess. Commodities are bound to get more and more scarce by summer's end, and prices are certain to go up. The sooner we move, the better."

"Father will be grateful, I'm sure, but what are your recommendations for transporting the goods, *if* we get them? My brother and I are ready to accompany any shipment, but I don't think the railroad is the answer, do you, sir?"

"Time will tell. I think not, but I'm not sure the river is, either. We may have to be inventive and disguise the shipment. Another difficulty will be the arrangements for your return home. It may take some time. But please, gentlemen, everything does not have to be decided today. Let's put our business talk aside until tomorrow."

He summoned the servant who had met them at the door. "Horace was about to go out for supplies to make a *ràgout de rògòon* for supper. That's a Creole version of kidney stew. Let me introduce you to mouthwatering local fare here at home and then we shall walk to see some of the sights of the French Quarter."

Philip raised his eyebrows and a smile reached his eyes in eager anticipation of a tour.

The next day, after a long, tense session in the hotel rotunda, Henry finished his letter to Maria.

Hotel St. Louis, New Orleans
30 April 1861
My dearest Maria,
I must try to be brief, if that is possible with all that I have to tell you. Our cousin is waiting downstairs to make certain this letter gets sent with the post. The trip by rail was long and frustrating. Every station was jammed with soldiers traveling north, so we took a steamboat from Tennessee to New Orleans. The timing was certainly not good, but the contracts that Cousin Philip will fill for Father are the redeeming result. Also the warm and gracious welcome we received! We saw a little of the city last night.

Today we attended auctions in the fascinating and beautiful rotunda of our hotel. One of them was a slave auction, which was very upsetting to me. Slaves were being sold like so many cattle. I witnessed a family being torn apart with no regard to a mother's cries. It was more than I could bear to watch, so I excused myself to retreat to our room while Philip stayed with our cousin to wait for the dry-goods auction.

This city is much different from New York, and far different from Washington City. New Orleans is preparing for war. Be thankful you are safe at Evergreen Park. Cousin Philip has been here for twenty-three years and speaks French as well as he does English. He has had an honorable and prosperous business career in one of the leading houses of trade. Although he never married, he is rich in family and friends.

You are so often in my thoughts, dear Maria. I wish that I could say when we will be together again. Let's hope that this does not become a summer of waiting. Our cousin insists we come stay with him until he can arrange a return for us. He may be able to secure passage on a mail steamship, which would bring us up the coast to New York! Perhaps then, I can ask your father for your hand in marriage.

*From New Orleans—*Je t'aime,

Ever yr devoted,

Henry

Chapter Fourteen

Maria lit oil lamps in the dining room as the deep violet of twilight gathered. Annie placed a vase of early lilacs on the table. Their sweet aroma scented the air.

"Shouldn't Carolyn be here by now?" Annie asked. "You know Papa gets upset when supper is not served on time."

"He will just have to be upset with Mr. Grisham then," Maria said. "Carolyn's father is driving her here, and I'm sure they will be here any minute. Besides, it's just the five of us tonight. Sarah took Andrew and Libby to Aunt Jane's for a visit, so Papa asked for a light supper."

Annie put her hands on her hips. "Well, Jo and I knew nothing about that. We took a long walk this afternoon and spent a lot of time gathering flowers."

"And they are lovely, Annie, but be a dear, now, and go down to Bridget. Ask her to hold off until six-fifteen, please, and then let Father know."

"Oh, all right, but you know Papa will not be pleased." The tall case clock struck the half hour past five as Annie ran downstairs to the kitchen. Maria went to the back parlor to watch from the window for the Grisham carriage. She retrieved a small leather-bound book she had left on the library table. An inscription on the flyleaf under *Poems by William Wordsworth*, was written in a firm masculine hand: *For Maria, from H.C.S.* She opened to a page marked with a ribbon.

She was a Phantom of Delight
When first she gleamed upon my sight . . .

A rap sounded at the door. Maria clutched the book to her breast and hurried to the door. "Carolyn, I didn't hear you drive up. Did your father leave already?" she asked, drawing her friend into the back parlor.

"Yes, he had to hurry back to Mama. So much has happened, Maria. Papa dares not leave my mother alone when I'm not in the house. I have so much to tell you. Do you suppose Martin will be able to bring me home later? I told my father to count on it."

"Of course he will take you home. I've much to tell you, too, but there's barely time before my father comes in for supper, and I really don't want to talk about Dr. Simms in Father's presence."

Maria took Carolyn's hat and gloves and pressed the book of poems into her hands. "This was a gift from Dr. Simms before he left for New Orleans. Just see the poem that's marked with ribbon, while I go check on Annie."

Maria opened the pocket doors, moving quickly through the front parlor to the windows. She looked out just as Annie and Horatio crossed the lawn that separated his office from their house. She called down the stairs to Jo and Bridget, then hurried back to Carolyn.

"Papa is coming now, and I really hope we can keep our conversation light for your sake, Carolyn. I'll try to steer Father away from any war talk, but please don't take offense if the subject of slavery comes up." She linked arms with Carolyn and brought her into the dining room.

Jo was helping Bridget arrange platters of cold chicken, ham, cheese, and bread, as Annie and Father entered the dining room.

"Well, well, I see your guest has arrived, Maria. Welcome, Miss Grisham," Horatio said. "Please sit, everyone. No need for formality tonight, my dears. I'm afraid I must get back to the office right after supper. Some pressing business must be finished."

Maria breathed a sigh of relief. "Jo made a special dessert for us tonight, Papa, Annie's favorite, blancmange."

"Maria is teasing me, Papa, because Jo had to take over the pudding. I can't ever get that pudding to set when I make it. Either that, or it gets burnt."

"No matter, my Miss Anna. The pudding will taste good, thick or thin, but I may have to ask you to save mine for later. Please pass the meat and cheese, Jo."

Everyone ate in silence, except Annie, chattering between bites about a sampler Jo was helping her with. Maria was relieved that her father seemed distracted and was treating Caroline pleasantly after all. Her eyes widened when Horatio's voice rose, interrupting Annie.

"How are your parents, Miss Grisham?"

"My father is well, but Mama is suffering with the vapors. Nothing serious, of course—that's what the doctor says. I personally think she's just plain worried about our relatives in the South. My aunt Persephone is ailing, and being ancient as she is, and a little craz—" Caroline's mouth suddenly pursed in a tiny O. She stopped and took in her breath, her eyes flicking from Maria to Judge Onderdonk.

"Excuse me. My aunt Pers is in her dotage, and Mama wants so much to see her once more before she passes on to Glory."

"If the train service were not so abominable, sounds like a trip south would be in order for your father." Horatio cocked one eyebrow and looked steadily at Carolyn. "But, of course, there's that trouble with the soldiers and the rioters at Baltimore."

The room grew suddenly quiet. Caroline cleared her throat. "Well, sir, my father plans to take Mama as far as Baltimore, anyway. Our cousins will meet the train and take her to Fairleigh Plantation. Father's office is much too busy just now for him to stay in Maryland, so he will take the return cars back to Brooklyn."

"Speaking of being busy, I'm afraid I shall have to excuse myself now, ladies. I'll be in the office if you need me, Maria, and don't forget to save me some blancmange. Enjoy your supper, everyone."

Jo served the dessert as soon as their father left the house. "Mmm, this is really good, Jo," Annie said after her first mouthful. "Please promise you will help me again, next time I make it?"

"Only if you will allow me to take your crooked alphabet stitches out and start your sampler over," Jo said. "You want Sarah to be pleased with your gift, don't you? And you know she has a very judicial eye when it comes to cross-stitch."

"Judicial? Do you mean like Papa is a judge?"

Jo laughed, ruffling her fingers through Annie's hair. "You might say that, Annie. Come with me to the back parlor, and we can work on your sampler at the library table."

As Jo tugged Annie down the hall, Carolyn produced Maria's small book of poems from her reticule. "I didn't think you meant to leave this in the parlor. I barely had time to read the poem you marked. It's a lovely one, Maria."

Color rose in Maria's cheeks and her eyes sparkled. "I was so anxious about Father's table conversation that I forgot about my book. But *I* didn't mark the poem, Carolyn. When the book arrived, the ribbon marked that page." She raised her eyebrows and cocked her head. "So I guess it was meant to be a message to me from Dr. Simms."

"Well, I do declare. A romance is really blossoming then?"

"Yes, but I'm afraid it will be a long-distance romance for a while. Doctor doesn't know when, or how, he and his brother will get back from New Orleans. But when they, do," Maria lowered her voice to a whisper, "he plans to ask Father for my hand in marriage."

Caroline squealed with delight until Maria shushed her with a finger to her lips. "Only Jo and Andrew know, Carolyn, and I'd like to keep it that way. You will keep my secret, won't you?"

"Of course I will, but why is it you want no one to know?"

"Because, when Henry does return, there's a possibility he may volunteer his services to the government as a surgeon. Papa would never give his blessing if that happens."

"Oh, Maria, I'm happy he wants to marry you, but it would be perfectly horrible if your father would not approve. Doesn't he like Henry?"

"Yes, I think he does, and I think he respects the Simms family too, but they have very different ideas about the war and . . . and slavery, and especially about President Lincoln."

"Well, I should have guessed as much, at least about Henry's feelings about slavery. Else why would he have been at Queen Street? I have something to tell you about myself that is kind of like what Dr. Simms may do. At least it's related."

"Whatever do you mean?"

"My father showed me an article that was printed in the *New York Times* this month. It was a call to women to attend a meeting at Dr. Elizabeth Blackwell's Infirmary in New York."

"Did you say *Dr.* Elizabeth?"

"Indeed I did. That's the clinic we heard about at the Friends Meeting House, remember? Papa says Dr. Blackwell has long been an advocate for women doctors, since she is the very first American woman to become one."

"I wonder if Dr. Simms has heard of her?"

"What I wonder is whether Dr. Simms would approve of female doctors at all. Most men don't, you know. Dr. Blackwell was clever enough to see that her infirmary be advised by a board of prominent male physicians in New York. Your Henry Simms would do well to lean on the side of progress, and find out what's going on with people like Dr. Blackwell."

"Yes, I suppose that's so, but he's not *my* Henry Simms yet, and we haven't even talked about his medical practice or serving in the war. I only know about the possibility of that happening because Andrew hinted about it. Besides, I don't see how you fit into all of this, Carolyn."

"You have to understand what's happening since the rebellion started. Dr. Blackwell and her sister are trying to manage relief efforts for the soldiers, much like we heard about at the Friends lecture. Except these supplies will be gathered for the soldiers, not the infirmary."

"I don't understand how it all will come about."

"That's what I'm trying to tell you. The doctors want to organize women around the country into a central association. It's to be called the Women's Central Association of Relief. I think that is so exciting."

"It sounds something like the Ladies Military Blue Stocking Association. Sarah and I joined that effort to knit stockings for the soldiers. Papa couldn't very well object when we said that our mother always encouraged us in our pursuits for the less fortunate."

"Good, Maria. Women *can* do something to help, and it seems that a lot of women think the same because the first meeting held at the infirmary was so well attended that Dr. Blackwell is calling another one at Cooper Union. It's to-

114

morrow, and I plan to attend."

"Goodness sakes. All those women came together to collect supplies for the soldiers?"

"That's only part of what they will do. According to the article in the paper, they intend to appeal directly to the U.S. Army's Medical Department. They want to train women as nurses for the hospitals and battlegrounds. That's what I meant when I said my plan was something like what Dr. Simms may do."

"Do you mean that you would . . . that your father would actually allow you to—"

"Yes, and yes," Caroline said, leaning across the table to grasp Maria's hand. "I intend to register to be trained as a nurse for the military."

01 May 1862
Dear Maria,

The meeting at Cooper Union was crowded with women. There was hardly room to stand and hear, but the exciting result is, I have good news! I want you to be the first to know that I have been accepted into the nurse training program and more than likely will be sent to Washington City before summer's end.

I went to register at Dr. Blackwell's Infirmary the day following the meeting. If not for Papa's letter of reference, I would not have been accepted. They were looking for much older women and you know I'm only two years older than you. Papa vouched for my ability and sent a generous contribution for the cause. Of course, Mama hasn't been told, and probably will not be told *until my father has her safely at Fairleigh Plantation. She is determined to go south, so my parents leave tomorrow for Baltimore. I begin my training the very next day! I won't have much time to write again, so I ask for your prayers,*

Maria, that I can be strong in spirit and learn quickly. I will miss you.

With affection,
Carolyn

Evergreen Park
May 1862
Carolyn seems to be able to bend the rules to suit her will, but I always borrow trouble when I try the same. If only I could trade places with her. Of course Papa would never agree to anything like that. I feel almost useless here. Mother would understand my wanting to do something brave and useful for the war. It seems I'm destined to wait and worry.
Maria O.

Chapter Fifteen

"I talked to Cousin Philip while you were off with your friend from the British Shipping Company," Henry said. "We're going to leave on the June mail boat after all."

"What kind of boat is it?"

"It's a steam sloop bound for the Gulf Coast of Florida. The boat's pilot is sick, so we're bunking in his cabin."

Philip looked puzzled. "What about the wool?"

"Cousin disguised it in cylinders marked 'rugs,' and stashed it in the hold. We leave day after tomorrow."

When the brothers stepped into the mail boat's cramped cabin, Philip made a sour face. The pilot's quarters had only one bunk. A sagging canvas hammock had been rigged, taking up the rest of the cabin's open space.

"Still thinking about sailing abroad, Philip?" Henry teased. "Don't worry, we'll take turns," he said, pointing at the bunk. "At least you'll be sleeping in luxury half the time."

Philip nodded and dropped his valise on the bunk. "I'll go first and make sure it's all right," he said, grinning slyly at Henry.

"Welcome aboard the U.S.S. *Belle*," Captain Pease said, when the brothers stepped into the wheelhouse. "We'll be putting in at Tampa to take on and deliver mail, then with the wind behind us at first light, we sail for Key West."

"Our cousin told us that once we leave the Keys, the *Belle* sails in and out of major ports along the Atlantic seaboard all the way to Halifax. When do you think we might reach Baltimore, Captain?" Philip asked.

"Good question, young man, but no easy answer, to be sure. The *Belle* is a barque-rigged steam sloop, ya see . . . She can sail under canvas, but the ship's steam engine can push her along at fourteen knots. That will put us in good stead along the Florida Straits and nor'east into the Atlantic." He paused and rubbed his chin whiskers. "Barring foul weather, wild currents, shoals and reefs, that is."

The captain looked from Philip's puzzled face to Henry's serious one. "All that, and add blockade runners, privateers, and Union boats chasing after them. A party just can't rightly predict, yuh see?"

Captain Pease drew deeply on his pipe and chuckled softly at Philip's worried look. "Never ya mind, lad. No need to give trouble a shape until it casts its shadow. When we pass the Keys and sail nor'east to Cape Florida, we should be able to steam along from New River to Savannah, with four stops in . . . oh, 'bout ten days. I've done it with smooth sailing in a few less, but there's no telling this time round. I've not made the Straits run without a pilot, and I'd be reaching for the wind on the time we'll get to Baltimore."

Brisk winds served them well under sail down the Gulf Coast. The *Belle* passed offshore, south of the Dry Tortugas, dropping anchor in Key West Harbor without incident.

Fort Taylor and the city of Key West were in Union hands. The port of call was a short overnight, time enough to deliver provisions and take on mail and water.

Philip tried to sleep in the narrow bunk, but his stomach was queasy. The creaking sounds didn't help, and the roll of the boat made him dizzy when he closed his eyes. "Did you listen to those stories the crew told during supper?" he asked Henry. "Pirate ships, Indian raids, and shipwrecks. It's sure scary enough. Do you suppose they were just yarns?"

"I think they were true about those days they spoke of, but I'm more concerned about tomorrow with the bad weather forecast Captain Pease told us about. Try to sleep, Philip. We may need our wits about us before dawn."

The mail boat pushed cautiously along the Florida Straits in foul weather before dawn. At first light, on his first trip topside, Henry watched as the sloop steamed slowly past the Keys in fog and rain. More wind and the roll and pitch of the boat sent Henry on deck for the second time to empty Philip's slop bucket. "It's a wonder I'm not seasick myself," he muttered, "watching him retch most of the night."

Now there was a high sea running with a fresh gale shrieking in from the south. He carefully made his way, holding tight to a lifeline the boatswain had rigged along the foredeck.

The sea heaped up in high waves breaking into spindrift, making visibility poor. The mail boat rolled on a course north by northeast, passing the upper Keys' shadowy forms, barely visible amidst massive green waves that bullied onto the deck.

The crewmen were sending down the sails, securing them on deck to reduce windage aloft. Henry could see two white lights starboard, shrouded in spray and fog. The *Belle* was approaching a lightship riding at anchor in the roiling sea. He heard the captain shout from the wheel, "Attempting to pass close aboard. Stand fast."

Struggling to pull himself along the lifeline, Henry heard a bell sounding, faint above the shriek of the wind. The bow lifted and smashed down in an explosion of sea spray. A shattering, cracking sound came in chorus with the wind and a tremendous jolt threw Henry off his feet. The bucket flew into the air and his body slid and slammed into the bulkhead. Searing pain tore through him before everything went black.

Henry awoke in his berth in the dimly lit cabin. Black spots danced before his eyes when he tried to focus on Philip standing over him. The air was steamy with a foul stench of vomit.

"Thank God you're awake, Henry. That jolt when we were thrown against the lightship scared me out of my misery, and the next thing I knew the first mate was carrying you in here. I haven't been seasick since."

Henry gently touched his jaw and winced.

"Nothing's broken there, Henry, but you've one beastly lump and cuts on the side of your head. The first mate says to lie still as possible. He's set your leg in a splint."

"My leg?" Henry's hand probed along the length of his body. He groaned when he reached his left knee.

"Your leg hit a stanchion when you slid along the deck. Ship's mate says it may have slowed you enough to save your life, hitting the hull as hard as you did."

"Good Lord," Henry said, gingerly feeling the bandages wound around his forehead and touching his face from ear to chin. "For all the cracking sound I heard, it's a wonder my teeth aren't all broken."

"What you heard was the shattering of lamp chimneys on a lightship's foremast. Captain says the *Belle*'s stern was thrown on a giant wave, into the side of the lightship. No serious damage, other than the lights on that ship. I think he called her Carrysfort Reef. We've weighed anchor near the lightship. Captain Pease means to wait out the storm before heading up the east coast of Florida."

"Can't say I'd argue with that, but I'm afraid I shall be my own worst patient." Henry tried to reach for the side of the bunk to ease the blanket away from his leg. "Can't stand this weight on it," he said.

"You'd best lie still, Henry. I'll take the blanket. It may be a long wait, but for a change, looks like *I'll* be tending to *you*."

Two days later the mail boat left Carrysfort Reef. After mail stops at Miami and New River on the Florida coast, she chugged north under steam, headed for Savannah. Between that city and Charleston, they were safely guarded by Federal gunboat patrols in Port Royal Sound. Captain Pease eased the *Belle* into the Union-held base, Hampton Roads, for fuel, food supplies, and mail. Next stop, Baltimore.

More than two months had passed since their departure from Washington City, leaving Henry and Philip little prepared for the pandemonium that greeted them at the docks in Baltimore.

"Hold on Henry," Philip said. "Lean on that cane that Matey made for you and wait right here with the 'rugs.' You've been guiding me around since we left Washington. It's high time I took my turn. I'll find a hack to take us to the train depot."

Cars going south at the Baltimore rail station were filled. Soldiers, citizens, stores and supplies; every coach occupied.

While Philip sent a wire to their father, Henry bribed the cargo master to stash their precious cargo of wool in the baggage car. Another silver piece, and a sympathetic porter found a seat for Henry on the last car headed for the capitol. Philip squeezed in amongst the less fortunate travelers standing toe to toe at the end of the car.

Chapter Sixteen

Maria turned the letter over and broke the seal as soon as she saw the postmark, Washington City. The tension-filled months of waiting for Henry's return had seemed endless to Maria. But this was not a letter from Dr. Simms.

30 July 1862
On train en route to Washington
Dear Maria,
 Weeks have flown by with no opportunity to see you or let you know about my training program. Regulations and more regulations! Hygiene, the dressing of wounds, the use of tinctures and medications—even the clothing we must wear, and the food and stimulants we must be prepared to give the soldiers. Duties I never dreamed would be mine will soon become real.

 I know there still exists a prejudice against "refined ladies" working in military hospitals. But at last, our government has given military recognition to female nurses, where heretofore nurses were all men! I am being sent to the Superintendent of Women Nurses in Washington City, a Miss Dix. From there, I will either be located in a military hospital or—imagine this—I could be assigned to work aboard a hospital ship! The Army has turned over some passenger steamers to the Sanitary Commission for evacuation of wounded soldiers from the peninsula to the city hospitals.

We will soon arrive at the depot, so I must say good-bye. I will try to send word as time permits, and let you know where to write to me. I would ask that you keep me in your prayers, Maria. Something tells me I will need them.

Ever your trusting friend,
Carolyn

Chapter Seventeen

Virginia saw the hack drive up to their door "They are here," she called out to her father as she flung open the front door.

"God have mercy, you're a welcome sight," she said, watching as Henry clumsily tried to step down from the hack. "What's happened to you? You look almost as bad as some of the patients in our house."

"Patients? What do you mean, patients?" Henry asked as he tried to walk up the steps without leaning too heavily on his cane.

"Well, our house looks like a hospital ward. Father has given accommodations to six wounded soldiers, until quarters can be obtained for them in one of the hospitals. Your bedroom has cots set up with soldiers in them. The two most severely wounded are in Father's study. But, Henry, you haven't told me what's happened to you. What's wrong with your leg?"

"There was a storm at sea and Henry took a bad fall," Philip said, coming up to give Ginny a hug. He pointed at Henry's leg. "It's broken."

Henry gave Philip an exasperated look and shook his head. "My leg is mending. Please don't make anything more of it, Philip, for Father's sake. Let's just get inside, Ginny. Please send Massie out to bring our cargo to the storage room."

Edward Simms was wringing his hands and pacing the parlor when Henry limped into the room with Philip. He rushed to their side, putting an arm around each of his sons. He looked down at Henry's cane. "You didn't tell me you were injured, Henry. Now I feel even worse about this whole mess we're in."

"No, no, Father. It's nothing serious. Just a mishap on the steamer. Proves I wasn't meant to be a sailor, that's all. I'll be fit in no time."

"I'm so grateful you are home and for what you did, but grievously sorry I put you through it. Who would ever have believed it would come to this? As sad as I am for you, what you see here in our home is the result of a dreadful loss to the nation—a terrible battle at Manassas Junction, Virginia."

Edward did not take heed of his sons' shocked faces. He continued to speak as though he had memorized the *Intelligencer* newspaper. "Our Union Army advanced on Confederate troops stationed at Manassas, but Rebel reinforcements came and our boys had to retreat toward the city.

"Whole processions of wounded came in, and hospitals are set up everywhere. Strangers from the North come flooding in to the city every day, looking for their loved ones." His voice broke and Philip led him to a chair.

Henry put his hand to his father's brow. "Please, Father, you shouldn't excite yourself so."

Edward looked up, a pretense of calm returning to his face. "Oh, how I wished you were here with us, Henry. I'm all right, but your mother has been unwell. Virginia has put in countless hours tending the soldiers while Georgiana and Edwina care for your mother and help Elizabeth run the house. We need you." He turned to Philip. "Both of you."

As much as he wished to be on his way to Brooklyn, Henry knew, that for now, it was out of the question.

Virginia Simms brought a tray to the bedside of a young

Union soldier in Henry's and Philip's room. She stood stock-still, gazing at the cot the boy lay on. A torn scrap of cloth with a canton of blue stars and faded red bars was spread in sharp contrast across the crisp white bed sheet.

The soldier had unfolded the tattered, blood-stained flag over the empty space left by his missing leg.

He looked up at Virginia, then down at the flag. His hand rested on the canton. "When my leg got blown off I captured this flag, an' I wish fer my ma to have it."

Virginia's heart felt as though it would burst. She hastily put the tray down. "I'm sure your mother would be proud to have it," she murmured.

Virginia watched as the soldier's fingers traced the ragged edge of the Rebel flag. "Would it be too much trouble, Miss, to send my journal and this here flag to my ma in Ohio? I wouldn't want to worry her none, so I'd be mighty grateful if you could write a letter for me. I just want to tell her my wounds are healin' and I'm fixin' to be sent home real soon."

He turned toward Virginia and sudden tears fell from his eyes, making a dark blob on the cover of a small leather journal next to his pillow. "Even if it ain't so," he said, picking up his journal and offering it to Virginia. "Her address is in the back."

Virginia took the small book, and started to fold the battered Stars and Bars. "Of course I will, and I'll pray that your message comes true quicker than you think."

Later that day, she did write the letter for the soldier, but first, with only a slight bit of guilt, she read some of the passages from his journal.

April 16
Hiked thirteen miles and pitched tents. Struck our tents and marched eight miles to Leeks farm to camp. Went to a

farmhouse with sugar and shortening and had four cakes
baked by a Secesh lady whose sons were in the Reb Army!
Made our beds with Secesh feathers. Reveille at two a.m.
Moved back ten miles to old church. Rebs shelled our regi-
ment. Charged Rebel skirmishers. Slept in thicket on a hill.
Passed battlefield of yesterday. Our boys burying dead.

April 20
Camped on south side of river. Took baths, gobbled young
porker. Band played "Yankee Doodle" at night near our
line. Rebel lines are twenty-forty rods distant. Our pickets
ceased firing. Swam across the river and traded coffee for
tobacco with the Rebs. Sang songs around our campfire.
Pretty soon the Rebs across river joined in, and "Lorena"
could be heard clear down to the next unit.

Virginia was preparing to wrap the small package at her
father's desk when the study door opened and Henry came to
her side.

Her tears came unheeded, wetting Henry's face as he
kissed her cheek. She held up the ragged Rebel flag, and
blurted out the soldier's story before Henry could ask what
was wrong.

"He's asked me to send them to his ma with a letter. I read
a bit of his journal," she said, as she tucked her letter inside.
"They are fighting one another one day, and singing and bar-
tering goods the next. It's so hard to understand this war,"
she said, shaking her head.

"I can understand the boy's feelings. He fought for
freedom under our Union flag. I'm feeling a sense of duty to
our flag, too. My time spent with these soldiers has convinced
me. As soon as I've had a little more experience, I'm going to
serve the best way I know how, Ginny. If the war keeps on I'll

offer my services as a surgeon."

Ginny put her hands on his shoulders. "I understand, and I think Father will be proud if you do volunteer. But what of Maria?"

He heaved a sigh and shook his head. "That's the hard part. I believe she will bide with me in this, but I doubt her father will."

Henry's leg was mending. Happy to walk with only a slight limp, he was relieved to let Philip take his place helping his sisters with the soldiers and lending a hand to his father at the bank. He felt badly about leaving his mother. Although her condition remained the same, she had tremendous spirit and faith, never thinking of herself. She urged Henry to get to his practice, back to New York. It was time to tell his father his plan.

"I hope to develop a good start with my medical practice in Brooklyn as soon as I return to New York. Of course, you knew that, Father, but then, if the war continues and I'm needed, I feel honor bound to come back and report to the Surgeon General for duty. I'd like to volunteer as a contract surgeon. I hope that's not disheartening to you."

"There's no doubt you'll be needed, son. After watching you with the poor lads here in the house, I guessed as much. I prayed it wouldn't be necessary, that this war would end and—" Edward raised his hands in a hopeless gesture.

"We are all praying for that, Father, but it doesn't seem likely any time soon. Promise you will let me know if Mother's condition worsens?"

Edward nodded. "Your mother will miss your loving care, but let's hope that if what you intend to do comes to pass, you will be sent near enough home to come see us."

Chapter Eighteen

Martin drove Horatio and Maria to meet the late afternoon stage. Maria's lips curved into a radiant smile when Henry alighted from the stage and reached for her hands. He held her with his eyes as steadily as if his arms were holding her close. Their eyes spoke the words that their hearts could not.

She held on to his hand as Horatio thumped Henry's shoulder in a hearty greeting. She did not let go as Henry climbed into the carriage behind her. Henry squeezed her hand and tried to talk to her, but the judge plied him with countless questions during the short drive to Evergreen Park.

"Tell me about this leg injury Maria mentioned. How will you manage in your office?"

"It's nothing of concern now, sir. Just a little lameness until it's fully mended."

"Maria tells me you were successful with your father's quest in New Orleans. I certainly commend you for that, but I cannot condone the use that will be put to the wool you brought back. This buffoon they've chosen to lead our country has led us into a terrible conflict. I feel an allegiance to the preservation of the Union, but not at the cost of a war."

Horatio leaned forward, spreading a hand on each knee. His eyes narrowed as he spoke slowly in a low, conspiratorial tone. "Was your New Orleans cousin helping out of loyalty to your father, or was he really in favor of secession?"

Henry shot a quick glance at Maria. "If you speak of my

father's cousin Philip, he stands for preserving the Union. So of course he helped us, without question." He paused, rubbing his side-whiskers. "But I think you should know that another, more distant, cousin of my father actually drafted the secession bill for Louisiana."

Horatio was suddenly silent. Maria looked from her father to Henry. *Why ever did he say that?* After a long pause, Maria broke the silence. "But Dr. Simms, who is this cousin you speak of?"

"He is Thomas Jenkins Semmes, resigned from the U.S. government and presently Confederate Senator of Louisiana."

Martin reined in the horse.

Horatio tilted his head back as though he was searching his memory. "Thomas . . . Jenkins . . . Semmes." His words rattled off the carriage top in slow time with the horses' hooves. The carriage rolled to a stop.

Maria's startled gaze roamed from Henry to her father.

"Can that possibly be a relative to the Captain Jenkins my father befriended during the War for Independence?" Horatio asked. "The captain was a Southerner, I'm sure."

"Yes, sir, I believe this cousin of mine is the grandson and namesake of your father's long-time correspondent, Captain Thomas Jenkins," Henry said. "Thomas's mother was the captain's daughter."

Maria was engulfed in a swirl of conflicting emotions. She tried to read her father's face. How could she know if his reaction was approval, disapproval, or whether he was simply shocked? Horatio exited the carriage, followed by Henry.

She managed a smile when she took Henry's hand to step down from the carriage. As they walked up the steps of the veranda, she whispered to him. "You remembered what I told you about my grandfather's correspondent, the sea captain. *I*

130

am happy to think that Grandfather Joseph sort of links us together." She paused to search Henry's eyes. "Through Thomas Jenkins, I mean. But I wonder if Papa will feel the same."

They entered the house in a swirl of happy greetings. Evergreen Park seemed a world away from the chaos Henry had left in the South. As soon as Maria was out of earshot, he sought a quiet moment alone with Horatio.

"I hope it comes as no surprise, sir, that I wish to ask for Maria's hand in marriage—a betrothal, that is. I'm sure you have guessed my feelings for her, but I must be forthright with you. You see, sir, these past two weeks, helping with the wounded soldiers at my father's home has convinced me that I should do more with my skills. If the war continues much longer, I will volunteer my services to the Union as a surgeon."

Horatio looked like a thundercloud. "Hell's fire, young man! If you are asking for my blessing for a wedding, I'll not agree to your marrying my daughter and going off to war."

"I don't mean right away, sir. I intend to gain some experience in my office at Brooklyn first. A betrothal is what we—"

"If I were your father, I'd never approve of your doing service for Lincoln's Army."

There was a long pause. Horatio's eyes softened a little as he looked into Henry's shocked face.

"But I'm sure your father doesn't feel as I do about Lincoln, or the war. I have nothing but respect for your family. Perhaps I will be able to welcome you *someday* into the family, but any engagement, or wedding plan, will simply have to wait."

Henry's shoulders sagged. "My sentiments, *almost,*" he said, "about the waiting for a wedding, that is."

Henry's confidence waned with his next thought. They

had both wanted a betrothal. Explaining to Maria about her father's answer would be difficult enough, never mind what his plans were for duty on the battlefields.

When Dr. Simms was not with his new patients in Brooklyn, he spent glorious Sunday afternoons courting Maria in the "country," as Henry liked to think of Evergreen Park.

Judge Onderdonk saw to it that the strict rules governing meetings between single men and women were closely followed. Henry and Maria were never without the company of one or more of her sisters. Horatio made certain of that.

Out of respect for Maria's father, Henry kept his silence about the war. Neither could he bring himself to speak to Maria about his plans. War was on everyone's minds. It hung over them like a dark gray cloud. Although Maria did not speak of it, she guessed that Andrew's suspicions were right. She tried desperately to hold back time.

Chapter Nineteen

"A letter came from my sister Georgie with some surprising news. Actually, the events are disheartening for my father, more than the rest of the family, but nonetheless surprising. Do you remember my telling you how my brother, Philip, was so enthusiastic about the steamboat we took to New Orleans?"

"Yes, you said it made him want to travel abroad on a steamship," Maria said.

"Well, he met a fetching young lady aboard the boat the morning we arrived in New Orleans. Turns out that Miss Rhoads was from Alexandria, and since we returned home from New Orleans, he has been courting her. Father is not too enthusiastic about that, but now there is a new scheme of Philip's which has Father more agitated and anxious than ever."

"Well, it's no small surprise about Philip's lady friend, but why should his courting her be disheartening to your father?"

"Because, her family are Secessionists, and the young lady's brother is fighting with the Confederate Army. Be that as it may, Philip is now talking about taking a job with a British shipping firm."

"A *British* shipping firm?"

"It's a long story, but I'll try to make it brief. While Philip was in New Orleans, he met a British investor named Charles Symington. The wealthy Englishman took a liking to Philip.

That much, I remember, and I've pieced together the rest of the story from bits told me by Georgie."

"Your brother Philip has always seemed to be Georgie's favorite. I can't imagine her being anything but happy for him. Did she tell you so?"

"Well, yes, but that's getting ahead of the story. This fellow, Symington, is principal owner of a shipping syndicate that is making huge profits on luxury cargoes shipped from England to America. Through correspondence, Philip was offered a position with the syndicate."

"But surely your father can't be upset that Philip has an opportunity to have a good position far away from this horrible war?"

"I don't think you understand my father or the whole of it yet, Maria. Syndicate-owned ships bring cargo through Nassau for runs to the port of Wilmington, North Carolina. Their luxury cargoes bring large profits by auction, and the ships return with cotton for the British market. Philip was hired as an owner's representative, to sail back and forth from Liverpool to Nassau with cargo."

"I still can't see how that taints his loyalty."

"Because, once the ships reach the islands, Philip will supervise the transfer of cargo from ocean freighters to blockade runners. That cargo ends up in the holds of ships selling to the Confederacy. That is why Father fears Philip is changing his loyalty."

Henry paced back and forth. "He reacted bitterly to Philip's decision to take this position. He knows that sympathy for the Confederacy runs strong in the islands. The port of Nassau is a notorious nest of Rebel sympathizers."

"But your own relatives are divided in their loyalties. Eddie wrote to me about your father's cousin, Raphael Semmes, being heralded by the Confederate Navy for his gallant capture of our Union ships!"

"I know. Father told me about it. One good thing is my sister Georgie stands steadfastly by Philip. She's fiercely loyal to him. She gave Philip a parting gift, a silver pocket compass. Attached to it by a silver chain is a holy medal of Our Lady, Star of the Sea. Georgie firmly believes that if the compass doesn't show him the way, the Mother of God surely will. I wish I had her faith, Maria. I really don't know what to do about my father."

"We can pray. I think that all we can do is pray that this war will end, and God will bring us all together soon."

On the heel of Georgie's letter, an urgent telegram came to Henry's office:

> *Can you arrange to come home to consult with Dr. May about Mother? She is failing. Since Philip left, Father has become very depressed.*

Henry left on the next morning train to Washington. When he arrived, his sisters tried to prepare him for the worst.

"We didn't tell you that Philip left because at the time we didn't know how serious Mother's condition was," Georgie said.

Eddie clung to Henry's arm. "Dr. May has been making weekly visits. He gives Mother laudanum to ease her pain, but there is little to be done for the tumor growing in her body." Her voice broke. She gulped a sob.

Virginia put her arms around both of them. "At first, Father didn't want us to send for you. Mother doesn't have long, Henry, and we thought you should be here for her, but also for Father. Philip's leaving broke his spirit. Maybe you can reason with him. We've tried over the past weeks, but he turns a deaf ear."

Henry was furious with his brother. At the same time, he was sorrowful to think that Philip would probably never see their mother again. He found his father in the study, sitting at his desk, staring out the window.

Edward didn't rise for his usual greeting. He merely clasped Henry's hand in both of his. "I'm glad you are here, son. Almost two months have passed without a word from your brother. Nor can he be summoned."

"But Georgie tells me that Philip actually left for England long before Mother's illness turned serious," Henry said. "He probably didn't realize—"

Edward raised upturned hands in front of his face, shook his head and stood abruptly. "Just come to your mother's side, son." He took Henry's arm. "You are here, and that's a blessing."

Henry sat at his mother's bedside intermittently for two days. Before dawn on the third day, Mary Catherine Simms died in her sleep

January 1862
390 C Street, Washington City
My dear Maria,

A telegram from my sisters prompted my hasty departure for home, without time to send word to you. Nor have I had an opportunity to tell you of the grief surrounding me these past ten days. When I arrived here, my mother was gravely ill. There was nothing to be done but comfort her in her last hours. A funerary wreath hangs upon our door. Mother died three days ago. I feel certain she rests in our Heavenly Father's arms.

Philip's absence compounded my father's grief, and I shall tell you about that at another time. Mother's wake and funeral

mass drew crowds of mourners, a tribute to the good and loving person that she was. I will stay on a few extra days to try to help my father through this, but I must get back to my patients before the month ends. My heart and hands are full. Please keep us in your prayers,

Ever your devoted,

Henry

The thoughts played over and over in Henry's mind on the train trip back to New York. *The more I think about it, the more I think Father may be right. Philip's job with the shipping line could be serving the Southern cause. It's hard to believe that the prospects of getting rich masked what this job is really about. I would think he'd know that blockade runners are a reckless lot of profiteers!*

Henry's new practice of medicine left him precious little time to travel by stage to Evergreen Park. He could only manage to spend a few hours with Maria on Sunday afternoons.

On the last day of February, a colleague called at Henry's Court Street office.

"The Surgeon General of New York is trying to organize an auxiliary corps of surgeons to go to Washington, Henry. The government really needs more contract surgeons. I know you haven't had much time to establish a thriving practice, but I think you should sit for the examination. If an older fellow like me can pass it, you surely can."

"My practice is growing, but not in the direction I had hoped for. I can honestly say I need no prodding to make this change."

Henry passed the oral and written examination in New York City, and agreed to be ready to leave with a contingent of doctors by the end of March.

Unfortunately, there was no opportunity to be alone with Maria to tell her his plans. The whole Onderdonk family gathered in the parlor when Henry came to call.

Before Maria could react, her father seized the moment.

"Dr. Simms, I believe you've made a foolish choice. With more and more doctors leaving for the military, your practice here could become very lucrative. I'm sure you know that the government will pay you poorly. Can you actually see yourself under horrible conditions in military hospitals or on the battlefields? From what I hear you will be complained of more than complimented by the regular Army surgeons."

"I'm not looking for compliments, sir. I'm going in full faith that the Union cause is a noble one. My time in Washington convinced me that I must take my turn to serve, and nothing can change my mind."

Sarah, Jo, Maria and Henry attended a prayer service with Judge Onderdonk on a blustery cold Sunday afternoon, Henry's last day at Evergreen Park. After the service the carriage ride home was solemn. Her father's disapproval of Henry's leaving added another measure of sadness to Maria's heart.

Martin reined in the horses at the stables and swung down from his seat to open the carriage door. Horatio climbed down and turned to give a hand to Sarah and then Jo. "Come along, my dears," he said, taking each by the arm. "It's a chill wind blowing in off the bay, and we'd best get inside quickly. We'll leave Maria some time for good-byes."

Henry's eyebrows raised in surprise. He took Maria's arm and they walked quickly away from the stables on an old farm path skirted by towering pine trees. The soughing of the pines was a melancholy sound.

As they neared the narrow neck of land that overlooked the bay, Maria stopped at a ridge of locust trees.

"Cow Bay," she said, looking off at Long Island Sound. Water the color of dark slate blew in foamy breakers against the shoreline below. She pointed past the ridge of trees. "The bay is what my grandfather Joseph watched while guarding our land from Tory whaleboats during the war. He had to stay and work his father's farm, but I know he wished to go off to war as much as you do, Henry." Tears prickled her eyes and her lower lip began to tremble. She quickly averted her gaze.

Henry drew her away from the sandy path, into the shadow of a tall tree. Setting her gently back from him, both hands on her shoulders, he brushed her eyelids softly with his lips, tasting the salt of her tears. "Maria, Maria," he murmured, pressing his lips to hers with infinite care, and disarming tenderness.

She reached her arms around his neck, resting her head on his chest. "I hoped you wouldn't go."

"I don't want to leave you to go to war," he said, "But how can I do otherwise?"

Maria brushed away her tears and met his gaze, nodding her head. "I know."

"I will carry you forever in my heart, Maria, and we will be together in our faith."

She looked deeply into his eyes as though she were trying to imprint his face on her mind. She swallowed against the knot that rose in her throat.

Henry pulled her close and held her fast. "Something the reverend said today about prayer has stuck in my mind," he said, kissing the soft spot below her ear. " 'God sees all, and hears all our prayers. He will answer and make us feel things in our hearts.' We have our faith to listen, my dear, don't we?"

Maria felt the beating of his heart through the rough wool of his coat. Words caught in her throat, and she could only nod her head against his shoulder.

They turned back toward the house, walking hand in hand on the old footpath. The shadows of the tall pines grew longer as the sun dropped in the western sky. By the time they reached the carriage where Martin waited, the wind had died. Darkness wrapped them in the stillness of a clear, starry night.

Maria pulled off her glove, pressed two fingers to her mouth and touched them to Henry's lips. Her hand squeezed his, then let go as he climbed into the carriage.

She ran to the porch stairs and watched Martin pull away, the carriage lanterns sending wobbly streams of light along the darkened lane.

That night Maria looked out her window at stars fading to a full moon. She wrote a single line in her diary.

March, 1862
Please, Lord, take Henry into Your keeping and bring him home safely to me.

Chapter Twenty

The thunder of big guns rattled the house windows in Williamsburg, Virginia. Relentless rain turned the streets into a sink of mud. Baggage wagons sank up to their hubs in the mire, stalling the regiments of Confederate General Johnston's retreat toward Richmond. The bulk of Johnston's divisions had already left, but the rear guard was not strong enough to keep Union forces back. By midday reinforcements came pouring in from the retreating Rebs, charging a line of Union soldiers. A fierce battle raged in the driving rain.

Dead and dying blue- and-gray-clad bodies lay in all directions in the field and woods surrounding Fort Magruder. The fort was deserted with the exception of wounded soldiers quartered there. There were no ambulances for the wounded, and those who couldn't march were left in Williamsburg as prisoners of war.

Hospital of the Methodist Church
Williamsburg, May 10, 1862
My dear Maria,
I am now quietly located in the village of Williamsburg, about fifty miles southeast of Baltimore. This is the first opportunity I have had to write since my hasty departure from Brooklyn. I have constantly engaged in camp duty since Monday, sleeping at night on the damp ground, with nothing

but my overcoat for a blanket, but with this I feel satisfied when I compare my condition with those around me.

You have doubtless read of the decisive victory of the Union forces at the battle of Williamsburg. I feel my weakness of descriptive genius when I attempt to depict the terrible scenes around me. The wounded and dead are lying about in scores, and the groans of agony that arise on all sides are lamentable. We arrived in due time to be of extreme service to the wounded and sick. I cannot say how many operations we have performed, since our hospital report is not yet complete. The wounds are mostly of a serious nature, being confined to the head and chest of the Confederate soldiers, and to the lower extremities of our men. In the hospital to which Dr. Ayres and myself are in charge, the wounded are nearly all Rebel soldiers, about one hundred sixty in number, and under the circumstances are doing fairly. About sixty-five have died and many more will die, thus relieving us and them of pain.

I am weary of body and mind, so I shall close until the morrow.

11 May 1862

The inhabitants of the village have nearly all fled, but a few Secession ladies are still remaining. They visit the sick twice daily with refreshments. The wards and the beds of the sick are strewn with flowers, which I have just given orders to be immediately discontinued, since the smell is anything but healthful after remaining a short time in the hospital. A Secession lady, as she calls herself, has just been giving me a piece of her mind, saying that I was not studying the comfort of the sick in refusing her to distribute her bouquets to the wounded men. She then made a face at me and left. It is too bad that, considering our mission is one of mercy, she should act in this manner.

The house in which we are quartered has the appearance of

having been inhabited by persons accustomed to the good things of this world. The village is under martial law. No soldier or citizen allowed out after nine o'clock without having the countersign. Yesterday Dr. Ayres amputated both legs of a Negro who had been deserted by his owner and left to the mercy of our men. He is, however, doing well. The colored seem perfectly happy in their abandonment by their masters and heartily wish that they may never return. They are extremely kind and are at our elbows to know if we can give them anything to do whereby our comfort may be increased. We are about to leave to attend the wounded that have been brought to our hospital. When I return I will resume this letter.

Late evening

The cruel reality of this monstrous war is in witnessing the irony that befalls the dead and dying. All around Ft. Magruder, the Rebels had buried cannon shells attached to wire fuses intended for the enemy after the Confederate retreat. Men and horses riding over the shells would activate and explode them.

A thunderous explosion at the edge of the trees shook the mud-streaked body of a wounded Yank and his dead horse. At the deafening sound, a Rebel instinctively threw himself over the Yank's body. Tree limbs, horseflesh and blood rained down on him. An airborne chunk of iron buried itself into his back by the explosion of that horrible device planted by his own men *before their retreat. The Union soldier he was attempting to take prisoner survived, but the Rebel died. I tell you about this because I have reason to suspect he may be related to Philip's lady friend from Virginia. He has the same family name, Rhoads.*

I find the mail is past closing and if this is not out today, you may not receive it in a week. Give fond regards to your

family and know that you have my deepest love.
   Henry

Before Harper's Ferry fell to the Confederates, Henry volunteered to leave field duty and escort a trainload of wounded being sent to Washington. Part of his mission was to check on a shipment of medical supplies that were long overdue and, hopefully, manage a visit to his father's home.

Half of the wounded soldiers the Simms family was caring for had been transferred to hospitals. The young soldier who had lost his leg had been sent home with special arrangements made by Edward. Henry's sisters spent their days making bandages and preparing food to bring to temporary hospitals set up around the city.

No word had been received from Philip and though Henry tried, he could not seem to lessen his father's worries.

"From all I've seen of the wounded and dying these past weeks, Father, you surely wouldn't want Philip on the battlefront."

"No, Henry, it is not my wish to lose a son to battle. I've never forgiven myself for all the suffering you endured on that trip home from New Orleans. But there are other ways Philip could have served. His choice will never be right in my eyes."

Henry spent a restless night in his old bed. When sleep finally came, it was full of disjointed dreams of Philip sailing on the high seas, and of soldiers screaming in agony in the surgeons' field tent.

The next morning he went to the Sanitary Commission to check on the long-awaited medical supplies for the field hospital. The Surgeon General had left an assignment for him that Henry never expected.

Chapter Twenty-One

Maria looked out her open bedroom window, past the haystacks at the end of the kitchen garden, to the woodlands behind the stable. A hazy sun climbed in the eastern sky, now and then covered by gathering clouds. Summer heat descended with a vengeance, and the air was heavy with the promise of rain.

She chose a wide straw hat, tied its ribbons under her chin, and lifted a basket from the small writing table. It contained her diary, writing materials, and her rosewood box. She lifted the wide skirt and petticoats of her coolest summer dress to descend the stairs.

The house was quiet. Sarah and Andrew were staying with Aunt Jane and the younger girls had gone berry picking with Bridget. Maria stepped outside and made her way across the carriage lane. She turned down a wooded path that led to her favorite childhood retreat, the evergreen glade behind the stables.

From the stable doorway, Martin waved a greeting. Maria was his favorite of the Onderdonk girls. He cocked one bushy eyebrow as his chin came up with an impish grin. "Are ye goin' to a fairy party now, Miss Maria?"

She didn't need to puzzle long over his question. She laughed softly as a scene came to mind of a long-ago birthday, her seventh.

Martin and Bridget had led the three older sisters into the evergreen glade. "Into the woods we go now, lassies, on this fine day," Martin had said. When they reached a wide circle amongst the trees where the undergrowth had been cleared, Martin swept his arms out to reveal two tree-trunk benches and a crude little table he had fashioned by hand. "And here at yer table ye shall have a right nice party with the wee folk who dwell in the woods. Sure 'n they'll bring you luck in your seventh year, my Miss Maria."

Bridget's basket held plates and forks and a small cake iced with white frosting and raspberries, Maria's favorite. She smiled as she remembered that happy day, and waved to Martin over her shoulder. "On my way to the glade to do some writing, Martin. It has to be cooler there," she called.

The dense undergrowth under the lofty spruce and fir trees surprised Maria. Hawthorne, woodbine, and fern intertwined and narrowed the pine needle path. She picked up a broken pine bough and held the fragrant needles to her nose. *Libby and Anna must have nearly abandoned this spot. But then, Annie is much more worldly than I was at her age.*

Farther along, the undergrowth thinned to a stand of hemlocks. Their lacy boughs formed a canopy over the crude table and benches, just as she remembered it. Maria brushed off the table and benches with the pine bough. She emptied the contents of her basket onto the small table, and sat on the bench. Taking up her leather diary she held it to her breast. Summer trips with their father had ended with the war, and Maria's diary had become a journal of her private longings. She dipped her pen into a small bottle of ink and dated the entry.

15 July 1862
The forest is blissfully cool. I hear only the birds and squirrels darting among the pine cones. It hardly seems that a decade has passed since Sarah, Jo and I played house here

at the little table Martin made for us.

God willing, I will have my very own house and a fine table to keep for Dr. Simms one day. If only life was as simple as it was when we were children. This war is a beast ravaging our lives. Everyone is discouraged and losing faith that our nation will ever be reunited.

Mother used to say hope is sweeter than despair. Hope for me is bittersweet, but my faith in God is strong, and I feel certain in my heart that someday Dr. Simms and I will be together.

Maria O.

She felt a heavy sadness as she reached for the rosewood box. The little note from Father was still tucked inside. "For your treasures." *These are my treasures, my letters and my diary.*

Grandfather Joseph's letters from the sea captain were on top. Her fingers stroked the yellowed packet. She could almost trace the red cockade through the thin parchment of the topmost letter. Captain Jenkins's widow had returned the brave little symbol of loyalty to Maria's grandfather after the War for Independence.

Papa's feelings about Dr. Simms must have softened, else he would never have given these letters to me.

Maria recalled the sparkle in her father's eyes. "Someday these letters will unmistakably declare your heritage to your children. I hope you will treasure them as I have."

She clasped Henry's letters to her breast and closed her eyes, letting her thoughts drift into daydreams. She was dancing in Henry's arms, and his disarming gaze held her captive.

She did not hear footsteps on the pine needle path. At the calling of her name, her eyes flew open and she rose from the bench to see Martin walking back along the path toward the stable, waving his cap over his shoulder.

As if she had conjured the man from her dreams, there stood Henry at the edge of the circle. She felt that lift of the heart she always felt whenever he was near. Was this fantasy? But I must be dreaming . . . Where? How? "Dr. Simms!"

In two long strides he was in front of her, reaching for her hands. They both stood very still for a long moment. There was one deep look between them, and then it seemed something magical pulled them into each other's arms.

His arms wrapped around her, crushing her to him. Her full skirts bobbed back and her hat fell askew. She pressed her cheek into his shoulder and felt his lips bury in her hair. He slowly released her to cup her face in his hands. His mouth covered hers with such tender urgency she was barely able to catch her breath.

"Forgive me, Maria, but I've yearned to do that for such a long time." He swept a tress of hair from her brow, following the curve of her cheek with the back of his fingers.

She put two trembling fingertips over his lips. "Please don't apologize. I . . . I must confess I've dreamed about the same. I can scarcely believe I'm not dreaming now. How did you get here?"

"I was waiting for a transport of supplies in Washington City when I was asked to board a transport ship bringing wounded home to New York. I jumped at the chance that I might have time to see you. A gent I met at the Flushing ferry was kind enough to give me a ride straight here." Henry flashed an endearing smile. "I told him I was hoping to visit my sweetheart in the little time I had."

Color warmed her cheeks. "Thanks be to God, Martin was the first to see you arrive." A flood of tenderness washed over her. "Martin knew I was here in the glade alone," she said, touching her fingers to Henry's cheek, "but we . . . we mustn't stay—"

Henry caught her hand and enfolded it in both of his. "I can only be here a few hours, Maria. Please allow me one more moment alone with you. I must speak my mind."

Maria stepped back, smoothed her skirts nervously and met his gaze.

Henry reached again for her hands. His eyes held glints of amber. "I must tell you what you mean to me. My love for you has grown since the day we met. Mine is a deep, abiding love, Maria. It is so strong that when I leave you, I carry you forever in my mind and in my heart. Sometimes, I long to look into your eyes and touch you. In my dreams I hear you say that you will be mine when this war has ended. I need to know that it's not just a dream."

She took a deep breath. "Just before—" she said in a hoarse whisper. She cleared her throat to begin again. "Just before you came into the glade I wrote in my diary that we *will* be together in our faith and our love."

A sudden wind lifted the hemlock boughs overhead. Maria looked up and shuddered at the sound of thunder rumbling. Henry reached out to pull her once more into his arms, but she drew back. "We have to get to the house before the rain comes."

With trembling hands, she began to pack up the contents of her basket, her mind whirling. *In a way, I'm thankful for this storm. It strengthens my resolve not to linger here. My heart is pounding just from the nearness of him.*

She handed the basket to Henry, covering his hand on the basket's handle with hers. "This rosewood box holds all my treasures. Grandfather Joseph's letters, your letters, and my diary."

Maria took a deep breath and leaned against Henry to

steady herself against the strong wind blowing through the glade. "If we hurry, we'll reach the house before we get soaked. I've discovered one of Grandfather's letters that I must show you."

Chapter Twenty-Two

August 1862
*Sometimes I think it's folly to puzzle God's will, but I don't
feel that way today. Dr. Simms said we would be together
in faith, and I believe God's hand brought Henry here to
me. I can still feel his strong arms around me. His lips were
so gentle. I couldn't keep it all inside, so I told Jo about the
glade. She's almost as happy as I am.*
Maria O.

Bridget entered the bedroom carrying a pile of clean linen just
as Maria finished rereading her diary. She quickly put it into
her treasure box and closed it in the drawer of the writing
table.

"A letter just came in the post for you, love," Bridget said,
waving an envelope in one hand. She put the sheets down on
the writing table and handed Maria the letter. "You may want
to take it downstairs to read if you don't mind. It's changing
the bed linen I'm here for."

Maria turned the letter over and over. The address was
barely readable on a water-stained, rumpled envelope, but
the handwriting was unmistakably Carolyn's. "It's a wonder
this letter reached me at all. This was written weeks ago," she
said aloud as she left her room. Downstairs in the back parlor,
she opened it and noted the date.

The Daniel Webster, *U.S. Floating Hospital*

28 July 1862

Dear Maria,

No doubt you are wondering what I am doing aboard a ship. At times, I question it myself, but believe me when I say that I believe God sent me here for a reason.

All that fuss that was made about the impropriety of "young" persons serving as nurses was foolishness. Miss Dix was adamant at first about my being too young, but after observing my work she changed her attitude. The soldiers are polite and obliging. But I would brook no nonsense from them even if their conduct were otherwise.

When I arrived in Washington, I was assigned temporarily to the North Capitol Lodge for Invalid Soldiers. I heard the soldiers talk about the hospital ships that brought the wounded to Washington. At my request, Miss Dix agreed to transfer me, and I have just now snatched some precious time away from duties here on the Daniel Webster to write to you. Our ship is anchored on the Pamunkey River in Virginia, along with six large steamers receiving the wounded from the battlefield.

There is no escaping the horrors of the sick, wounded and dying all around us. Every foot of the stateroom floors and belowdecks is more than filled with both Federal and Confederate soldiers. At first, to see the carnage that bullets and cannon shells rent was horrifying. I have learned to put away all feelings and have no time to consider missing the comforts of home. We have worked continuously for two or three days with very little sleep. Cleaning wounds, changing dressings, and trying to bathe their battered bodies. I have closed the eyes of many dead soldiers. Much of our time is spent preparing and serving beef stock to the poor fellows, keeping cots and mattresses clean with linen, and emptying slop pails.

Please do not think I'm complaining, because I really feel as though this is where I am meant to be. When I think of you, I wonder if Dr. Simms is nearby in Washington, or if our paths will ever cross.

I have no more time to write if this is to go off with the ship's mail. Please keep the poor soldiers and me in your prayers. Know that I think of you often and count you as my dearest friend.

With affection,
Carolyn.

"I scarcely believe this," Maria said aloud, folding the pages back into the envelope. Thoughts and emotions in turmoil, she hurried back upstairs with the letter.

Bridget passed her in the hall. "All's finished in your room, Miss Maria," she said, eyeing the envelope in Maria's hand. "Your letter looked like it came through the misty moors over the sea."

Maria ignored the comment, closing her bedroom door firmly. She stopped to stare at a small daguerreotype of her mother on the dresser. *If only I could be calm and patient like her.*

Holding the small silver frame tightly, she closed her eyes, picturing her mother's long, graceful fingers playing the pianoforte. She remembered those patient hands braiding Jo's hair, teaching Annie to cross-stitch, and cooling Andrew's fevered brow. *Mother's hands were never still. She would understand my useless feelings and my longings.*

Maria touched her fingers to her lips and brushed them across the small photograph. When she placed Carolyn's letter in her treasure box she pulled out her diary and the letter that arrived after Henry's surprise visit.

Willard Hotel, 09 September '62
Washington City
My Dear Maria,

After a tedious and sleepless night, I landed safely in Washington and reported for duty to the Surgeon General. Since we had seen field duty at Williamsburg, the major part of our delegation has been assigned to duty at Georgetown College Hospital. Good news in a way. I'm near Father.

I returned safely from the battlefield on Sunday morning and was anxiously expecting to hear from you, but no mail arrived.

I need not detail to you the scene as presented to us when we reached the field of action with our ambulances. This can be better imagined than described. There were at that time about nine hundred dead soldiers lying still unburied, and the odor from the decomposition thereof would sicken the stoutest heart and discourage the most valiant, to see how our forces had been led to slaughter.

In the field hospital quarters, which embrace an open field, were lying near two thousand dying and wounded men. We filled our ambulances and returned to Washington. The city is in an intense state of excitement since the Confederate forces invaded Maryland. Father's house is once more in disorder. He's accepted more wounded soldiers.

I miss the peace of Evergreen Park and you, my dear. I treasure those moments we had together. At last I know you are truly mine, and I can hold you forever in my heart.

Your devoted,
Henry Simms

Maria opened her diary. "And I miss you, dear heart," she whispered. She dipped a pen into the inkpot and wrote the date in her diary.

Evergreen Park
17 September 1862
This ugly war is wearing everyone down, most especially
me. I received a letter from Carolyn. She is doing something
noble and worthwhile, while I sit here feeling helpless. The
bloodshed on the battlefield that Dr. Simms described was
so shocking that I tremble to think about it. Thousands of
lives lost. My anguish is the fear of losing him, too. I must
not read that letter again, as I am inclined to do with most
of his letters. I've made a vow to keep my sadness from any
lines I pen to him from now forward. I must remember to
keep my writing hopeful.
Maria O.

Maria took writing paper from the drawer.

Evergreen Park, New York
My dear Dr. Simms,
I have not been allowed to be lonely since you left. Sarah
and Jo take turns thinking of things for us to do, but all of it
seems so ordinary when I think of what my friend Carolyn is
doing. I continue to receive letters from her. She is now serving
as a nurse on a hospital ship in Virginia. She mentioned you,
and if you should ever see her, would you please let me know? I
worry about her, too.
The leaves are turning early with cool nights and glorious
sunny days. My brother, Andrew, is doing very well at school,
but lately he talks about joining the Navy as soon as he's old
enough. Of course, Father takes it lightly, because he believes
the war cannot possibly last that long, and because Father has
great plans for Andrew to become a lawyer.
You may recall my telling you that my cousin Joseph
(Uncle James's son) left the farm last year and joined the in-

fantry. Joseph believes they are going to Maryland. I know that is close to where you are. I pray that you do not see him— as a casualty of any battle, that is!

Your last letter about the battlefield at Manassas was so painful to read. I am fearful for you, as I am for all my loved ones. I want to believe that as God has joined our hearts, He will surely bring us together soon. Our pastor says, "We can see a brighter day through the eye of faith." I am longing for that brighter day.

The girls miss you and send prayers, as do I.

With much affection,

Maria

Sarah read every newspaper account that her father brought home. She was in the parlor reading an article aloud to Jo.

"The September nineteenth issue of the *New York Tribune* ranks the battle at Antietam as the greatest fight since Waterloo. A photographer captured these horrifying details:

" 'The carnage was staggering. Both armies began to gather up their dead and wounded as darkness fell. Cries and moans filled the air as both sides searched the fields and woods by candlelight. Broken caissons, wagons, dead mules and horses clogged the roads. Thousands of blue- and gray-clad bodies lay dead in the lanes, fields, and woods along Antietam Creek.' "

Maria stood as still as a post in the parlor doorway. She cleared her throat, her face a pale mask. Jo turned a startled face to her. "Oh, Maria, we didn't know you were there," she said.

Sarah dropped the newspaper and went to Maria's side, urging her to the library table. "I wouldn't have wanted you to hear that. Truly, I wouldn't. I know how worried you are, and I'm so sorry. I didn't know you were in the hall."

Jo's eyes darted to the small book Maria clutched in her hand, *Poems by William Wordsworth.* "I have an idea," she said. "Remember how we used to read your travel diary aloud? If you wouldn't mind, Maria, could we read some of the poems from your book? Surely it would help us think about pleasant things, instead of the ugly old war."

Frightening dreams tormented Maria's sleep that night. Soldiers with outstretched arms were crying out to Dr. Simms on the battlefield. The scene shifted to Carolyn scrubbing bloody cloths in a basin on the deck of a ship, crying as she scrubbed. Maria called out in her dream and thrashed in the bed until her nightclothes and the counterpane were a twisted tangle.

Awakened by Maria's cries, Sarah shook her sister gently. Maria woke with a start, wrapped her arms around Sarah and sobbed out the horror of the dream.

"Shhh, hush now. Everything is all right, Maria. You just have to stop thinking about those battles. You are making yourself sick with worry and it will not do one bit of good. I know you have sworn your love to Henry, but whatever happened to faith and hope?"

Maria clutched her pillow. "I do have faith, Sarah, but hope is the cruelest of virtues. I can't help worrying that something terrible is going to happen."

"Offer your worries up to the good Lord. That's what Bridget says to do, and God will surely send you courage in return."

Chapter Twenty-Three

Evergreen Park
January 1863
Sarah and Jo have been especially kind to me lately. They
seem to have a much stronger spirit than I. I know that
Sarah is really just trying to take Mother's place, but even
as she tries, her nature is not at all like our sweet mother's.

Jo and I have been helping Bridget with fall canning.
Anything, anything, to keep our hands busy. Carrots, snap
beans, beets, tomatoes and the last of the corn are all ready
for the cold cellar shelves. We put up so many jars of pear
compote that I wished I might never peel another piece of
fruit. I know I should be thankful that we have the garden,
but I would much rather be feeding soldiers or even nursing,
as Carolyn does. No doubt Dr. Simms's sisters help with
household chores too, but they still find time to care for the
wounded soldiers in their home. I'm tired of dreary old knit-
ting of stockings for the Blue Coats. I know I could do more.
If only I could be in Washington City.

"What cannot be changed must be endured." That's
what Sarah said when I told her what my wishes were.
Maria O.

Cousin Andrew pulled a folded newspaper article from his
frockcoat. "According to this newspaper, he's freeing all slaves
in the enemy homeland and provoking outrage in the South."

He tightened his jaw and slapped the paper against his palm, then opened it to read. "Hear this, Uncle:

" 'As of January, 1863, all slaves within any state in rebellion against the United States shall be free. Contrabands in increasing numbers are being employed by regiments quartered around the city. Maryland slaves have come across the Eastern Branch Bridge, and their masters come after them seeking redress.' "

Andrew laid the paper beside the tea tray. "Lincoln's Proclamation confirms the government's opposition to slavery, wouldn't you say?"

"Please sit and take some tea, Andrew," Judge Onderdonk said, hitching forward in his chair. He gave a cursory glace at the paper, and stroked his beard.

"Yes, it seems so, according to that article. Yet my friends in Washington tell me that many of the Federal troops there are hostile to the emancipated slaves. They chase them and stone them in the streets. I certainly don't approve of the troops' action toward them, but I still have my doubts about abolishing that peculiar institution. Freeing slaves gives them freedom they are ill equipped to handle and puts a burden on society."

"I hear you, but I would be interested in hearing Henry Simms's point of view on what's happening in the capitol city," Andrew replied. "I'm sure he would give a candid reply."

Sarah and Maria exchanged glances. "Have you had any letters from Dr. Simms, Andrew?" Maria asked.

"Not in the new year. The last letter I received was mid-December. He wrote about his brother Philip coming back to the States. Henry inquired about a factor I know in the city of Wilmington. It seems Philip may be in need of one. Has he mentioned any of this to you, Maria?"

"No, not in his last letter, but his sister Georgie wrote to me about Philip. Doctor has little time to do anything beside his duties at the Georgetown Hospital. When he has any spare time he makes rounds at his father's house and at other places set up as hospitals around the city."

Andrew gestured with an open hand. "He did not go into much detail about his work in my letter, but he did mention that many private families had taken wounded into their homes."

"You may be interested to know about the last letter I received from my friend, Carolyn Grisham. She is also nursing wounded soldiers," Maria said, sparing her father a quick glance, "aboard a hospital ship in Virginia."

Andrew arched a brow and also cast a look at his uncle. Surprisingly, Judge Onderdonk's face showed no emotion.

"Well, that is surprising news, Maria," Andrew said. "How did Carolyn ever manage that?"

"Her father agreed to her training as a nurse under Dr. Elizabeth Blackwell in New York. After her training, Carolyn was sent to the Sanitary Commission in Washington City, and from the capitol Miss Dix sent her to serve aboard a hospital ship."

Horatio cleared his throat. "I will never understand Attorney Grisham's approval of that turn of events," he said, shaking his head. "The idea of a refined young lady serving as a nurse is beyond my comprehension."

"But, Father," Sarah said, "Dr. Simms's sisters have been doing the very same thing ever since Mr. Simms took wounded soldiers into his home."

Horatio raised shaggy brows and pursed his lips.

Andrew spoke up quickly. "It is difficult to see ourselves in the shoes of those most affected by the war, but I'm sure Henry's family feels justified to do whatever they can for the cause."

Horatio harrumphed a few times. He finished his tea, pushed his chair back from the tea table and remained unusually quiet.

When Andrew rose to leave, Maria accompanied him to the stable. "Were you surprised that Sarah stood up to Father today?" she asked.

"Yes, I was surprised. I do think Sarah was right to speak up about the Simms sisters. That's a privately controlled setting. When it comes to nursing, I'm not sure that I hold the same opinion as your father and I think your disclosure about Carolyn prompted Sarah. You know how I feel about your impulsive young friend, Carolyn. I understand you admire her, but—"

"More than that, Andrew. Carolyn is doing just what I wish I could do."

Andrew's brows shot up. "Do what she does? Carolyn is a plucky one, but I doubt there's any likelihood of your doing anything like that in New York."

End of dreadful March, 1863

I wish I were writing this diary page from anyplace except Evergreen Park. Late yesterday, after Cousin Andrew left, Uncle James brought Father a letter received from an Army officer. The soldier had marched with Cousin Joseph in the 59th N.Y. Regiment. It wasn't official, but the family took it to be. The letter said that our dear cousin Joseph was missing in the field of action at Antietam. I overheard the whispered prayer of Bridget when Father told the servants the news. " 'Sweet Jesus, let not death come in threes to this family.' " The lament sent shivers up my spine. My only comfort came from the preaching at Flower Hill church today. I prayed and prayed that the dear Lord will bring us peace soon.
Maria O.

Chapter Twenty-Four

Philip Simms looked up at the crude wooden sign. *Benjamin Channing—Master Pilot.* He straightened his shoulders and entered the small wooden shack at the end of the wharf.

"Philip Simms, sir," he said, giving a short nod. "I represent Symington Shipping. I need a safe passage back to Nassau with the *Lady Symington*, and you come highly recommended, Mr. Channing."

"Ben suits me just fine. Most folks call me Ben."

"All right then, Ben." Philip grinned to mask his nervousness. "In the past months I've made several voyages from England to Nassau, spending most of my time supervising the cargo exchange from our vessels to blockade runners. This will be my first and *last* trip back to Nassau. I'm told you've worked the run from Cape Fear River."

The burly, ruddy-faced man drew on a pipe and eyed Philip up and down "Yes, sir, true enough. I climbed aboard a riverboat when I was a young 'un and worked my way up from river rat to master pilot. Been piloting these waters longer than I care to count. Don't plan on signing on much longer."

"Exactly my feelings, too, Ben. Symington Shipping has taken two losses to the Federals in the last six months. They say runners almost never surrender under Federal fire."

The pilot's steady gaze never left Philip's face. "More Federal boats on the water now. Risky business, for sure."

"Most of my time's been spent waiting out returns of the runners from Wilmington. As I said, I'm looking for a willing pilot to take the *Lady* back to Nassau. I'm prepared to make it worth your while."

Channing knocked the ashes from his pipe against a spittoon and stood with surprising agility for such a big man. He nodded. "I'll sign on with you, Simms, for this one run . . . but not for paper, you understand. I only deal in silver."

"Coin of the realm it is, then, Ben. We leave at dark."

In the pitch-black night, the *Lady Symington* was pushing along. The slapping of her paddle blades and the throb of the engines were the only sounds as she slipped down the Cape Fear River. No lights were allowed, and orders were passed in whispers as the long, low side-wheeler hugged the shore on this moonless night.

She was a fast ship, a single mast, sloop-rigged, with funnels fore and aft. Her course was charted for Nassau. She was loaded with 1,200 bales of cotton for the British market.

Philip stashed most of his personal gain in the National Savings Bank of Wilmington before he left port, then he posted a brief letter to his sister.

April 10, 1863
Dearest Georgie,

Father will be happy to know that my conscience no longer allows me to continue with Symington Shipping. With Henry's help finding a factor, the auction of my goods from Europe brought an enormous profit on this last run our ship made to the states. In British sterling!

In the event anything should happen to me, I have banked a good deal of it in your name in the National Savings Bank of Wilmington. Added to my savings, this last earning may be all that I need to get out of this nasty business at last.

I wrote to Henry about my intentions, and I'm sure that is why he gave my name to the factor in Wilmington. I must clear up matters in Nassau and then, before this year ends, I plan to return home to Washington for good. Please tell Father of my intentions, and continue to pray for the safety of yr loving brother,

    Philip Simms

The most compelling reason for Philip's decision was his niggling conscience about Union loyalty. Earlier in the year, the Confederate government had attempted to regulate the importation of luxury goods by reserving half of all cargo space for government supplies. That meant arming the Confederacy. And that, Philip would not do.

His refusal to haul arms and munitions for the Rebel government, coupled with the increasing dangers to the fleet, convinced him to make this his last effort on behalf of Symington & Co.

The *Lady* had timed her departure to have a moonless night for the start of the three-day run to Nassau. The ship pushed cautiously down to the mouth of the Cape Fear River, New Inlet's entrance to the sea. Her lights were blacked out and the crew was tense and silent as they anchored at the mouth to watch and wait.

Philip stood on the foredeck as darkness resolved into shades of deeper black. Pilot Ben Channing sighted a pair of Federal gunboats inside the breakers. A seaman conveyed the message to the captain.

Captain Wiggins whispered orders to weigh anchor slowly. Her side wheels barely turning, the *Lady* inched along in the narrow inlet attempting to pass unnoticed..

A sudden flare from the Yankee boats lit the black sky, and

Philip crouched against the bulkhead. They were spotted! Instinctively, he clutched the silver medal attached to the small compass in his pocket. "Mother of God, star of the Sea, with Thy grace . . ."

"Hard to starboard," muttered Ben.

The rocket flare had done its job for the Union boats, illuminating the *Lady* against the night sky. Federals brought their guns to bear and fired on the fleeing ship. Pillars of white geysers rose up all around them. The ship shuddered from a first hit, close to the bow.

"Full speed ahead!" shouted the captain. The *Lady* steamed toward the open sea, paddles churning the black water. A roar of explosion followed a flash from the gunboat as a second hit rammed the forecastle.

Philip was flung to the deck, his head striking so hard, his vision blurred. Something warm oozed down his neck. The pain in his head was fierce. He tried to get up, but dizziness overcame him. Blackness closed in. A crewman rushed forward, lifted him under the arms and dragged him away from the carnage at the forecastle.

Many hours later, Philip opened his eyes to the weak light of an Atlantic dawn. He couldn't seem to focus on anything without dizziness. The throbbing in his head matched the steady drone of engines that told him he was still aboard ship. He prayed that the *Lady* was far south in the Atlantic.

The battered *Lady Symington* limped into the port of Nassau. Philip Simms was carried ashore. He spent several weeks in a hospital, recovering from a severe concussion and fractured backbone. It would be weeks before he could follow his plan to return to Liverpool and resign as ship's representative of Symington & Co.

As luck would have it, Charles Symington took pity on

Philip, not only because of the long recovery from his injuries, but because it was becoming obvious that the years of profit from the American war were coming to an end. Even the Confederates could see that the end of their rebellion was near.

Symington put Philip on a ship sailing to New Orleans. There he could seek refuge with his cousin. It would be a long journey home to Washington City.

Chapter Twenty-Five

July 4, 1863
Georgetown
My Dear Maria,
Crowds gathered on the grounds of the White House this
week, but not only to celebrate Independence Day. Excitement
roused to rejoicing at the announcement of a victory at a farm-
town in southeastern Pennsylvania called Gettysburg. My
father feels that the Army of the Potomac has at last given the
promise of success to the Union cause. It is high time, since you
and I know full well that this is the Rebellion's third summer.

My days blend into nights working in the hospitals around
the city. I scarcely have time to visit Father's home, but late
yesterday, a messenger boy brought two surprises from C
Street. One was a hastily written note from your friend, Carolyn. She sent it from her hospital ship to the Sanitary Commission with my name on it and 390 C Street. I assume you
probably gave her my father's address, because I remember
your asking me to let you know if I were ever to hear from her. I
suppose she thought that sending the note in that manner was
the fastest way to reach me.

Carolyn advised me about a village being built in Arlington
to provide housing for freedmen and contraband slaves. There
are so many Negroes in camps around the city that I have no
doubt a hospital is needed. Many of them are dying with
smallpox and typhoid fever. I've tried to help at their camps,

but there just aren't enough hours in the day. I do not know when I will have time to look into it, but Carolyn has asked me to inquire about a hospital for the freedmen. Since this is a mutual interest we share, I will respond to her as soon as I can.

The second surprise was a note from my sister, Georgie. She says that Philip is leaving the shipping firm and coming home. That is good *news, but I halfway expected it inasmuch as Philip wrote to me a month ago about needing a factor to sell his goods in the Carolinas. It is late, and time for sleep, so I shall close with a fervent prayer that even though we are far apart, we are always together in God.*

My love to you, dear heart,

Henry C. Simms

Henry moved from cot to cot, checking wounds. At the end of the longest row in the converted college laboratory, a nurse was trying to hold down a Confederate soldier attempting to rise from his bed.

"But I can see him. I know him . . . it's Henry," gasped a weak, gravelly voice. The soldier thrashed from side to side, waving one arm in weak desperation.

Henry heard the man's cry. It sounded like a voice from the past. Fear stabbed his heart as he approached the cot.

"Good Lord in heaven! Will? Is that you, Will?"

Henry had seen men blown apart by artillery fire, wounded men covered by dirt and blackened by powder, and terrible as that was, he'd not been shaken as he was now. This was his friend and old college roommate, Dr. Will Johnson.

Will's thin body and gaunt face were tragic enough, but it was the nature of his wound that triggered Henry's reaction. Hot tears burned Henry's eyes as he knelt beside the cot and reached to touch Will's shoulder. It was the first time Henry felt such strong emotion in all the months since the war began.

Tears fell uncontrollably from both men's eyes. Will was the first to speak in a low, strained voice.

"I'm a prisoner here, Henry, by choice. When I first joined the Confederate Brigade as a regimental surgeon, I was most curious about our general. His name was Paul Semmes. I tried to make a connection between his name and yours, but I never had the chance to inquire."

"No need to explain, Will. Rest easy now," Henry said as he gripped his friend's hand. "As fate would have it, there are Semmeses and Simmses on both sides of this unholy war."

A fit of coughing left Will's thin chest heaving. His voice was hoarse as he struggled to go on.

"It was the fiercest three days of fighting . . . oh Lord, it was horrible! Most of the wounded in my care at Gettysburg left in a long wagon train retreating with Lee, back to Virginia. I couldn't trust my survival on that long ride back. If I had chosen to go, they couldn't send me home to Georgia, anyway. My home is gone. My mother died six months ago and my father left our ruined plantation to go north to relatives in Philadelphia."

Will choked back a sob and Henry waited, dumbstruck.

"I ended up at the Feds' hospital at Gettysburg for a few days but, thank God, they honored my request and transferred me here by train. I lied, Henry. I thought your practice was here in Washington City, so I told them you were a relative."

Will winked through his tears and tried to aim a playful jab at Henry with his one good fist. "Impossible as it might seem, I thought to find you, Henry. I knew that good old Northern training we had in Philadelphia would pay off one day, and here you are, proof of the puddin'."

Henry shook his head in disbelief at the fate of his friend. Words felt thick in his throat when he examined Will's right arm, severed above the elbow. "Your spirit surpasses mine beyond measure, Will," Henry said after a long silence.

"Maybe one day when this bloody war is over, I'll find a job back at Jefferson Medical College. What do you think, Henry? One-armed surgeons ought to be able to teach at their alma mater, wouldn't you say? Honor and glory and all that rot."

Will's words sounded like the tolling of a bell to Henry. One-armed surgeons . . . He struggled to keep his feelings in check. His eyes focused on the mangled arm, his lips set in a thin straight line.

At last Henry raised his head slowly, attempting a smile. "That might not be such a bad idea, Will," he said with feigned enthusiasm, "but I have to get you some immediate attention. Perhaps I can manage a prisoner exchange. Doctors can excuse officers and grant a certificate of disability, as I'm sure you know. In the meantime, old friend, I know a couple of Simms ladies who would eagerly nurse you back to health right here in my home town."

Thoughts were teeming and tumbling through his mind as Henry left his rounds. There was so much to ponder.

What if Will's and my fates were reversed? I couldn't bear to return to my precious Maria so grievously wounded. Will served less time than I, and now his career as a surgeon is over. Dear God in heaven, grant me the wisdom to know Thy will.

Loyalty had upheld Henry in the field of action—until now. Loyalty to the cause, loyalty to his nation, loyalty to his father. But on this day, in his own city, that loyalty was badly shaken.

Maria stood in the hall near the gas light at the front door.

170

Bridget brought the letter to her just as everyone was getting ready to leave for church service. The moment she saw the seal, she tore it open.

> *Georgetown College Hospital*
> *August 20, 1863*
> *My Dear Maria,*
> *Making rounds here a week ago became a living nightmare that I hope never to repeat. Much to my horror, one of my oldest friends from medical school became a casualty in my care. Dr. Will Johnson was hit with a minié ball while tending wounded on the field of action at Gettysburg. His arm was amputated and I fear he may never practice medicine again.*
> *Will's plight became a signal that flashed in and out of my thoughts for days. It has brought me to a decision. I can no longer hold you only in my heart, dearest Maria. I wish to wait no longer for our marriage. I intend to speak to the Surgeon General about ending my contract service by this year's end. I want you in my life now, and if it works out, dear heart, I would like you to think about planning our wedding. That is, if your father will agree to our plans. In the meantime, my love is constant.*
> *I remain forever yours,*
> *Henry C. Simms*

I want you in my life now. Maria caught her breath in a burst of joy and tears.

Jo opened the back door and called out, "Maria, Father is waiting in the carriage. Are you coming?" When no answer came, Jo hurried up the hall.

Maria stood with shoulders slumped, holding the stairway banister with one hand, a letter in the other.

Jo peered around into her sister's face. "What is it? Why

171

are you crying? Has something happened to Dr. Simms?"

Maria raised her head, smiling through her tears, and held up the letter. "It's what is going to happen, Jo. Dr. Simms wants to end his service—to come home this year to plan our wedding." She threw her arms around her sister and whispered in her ear. "But please do not say anything to Father about this yet. I just need a moment to compose myself." She tucked the letter into her reticule, withdrawing a handkerchief. "Go to Papa, Jo. Tell him I'll be right along in a minute."

Horatio's stony silence on the short ride to church had the sisters keeping their own quiet thoughts. Jo looked askance at Maria several times. A smile never left Maria's lips.

As soon as they entered Dutch Church, Maria spied Carolyn's father sitting alone in a pew at the rear, his head bowed in prayer. No one could mistake Mr. Grisham's curly red hair. A flash of sadness coursed through Maria. How lonely the poor man must be. She clutched Jo's arm, thankful for the comfort of family.

The minister stood at the pulpit, the congregation singing from hymnals, as Judge Onderdonk ushered his daughters into their pew. Maria whispered to Jo while the last strains of the opening hymn were sung. "Did you see Mr. Grisham sitting back there alone? His wife and Carolyn are both in the South, you know. Both in harm's way."

Jo fumbled with a hymnal, nodding toward Maria. Sarah glared at them. The minister began to speak.

"To do God's will, we must have faith in His compassion. The Shepherd of our soul forgives and sets us on a righteous path . . ."

Maria's mind wandered. Her thoughts were ever interfering with her prayers.

"There are many fears that prevent us from seeking to

know, love and serve Him more faithfully . . ."

The line from Henry's letter played over and over in her mind: *I need you in my life now.*

"Out of His infinite love our Lord calls us to holiness. May all that we do and say work for the health, holiness and happiness of others. Especially we need to help those who are struggling in this dreadful war . . ."

Maria squeezed her eyes shut. *That's what I've wanted to do all along, Lord.*

" 'How narrow the gate and close the way that leads to life. And few there are that find it.' Brothers and sisters, reflect this evening on that passage from Luke and pray that our Savior will renew in us the spirit of prayer that draws us ever nearer to Him."

On her right, Sarah nudged Maria as the preacher asked the congregation to rise for the closing prayer.

"We must all strive to keep faith in Christ, for faith expresses itself in love. Let us pray that the good Lord will come dwell in our hearts, Amen."

Maria leaned toward Jo. "I do feel God's love," she whispered. "Let's hope Papa does, too."

Jo smiled with her eyes, covering her mouth with her gloved hand.

As they exited the church, Maria took her father's arm. "Papa, I see Mr. Grisham up ahead by his carriage, and I would like to speak with him. Will you wait for me? I'll only be a minute."

Horatio gave her an impatient look. "Go quickly, then. We waited for you earlier and were late for church because of it. Let's not repeat bad habits."

Maria hurried ahead to the carriages. "Mr. Grisham," she called as Carolyn's father climbed up to his seat. "Please wait. I don't mean to keep you, sir, but I wonder if you have had any word from Carolyn? My last letter from her came a month ago."

"It's kind of you to ask, Maria. I appreciate your concern, but I'm afraid I don't have very good news. In two days, I leave for Maryland to take my wife from her family plantation and bring her to the authorities in Washington City."

He hesitated, couching his forehead in the fingers of one hand, heaving a heavy sigh.

The sadness of the sound made Maria's breath catch in her throat. "What is it, Mr. Grisham? Is your wife unwell?"

He shook his head and reached for Maria's hand. "Mrs. Grisham is gaining her health back, but she is very distraught. It is not my wife who is ill—it's my Carolyn."

"Carolyn? I thought she was on a hospital ship."

"Yes, she was, but she had to leave the ship because of an illness she didn't identify. She's gone to Washington City. Carolyn has some fool notion about working and being cared for in a hospital in the capitol that we know nothing about. I mean to bring her home, Maria . . . if I can find her."

Chapter Twenty-Six

September
Evergreen Park
What could be worse than feeling trapped by my own help-
lessness? That would never have happened to Carolyn.
Carolyn faced the horrors of the hospital ship with such
courage. Even now, though her father says she's ill, she has
her own plan for survival. That's what I need right now—
courage and a plan. I know what I would like to do, and I
think, with God's blessing, it might work. If only I can con-
vince Papa.
Maria O.

Maria rapped lightly before opening the door to her father's office. Judge Onderdonk raised his head from the papers he was shuffling.

"Maria. What in the world brings you out here so early this morning?"

With her chin held high and her back straight, she walked to her father's desk. "If we were in a courtroom, Papa, I believe I would say I've come to plead my case."

"Please sit, my dear," he said, indicating the wooden bench at the side of the desk. Horatio gave her a fleeting smile as he stacked papers and placed them into a brown leather case. "Is it something you are needing, Maria? Trimmings for a hat, yard goods for a new dress, or perhaps more yarn for your Ladies' Blue Stocking Association?"

Maria twisted a handkerchief in her hands. "No, Papa, it's nothing like that." She paused and color rose in her cheeks. "It is important. It's something I desperately need to do for myself . . . and for God."

Horatio's eyebrows shot upwards. "Whatever are you talking about, child?"

"Papa, I'm not a child. I'm almost twenty years old, and there is something I really want to do. It's about the war, and well . . . I'll get right to it. For a long time, I have been yearning to do something important. Something God calls us all to do, help others. All I do here for the war effort is knit stockings for the soldiers. I would like to be able to help them in a real way. Dr. Simms's sisters invited me to come help with the wounded soldiers when Doctor first came home from New Orleans but . . ." She paused when Horatio's brows knit in a frown. "But now I have an even more urgent need to go to Washington. It's Carolyn—"

"Go to that war-torn city?" Horatio interrupted. "Why, that would be far too dangerous, my dear."

She bit her lip. Her voice caught a little, but she continued without pause. "Last evening Carolyn Grisham's father told me that Carolyn is very ill in a hospital in Washington. He is going to her. With your permission, I wish to go with Mr. Grisham. I know that I will be safe with him, and I'm sure Dr. Simms's father will help us once we get—"

"Come, come, my dear. You can't be serious."

Her back stiffened. She felt a flush of color creep up her neck. "I'm very serious, Father, and I ask your patience to hear me out."

Horatio sat back in his chair and folded his hands, "I am listening, Maria."

"Long ago Carolyn convinced me that slavery was wrong. I didn't have the courage of my convictions at the time, and I deserted Carolyn in the midst of her plans to help a runaway slave."

Horatio's back stiffened. He sat up abruptly, his eyebrows raised in astonishment. "How is it I know nothing about this? When did it happen?"

Maria's hands clenched. "It was almost two years ago, Papa, when I went to New York with Carolyn. You probably don't remember the day I came to your office not feeling well. You thought I cut short a shopping trip because of illness, and you brought me home on the ferry. I never told you about Carolyn's plan because she asked me not to. Nor did I tell you about meeting Dr. Simms that day."

"But, but—I thought it was Andrew who introduced you to Henry Simms."

"Actually, the Metropolitan Hotel supper dance with Andrew was the *second* time I met Henry. I met him first with Carolyn at an Anti-Slavery Association meeting."

"Anti-Slavery meeting!" Horatio's mouth thinned to a slash. "But . . . but, Andrew led me to believe Henry was a serious medical student with a bright future and I—"

"That is true, but Andrew knew nothing about Doctor's abolitionist activities. After you invited him to visit Evergreen Park I found that he and Carolyn and I shared the same sentiments, not just about slavery, but about the war to save the Union."

Horatio shook his head slowly, running his hands over the smooth surface of the desk. "I find this hard to believe. The war changed our circumstances, Maria, but I've not heard you speak of these things before."

"That's *part* of what I'm asking about today, Papa. Henry and Carolyn have both acted upon their desires to help the

Union, as you well know, while *I* have never been able to do so."

"I'm not sure I understand. What in heaven's name could you do?"

Maria's lower lip trembled, but she squared her shoulders and looked directly into Horatio's eyes. "I never thought I could talk to you about what I want to do, or that you would understand. Everyone knows that you sympathize with slaveholders, and you are definitely against the war and Mr. Lincoln."

Horatio bristled. He cleared his throat and fingered the papers on his desk. "Many of my associates oppose abolition, as I do. They view abolitionists as foolish visionaries. I admit, Maria, that some of my opinions are based on the political stance that I take, but I do not feel that I've forced those opinions on you."

A tiny bit of hurt flashed through her eyes, and she felt the sting of tears. "In a way you have, Papa. You refused to allow Dr. Simms and me to be betrothed before he left to serve the Union. That gave me very little to hope for."

"But he was going off to war! And I was only trying to protect you from eventualities that happen in wartime. It was never because I disliked Henry."

"Surely you must know that our love has held strong these past two years. His intentions have not changed. Nor have mine. I want so much to go to Washington, not only because my heart's wishes are to see Dr. Simms. I want to be there to help my friend, Carolyn."

"I can understand your desire, foolish though it is, but Washington City is under military government. Travel everywhere is restricted." He scowled and shook his head. "It's far too dangerous."

"Mr. Grisham will see that I get to the Simms house

safely, and in turn, Dr. Simms may be able to help us with Carolyn. *It can work,* Father, with a little assistance from Mr. Edward Simms and his daughters."

Horatio steepled his fingers in front of his mouth, closed his eyes and slowly shook his head.

Fear clouded Maria's eyes. *God, guide my words.* Standing slowly, she moved to the edge of the desk. She took a steadying breath and leaned forward, splaying her hands on the desktop.

"Remember, Papa, when the visiting minister at church gave the closing prayer yesterday? It was the reflection from scripture about the narrow door and the few that find it? Well, I believe that for each of us there is a door or a gate leading to a closer experience with God. I have the faith I need to open that door and I think it will lead me to Carolyn Grisham. I hoped that today you would give your blessing for this journey."

With a swift intake of breath, Horatio looked up into Maria's deep brown eyes, the image of his own. He opened his mouth to speak and promptly closed it. Seconds passed. Horatio looked down at dust motes glistening in sun streaks streaming across his black walnut desk. He stood slowly as Maria straightened. He took his leather case in hand, and met her gaze.

"You know that I rarely make hasty decisions, Maria. I will promise you, however, to speak to Mr. Grisham when I am in the city today. We shall see," he said, as he took her arm and ushered her out of his office. "We shall see."

The sentry stopped the carriage as it left Union Railroad Station. "What is your business here?" he asked.

Edward Simms stuck his head out of the carriage window. "I live just a few blocks from here, young man, but this should

179

state my party's destination *and* our business." He handed the soldier a written pass from Surgeon General Hammond to proceed to the Sanitary Commission Headquarters. It was dated 10 October 1863.

The soldier scanned the pass and looked in at the two ladies and the other gentleman in the carriage. He stepped back, and waved his arm. "Move on, sir."

Maria shivered with a sigh of relief and patted the gloved hand of Mrs. Grisham.

"Do you think the Commission people will know where my daughter is, Mr. Simms?" Carolyn's father asked.

"The Sanitary Commission does a little bit of everything," Edward Simms said. "Its inspectors look into all the camps and hospitals. They collect food and supplies and get them to the soldiers. My son, Henry, believes that they will know, if anyone does. Their headquarters is at the Home Lodge on Capitol Street, very near C Street, where I live. I generally walk these streets with ease, but we will do well to keep this carriage. We should be there in minutes."

"Were you able to speak to Dr. Simms about Carolyn?" Maria asked, wishing that Henry might have sent a word of greeting for her.

"Not exactly, my dear. Since the telegraph came from your father, all of my communication has been through the Surgeon General's office. Henry has been too busy to come to the house, but as soon as I got word to him, he sent a message with this pass." Mr. Simms held up a folded piece of paper. "Henry's message told me to take Mr. Grisham to the head-quarters of the Commission first thing upon your arrival."

It had been a long and trying trip, delayed a whole week because of track damage on the Baltimore line. Especially frustrating for Maria was the stop in Baltimore to get Caro-lyn's mother.

180

Maria gripped her reticule and stared out at the street. Soldiers, wagons, carts and drays jammed its muddy width. She hoped Mr. Simms had not noticed the disappointment in her eyes when he met their train.

"Here we are," Edward Simms said as the driver reined his horse to a stop, "just over there where that dray stands is the Sanitary Commission Headquarters. Ladies, we shall try to be as quick as possible, but you will be safe here with the carriage driver. I will alert the soldiers at the entrance that you wait upon us."

Maria could see soldiers lingering on the wooden walk. Some, limbless and bandaged, sat in chairs under a sign that read The Lodge for Invalid Soldiers. Negroes were loading a wagon with barrels, crates, firkins, and baskets.

She looked at Mrs. Grisham, sitting very still beside her. "Those stores they are loading look like supplies for hospitals. I wonder which one they are going to?" Maria said.

Mrs. Grisham stared silently into space. It had taken nearly three hours to travel between Baltimore and Washington and she had said very little on the entire train ride.

Maria understood that the woman's poor health was the cause of their delay in Baltimore. Mr. Grisham had to find accommodations for himself and Maria while they waited for her late arrival from the plantation. Damaged tracks caused further delay.

It didn't take long to realize that Mrs. Grisham had a very different temperament from Carolyn's. She had been either simpering or sour most of the time since she joined them. Nothing on this trip had gone as planned.

"I know the hospital ships need supplies," Maria prompted. "Your husband told me about Carolyn's last letters to him. She wrote that the *Daniel Webster* was in dire need of sheets and pads for the beds, and clothing for the men."

181

Mrs. Grisham raised her eyes to Maria. "I just cannot imagine my Carolyn cooking and washing dirty linen, doing all those servile things that nurses must do." Mrs. Grisham covered her mouth with a handkerchief and slowly shook her head. "No wonder she became ill," she said in a pinched voice.

"It could be that her illness is just the result of working so many hours without rest, Mrs. Grisham. I think Carolyn had become used to the suffering of the soldiers and all the work involved with their care. She wrote to me that she was really where she wanted to be."

Mrs. Grisham made a whimpering sound. Maria turned away, relieved to see the men walking back to the carriage.

Mr. Grisham's face had a worried look. Once inside the carriage, Maria sensed he was making a brave attempt to mask his feelings.

"Well, they certainly were efficient in there," he said. "They have a directory of all the hospitals and patient lists and such."

Mrs. Grisham looked beseechingly at him. "Carolyn?"

"Yes, dear, we think we know which hospital Carolyn went to."

"What do you mean, you think you know?"

Edward Simms reached a calming hand to Mrs. Grisham's shoulder, patting it ever so lightly. "My dear lady, we must trust in God and the good commissioners. They gave us all the direction they could. They told us that Miss Carolyn first insisted on being taken to Freedmans Village. The American Missionary Association runs things there, but—"

"Freedmen? You mean colored people?" Mrs. Grisham asked.

"Yes, Ma'am. There are camps and refuges for the former slaves all around the city. This place for the freedmen is a separate village governed by the War Department. It's just been built on the old Custis-Lee estate on Arlington Heights. That's just across the Potomac River from us."

"Dr. Simms knows about that place," Maria said. "He wrote to me about it after Carolyn inquired about Freedmans Village in a letter she wrote to him."

"At any rate, we are *not* going there," Mr. Grisham said, his lips forming a thin, hard line. "The village has houses for freedmen's families and a missionary hall and dispensary, but the Contraband Hospital is a single, rough wooden barrack. The Missionary Society staffs it with a few nurses and Quaker volunteers."

"But why can't we go there?" Maria asked.

Edward Simms looked at his hands for a moment, then from the Grishams to Maria. He took a deep breath before speaking.

"The sick and wounded, diseased, and aged colored who have been made free by the progress of our Army are flocking there from contraband camps." Edward nodded his head at Mrs. Grisham. "Men, women and children who go there are in every condition of horror. It is not a sight for ladies."

"We are not even sure Carolyn is still there," Mr. Grisham added.

Mrs. Grisham made a low moaning sound and reached for her husband's hand.

"Let me take you all home to C Street," Edward said. "My daughters are anxious to be of help, and heaven knows you could all use some rest and a good meal. We can start out fresh tomorrow."

Maria felt uneasy. She would be glad to see Henry's sisters, but something seemed amiss about Carolyn. And where was Dr. Simms? It was disappointing not to see him when they arrived at the train station. Maybe his sisters would have some answers.

183

Chapter Twenty-Seven

Shortly after their arrival at the Simms home, Georgie showed Maria to Edwina's bedroom. "There is an explanation for Henry's absence and all the confusion about Carolyn, but I'm not at liberty to tell you all of it just yet. Try to be patient until tomorrow, Maria. I will come here to Eddie's room and awaken you at dawn. Hopefully you will understand why we will all do our best to keep the Grishams as comfortable as possible for tonight."

At daybreak Georgie led Maria through a dark storage room to an alcove behind the Simmses' kitchen. A gas light flickered at the back door as Henry stepped out of the shadows. He placed his fingertips over her lips to muffle Maria's startled cry.

"Hush, dear heart," he whispered, drawing her close and pressing his cheek to hers. "I have been waiting for this moment ever since your father's telegraph."

"But Georgie didn't tell me that you—" She splayed her hands against his chest and twisted around to face Henry's sister, but Georgie had slipped out of the room. Maria turned to Henry with a puzzled look.

"My sister didn't tell you that I couldn't get here until today, because she was following Father's wishes," Henry said, taking both her hands in his. "I was needed in surgery all day yesterday and couldn't possibly get to the train to meet you. But I *have* longed to hold you in my arms."

For an instant her eyes betrayed her need to be in his arms too, but Maria shook her head.

"I *was* disappointed not to see you yesterday. I knew something was wrong when your father met our train. Things just did not add up on that trip to the Sanitary Commission either. Your father told us about the Contraband Hospital at Freedmans Village, and then we couldn't go there!"

"Let me explain, but first—" He lowered his mouth to hers and kissed her lips with infinite tenderness.

"I've dreamed about doing that for days," he said as his long lashes swept her cheek. "Please let us just be Henry and Maria from now on, all right?"

Despite the cold damp morning, Maria felt a tingling warmth spread from her lips down her neck. She pressed a hand to her heart and met his gaze. "All right . . . Henry. I'd like that."

Henry's eyes glinted in the lamplight. He stepped back and held her at arm's length. "I have been waiting for time off from the Surgeon General, you see. My father went along with my plan for him to bring the Grishams to the Sanitary Commission first. That was arranged yesterday, so that I could be the one to take you all in a carriage to Carolyn early this morning. I caught the first omnibus out of Georgetown to get here."

"I still don't understand, Henry. Why is Carolyn not at the Contraband Hospital?"

"It's a long story, but it wasn't possible for her to stay there."

"Not possible? But why?"

"Well, Carolyn had a stubborn notion that she could work there, nursing the freed slaves until she could no longer lift a hand. But the doctor at Contraband Hospital knew right away that Miss Grisham needed to be a patient more than she needed to be a nurse. She barely made it through one week."

"Is she really that sick, Henry?"

"I'm afraid so, Maria. Carolyn has typhoid fever."

Maria's hands flew to her mouth. "Mercy, no!"

"So many of the injured soldiers brought aboard the *Daniel Webster* were suffering with the fever that it is not surprising she became ill. The amazing thing is her spirit. She worked aboard ship right along with the fever and headaches."

"Then how did they find out?"

"One of the other nurses saw the mulberry spots on her skin. A sure sign. That was the end of her service aboard the hospital ship."

"I cannot believe all this happened in such a short time. I know it took longer than expected for Mr. Grisham to get all the travel arrangements made for us to get here. Then we were delayed in Baltimore waiting for Carolyn's mother. But, Henry, the Grishams know nothing about the fever. They only know that she is ill. What will you tell them? What will happen to Carolyn now?"

"That will be up to the good Lord. That was the reason for delaying the Grishams yesterday, so I could tell them. But believe me, I do not cherish being the messenger of this bad news. I have to try to prepare Mr. Grisham before I take them to see her."

"Where is she, Henry? You haven't told me where Carolyn is." Maria bit her lip, searching his troubled green eyes. "Or why it is that you and I are meeting back here in secret?"

Henry's brow relaxed and his mustache twitched with the start of a smile. He took her hands in his again, kissing one and then the other.

"Think about it, Maria. Georgie knew how anxious you

were to see me, and I to see you. She convinced Father to let us have these few moments alone at first light, before the serious business of the Grishams is faced. My sisters know how much I've missed you. It would have been awkward to greet you as I just did with everyone present. You understand?"

Maria felt her cheeks flame. She lifted his hand, pressing it to her face. "I have missed you too, Henry. I was so happy when your last letter arrived. To know that you don't wish to wait anymore was like an answer to my prayers."

"I still find it hard to believe your father allowed you to come to Washington. Do you think maybe his feelings are softening about us?"

"It's hard to tell *what* my father is thinking. I dared not tell him you were hoping to finish your duties early and return to New York, else he probably would not have let me come here at all." Maria tilted her head and pressed her lips together in a winsome smile. "I did tell him our love is strong, but not that you wanted me in your life now."

He kissed her again, soundly this time.

"I do. I do. But in the next few days there will be little time for me to kiss you, hold you close, or even walk with you."

"I'm thankful, Henry, just to be near you, here in your father's house. Did you know that Edwina is sharing her room with me?"

Henry enfolded her in his arms and smiled, then kissed the soft spot below her earlobe. He whispered into her ear, "I know, and I'm thankful too, more than you know." He stood back, holding her at arm's length. "I have only a few hours today, so I must leave right now to get a rented carriage at Pumphrey's Stable."

"When will you be back?"

"I should be back in about a half hour to bring you to Harewood Hospital. That's where Carolyn is. I want you to go quickly inside now. Have some breakfast, find Father and tell him that everything is arranged." He squeezed her hands. "And say a prayer that when I return, I can find the right words to tell the Grishams what to expect."

Dawn was brightening the sky and the first birds were calling as Edward Simms led Maria and the Grishams outside to Henry's rented carriage.

"Mr. Grisham will find the best doctor for our daughter, be sure of that," Carolyn's mother said to Maria as Edward helped her, and then Maria, into the carriage.

Maria knew better than to say differently. She held Mrs. Grisham's hand, trying her best not to ruffle her. The frail-looking woman had all but swooned when Dr. Simms told them about the fever. But then, in the next breath, Mrs. Grisham became rigid and obstinate. She refused to believe Henry when he explained that there is seldom a recovery from the disease.

Henry's talk with the Grishams played over and over in Maria's mind. Carolyn's mother seemed determined to prove the doctors wrong, but Mr. Grisham was much more understanding. It was difficult to meet his gaze when Henry told him. His sad blue eyes misted and he ran his fingers through his fiery hair. Carolyn was the image of him.

Mr. Grisham sat next to Henry on the driver's seat as they drove up Seventh Street Road.

"My father thinks that Harewood Hospital is one of the best facilities around," Henry said. "The hospital was built by the government on the old Corcoran Farm. It has fifteen large pavilions for the patients, as well as service buildings. I'm sure Carolyn is receiving the best possible care. The Sisters of Charity and the Sisters of Mercy work very hard there."

"Be that as it may, I simply have to try to bring my daughter home," Mr. Grisham said, lowering his voice. "I have not been able to get through to her mother that Carolyn may not survive this dread disease, so I must make every effort to arrange for safe travel back to New York."

Henry pursed his lips and flicked the reins, turning the horses up a winding dirt road. He decided to say no more. *Let them see for themselves,* he thought.

"There it is ahead, at the top of that hill, sir. The Corcoran Farm. You see that fancy big barn? That's where all the supplies and equipment are stored for the hospital. The long buildings in a horseshoe curve house the patients. I'll stop and try to find out which ward Carolyn is in."

Fear threatened Mrs. Grisham's hope that Carolyn would not be as sick as Dr. Simms had said. Her fear surrendered her to silence.

Henry stopped alongside a large vegetable garden where a man was supervising workers gathering the last of a cabbage crop. After speaking to the man, Henry drove in silence to the very last pavilion on the horseshoe curve.

"The supervisor knew right away where to send us when I mentioned that Carolyn was a nurse patient and not a soldier," Henry whispered to Maria as he helped her out of the carriage. "She's in an isolation ward."

Mr. Grisham helped his wife down from the carriage and guided her toward the entrance. A Sister of Charity met them and spoke quietly to Mr. Grisham before bringing them inside.

Row upon row of cots stretched out before them. A mixed stench of foul smells stung Maria's nostrils. The nun led them to a curtained corner of the long barn-like ward.

Maria stood with Henry at the open curtain while Mr. Grisham guided his wife toward a cot. Expecting the worse did not make it easier to face.

Mrs. Grisham's sudden, keening wail broke the silence. Maria squeezed Henry's hand and leaned into his side.

Henry whispered, "Carolyn may not know you. Be strong, dear heart."

"Carolyn, it's Papa," Mr. Grisham said. "Your mother is here to help you get well. Can you speak to us, dear?"

Maria and Henry moved closer. Carolyn's once flaming hair was a tangle of sweat-drenched rusty curls plastered to the sides of her sallow face. Her eyes, glazed with fever, seemed to stare into space. A telltale smell of laudanum hung in the air.

Maria heard Carolyn's raspy voice. "You shouldn't have come, Mama." Then silence. Carolyn's hollow eyes stared, half closed. Tears coursed down Mrs. Grisham's face. There was a long moment of silence.

Suddenly Carolyn's head twisted from side to side. Her eyes opened wide. She was trying to heave her body up, calling out, "It's all right, yes, yes. Nurse Carolyn is going to help you . . ." Her hand shot out from under the sheet and waved wildly. "Over here, Doctor, quickly. Oh Lord, Lord. Big John, my dear—"

As suddenly as she had attempted to rise, her shoulders slumped and her head sank back into the pillow.

Mrs. Grisham turned to her husband, sobbing. A nun stepped into the curtained space with a basin of water. She felt Carolyn's neck for a pulse, then wrung out a wet rag from the basin and placed it on her forehead. The Sister nodded to Dr. Simms and patted Mr. Grisham's arm.

"It's best to let Miss Carolyn rest now, sir. Please come with me," she said, taking Mrs. Grisham's arm and leading her away from the cot. Carolyn's father laid his hand gently on Carolyn's head. Maria could hear his soft, shuddering moan. As he turned to follow his wife, the forlorn expression on his face brought tears to Maria's eyes.

Trying to hide her own dismay, she brushed the tears away and stepped closer to the cot. She groped for Carolyn's hand. "Carolyn, it's Maria. Can you hear me?" Carolyn lay motionless, her eyes half closed again. There was no response.

Henry put his arm around Maria and drew her back a little. "I'm afraid it's no use, Maria. Delirium has set in and any conscious thoughts Carolyn might have will be few and far between. The good Sisters are doing all they can for her. Perhaps tomorrow she will know you."

For the next two days, the Grishams made the trip up Seventh Street Road in a carriage with Maria and Edward Simms. Carolyn showed no change.

At the end of their third visit, late in the day, Mrs. Grisham asked to speak with a Sister of Mercy. Maria followed them to a small dispensary that served as a surgeon's office.

Weak rays of sunlight slanted through a tiny window above shelves of bottles, basins and bandages. A single wooden chair was pulled up to a table laden with stacks of records. The nun urged Mrs. Grisham to sit as she took a paper from the top of the pile. Mr. Grisham moved closer to the table.

Maria watched from the doorway. The nun looked briefly at the paper in her hands and cleared her throat. "You wish to speak to me about Carolyn's condition, I'm sure." Mrs. Grisham gave a short nod.

"God asks us to be merciful, Mrs. Grisham. Your daughter showed all the mercy and compassion a body could when she worked with the colored who flocked to the Contraband Hospital. To the harm of her own declining condition, I might add."

Mrs. Grisham bristled. "So we were told, but do tell me why a merciful God will not let us bring our daughter home with us now."

"Because, my dear lady, Doctor has ordered it so. She is not to be moved because she is much too ill, and I do believe Miss Carolyn is where she wishes to be."

"But she doesn't realize that we could do so much more for her in New York," Mrs. Grisham said.

"Perhaps so, but we must leave this in God's hands. I have prayed with Carolyn, and heard her pleas to our gracious Lord. In lucid moments, your daughter still has hope . . . hope that she will get better and be able to continue nursing the poor unfortunates here in Washington City."

"Carolyn has hope?" Mrs. Grisham's eyes brightened for a second, then suddenly clouded again. "I know that my daughter has a certain loyalty to our *people*. She has never forgotten our way of life on the plantation. But this horrible war has changed everything. I just cannot accept that my precious daughter is willing to risk her life to . . . to—"

Mrs. Grisham's gulping sobs choked her words. She raised a handkerchief to her face, and burst into tears.

As her weeping grew louder, Maria shuffled her feet nervously. She placed her fingertips to her lips, silently willing the woman's crying to stop. *If only something would happen to make Mrs. Grisham understand.*

As if on cue, the room grew suddenly dark. Lightning flashed in the small window and thunder rattled the windowpane. Big raindrops splatted against it.

Maria cast a pleading glance at Carolyn's father. She moved swiftly to Mrs. Grisham's side, clasping her hand. Mr. Grisham took his wife's arm. Together they gently lifted her out of the chair.

"I think we'd best go along now, Mrs. Grisham," Maria

said. "A storm is brewing and I'm sure Mr. Simms will be anxious to get us home in the carriage."

Maria prayed all the way back to C Street that something would convince Carolyn's mother to leave her daughter in God's hands. Her prayers did not go unanswered.

Chapter Twenty-Eight

In the hours after the Grishams' departure from Harewood Hospital, Carolyn slipped into a coma. She died without ever awakening.

01 November, 1863
Washington City
When I left Evergreen Park with Mr. Grisham, I never dreamed that Carolyn was so deathly ill. Certainly not that she would be taken from us so swiftly. I can scarcely take it all in. One thing is sure. My dear courageous friend will never be forgotten. She will always have a place in the corner of my heart.
A Reverend Hardy presided at her burial. He did not know Carolyn, but he knew about her work. Very fitting words were quoted from the Psalm of David: "And the justice of your cause will shine like the noonday sun."
What a sad, sad day it was. I had become accustomed to Carolyn's mother's weeping, but it broke my heart to see Mr. Grisham's eyes cloud with tears.
As we left the graveyard, he gave me a small prayer book that had belonged to Carolyn. "You should have this," is all he said. Inside I found a folded scrap of newsprint dated February 27, 1860. It was an excerpt of a speech Abraham Lincoln gave at Cooper Union in New York. These words were underlined:

"Let us have faith that right makes might, and in that faith, let us, to the end, dare to do our duty as we understand it."

Carolyn surely lived the last months of her life by that oath. I believe that God has a purpose for my life, too. I pray that Carolyn's light will shine on in me. I need her daring to stay here in Washington City and not go home with the Grishams. I think I am strong enough to do this, but hope and dismay do battle in my mind. Today I am writing to Papa. Henry has promised to post my letter.

Maria O.

390 C Street

Washington City

Dear Father,

I wish the good Lord could wipe away the sorrow of this day. It grieves me to send this word that my dear friend, Carolyn, has died in the grace of the Lord. She was very ill with typhoid fever, and her decline was shockingly fast. I'm sure Mr. Grisham will tell you all about it when he arrives back in Brooklyn.

Carolyn served as a nurse with grit and fervor, and no one could begin to take her place. Certainly not me, but I am needed here in Washington, Papa. Mr. Simms has welcomed me to stay as long as I wish.

Cartloads of wounded have come into the city from the hospital ships. Henry says they are the survivors of a terrible battle in Tennessee. Henry's sisters, Virginia and Edwina, could use my help with the wounded soldiers the Simms family has taken into their home. I hope to be able to assist them, but a different opportunity has come up which may be more suited to me. Henry's sister Georgiana would like me to help her teach the children from the contraband camps to read and write. Space *for a classroom has been made in the basement of St. Aloysius Church.*

I am so excited about having the chance at last to help where help is needed. I know how you feel about slavery, but surely you wouldn't deny me the opportunity to teach the poor colored children to read and write. I think Mother would be proud of me for what I have chosen to do. I try my best to copy her example and imitate her virtues.

Please don't worry about me, Papa. I will come home as soon as Dr. Simms is released from his duties. Give my love to the girls and brother Andrew. Tell them I miss them, as I do you.

Your loving daughter,
Maria

A soldier lay on his side on a cot in Henry's old room. Virginia was showing Maria how to change the dressing of his wound. As Virginia peeled away the bloody bandage, Maria tried to focus on the display of family pictures on Henry's old dresser. Daguerreotypes of Henry's mother and a much younger Philip stood side by side.

The soldier's moans brought her back to the serious task at hand.

Virginia was cleansing the septic area where a bullet had gone clear through the muscle of the man's shoulder, exiting near his neck. The sight made Maria shiver. She drew in her breath and winced as though she were bearing the pain the soldier endured.

Virginia gave her a sharp look. The basin holding the bloody bandages trembled in Maria's hands. She swallowed down the knot in her throat.

Virginia swiftly secured the dressing with a torn strip of sheeting from her apron pocket. She tucked a folded blanket under the wounded shoulder and helped the soldier to rest against it. "There, that should make you feel better soon, Captain," she said. "Come, Maria. Perhaps some of Elizabeth's beef bouillon will help the Captain gain his strength."

Virginia paused at the top of the stairs. "I'm sorry that didn't go well for you, Maria. I'm sorry, too, about my scolding look. I try not to show emotion in front of the soldiers, but I know you have had little practice with things of this sort. Have you ever cared for an injured person before?"

"No." Maria shook her head, shamefaced. "I only wish I could do as you do. You are so calm and straightforward with the soldiers. I feel embarrassed for being so squeamish, but I felt a little sick in there."

"Please don't let it trouble you. I think it just comes naturally to me. Probably I have Henry's nature," she said, tilting her head and smiling at Maria.

"Do you think Henry will be disappointed in me?"

"Heavens, no. Henry loves everything about you. There is no room for disappointment. We are all happy to have you here. I do think that maybe it will be best for you to just help Elizabeth with the food trays for a while. You could help to feed those who can't manage on their own . . . just until you become more accustomed to things."

Maria nodded and attempted a weak smile.

"Besides, Georgie is anxious to get started next week at St. Aloysius, and I know you will do well there. Now, let's go get that bouillon for the Captain."

Washington City offered a dreadful spectacle to anyone navigating its streets. Army wagons and artillery rumbled through. There was a constant clamor of caissons and soldiers roistering and shouting. Trains and steamers carrying the dead and wounded rattled over Long Bridge or tied up at the Sixth Street piers. Injured soldiers jammed the city hospitals and even walked in the city's best districts. The streets had become intolerable.

Georgie and Maria hurried along North Capitol Street, headed for St. Aloysius Church. Soldiers were everywhere, patrolling from nearby forts, or on their way to and from nearby hospitals.

"It was one thing to sit at home in Evergreen Park, knitting stockings for them. It is quite another to see soldiers at every turn. Heaven knows how any of you have managed to keep your sanity," Maria said.

A horse and wagon moved dangerously close. The wagon was a blur of uniforms. Maria looked up, startled by men whistling and calling to them in a crude and unbecoming manner. Georgie pulled her bonnet lower over her face and clung to Maria's arm. "We can trust the ones Father has taken into our home, but these soldiers out here on foot and in wagons—well, it's best to look straight ahead. Papa wouldn't have let us risk the danger if he knew we were on foot today. We'll probably have to hire a buggy from now on."

Both girls were buttoned into warm cloaks against the cold November wind. Maria carried a heavy sack filled with slates, chalk and a few books that Mr. Simms had scavenged for them. Georgie's basket was laden with a pot of stew and biscuits from the Simmses' kitchen.

"Thank heavens it's not too long a walk," Maria said, as Georgie pointed out the wooden doors of a brick church through the trees up ahead.

The basement of St. Aloysius Church could be reached by a stairway behind a door in the vestry, or from a side door at the lower side of the church. The girls came in through the vestry. The basement room under the nave was damp, cold, and dark. Someone had arranged chairs around two long tables, adorned with a solitary oil lamp. The makings of a fire were ready in a box next to an old iron cookstove.

"Thank the Lord for tender mercies," Georgie said, as she eyed the stove and lit the lamp. "Put the slates in the center of this table, Maria, while I get the stove going. I think you will find some bowls and spoons in that corner cupboard. We'll need to warm and feed their bodies first before we can try their minds."

Soon Georgie had the firewood hissing and snapping under the stew pot. Bowls and spoons were placed on the second table.

Maria was leafing through a small book of Mother Goose rhymes when the door at the top of the stairs flew open to a group of children. They stood shivering on the stairs. A man's voice called out from beyond the door, "I'll be back roun' two bells, chirun. You be ready, Abram, ya hear?" The door closed behind them.

Georgie looked at a small timepiece pinned to a ribbon on her shirtwaist. "That gives us a little over two hours with them. I count six children," she whispered to Maria, "and they look like frightened scarecrows."

Maria stepped to the bottom stair. The tallest child, a boy, stood in front of the other children. He seemed to be shepherding the group. A worn Army coat hung loosely from his thin shoulders. It almost reached the top of his worn, dirty boots. He wore tattered, striped livery pants held up with a piece of rope.

Maria smiled at him and beckoned. "Come along, children. Come down near the stove and warm yourselves," she said.

The boy whipped off a battered kepi cap and bent his torso in what was surely meant to be a bow. His coffee-colored face broke into a grin that didn't reach his wary eyes.

The boy nudged a younger child who held tight to the hand of a smaller girl beside him. "Move on down, Willie," he said. "Don't you wanna see what's on those tables?"

"No need to be afraid, children," Georgie said, walking briskly to Maria's side. "You are in the house of the Lord and God will bless us all. I'm Miss Georgiana, but you may call me Miss Georgie."

She took the hand of the smallest child, and led her to the table nearest the stove. Maria watched as the others followed slowly until all six stood behind a chair.

Each child's clothes were more ragged and shabby than the next. On this cold day, none wore coats, except for the tall boy in the Army coat. Some had raggedy sweaters or jackets without buttons, pulled close around their thin bodies. The smallest girl was wrapped in a frayed and stained wool shawl that covered her from head to toe.

Maria took her place at one end of the table, Georgie at the opposite end. "Miss Georgie has brought some beef stew today. We will be eating before our lesson, children, so let's bow our heads and offer thanks for this food."

Maria could see from the corner of her eye that the tall boy bowed his head and the other children quickly followed suit.

"Bless us, oh Lord, for these our gifts, which we are about to receive from Thy bounty, through Christ our Lord, and please, dear Lord, be with us today as we learn, Amen."

Georgie bent to whisper to the little girl as she unwrapped the shawl from her head. Then, nodding to Maria, Miss Georgiana took her place to serve at the stove.

Maria took the hand of the girl child and directed the rest to line up behind her. Georgie ladled stew into bowls, topping each bowl with a biscuit.

The tall boy, last in line, eyed his bowl as he hurried to his

chair. The children gulped down their food like hungry rab-
bits eating stolen cabbages in a farmer's garden. Their dark
eyes darted left and right as spoons went from bowl to mouth.

The tall boy sopped the last of his biscuit in the gravy leav-
ings of his bowl, swallowing the morsel with a loud sigh of sat-
isfaction. He looked over the heads of the children to see if
they had all finished, then grinned again at Maria. "Thank
you kindly, Miz," he said. "That was most delicious."

Maria was surprised at his manners and at the big words
that he used. "You are most welcome. My name is Miss
Maria," she said. "What is your name?"

"I'm called A . . . bra . . . ham," he said slowly, emphasizing the syllables. "Marse gave me that name after my
pappy come to be his houseman. Marse Ian say my name
come from the Good Book."

"That's right, and a fine name it is. The Bible tells us that
the first Abraham was a great leader, the father of God's
chosen people. Our president, Mr. Lincoln, has that name as
well, and he leads our country. I'm guessing that you are the
leader of these children today. Am I right, Abraham?"

This time a ready smile brightened his eyes. "Yes'm, these
be the children of the house slaves of ole Marse. That be
Marse Ian McCormack. After he freed us, we come to
Washton City with my pappy. Pastor Higgins here gave my
pappy work in this fine church an' Pastor say we can have a
new life if we learn to read an' write."

"Indeed you may. You have a good start, Abraham."

"Yes'm. I be learnin' to speak proper-like in the big house.
I had it better than these chirun cuz I worked in the kitchen.

"Sometimes I helped young Master James. I listened when
the teacher come to the big house to teach Master James. My
pappy say, 'God give you ears to hear, son, so listen to they
words, and say them to yo'sef. Jus' keep yer eyes down, an

201

don' let 'em know you is listnin'. Seem like I spent a lot o' time listnin'."

The boy scratched his head and looked up at Maria with a smile. Maria couldn't help but smile back. She looked up to see Georgie's lips twitching.

"I'm glad to know you are a good listener, Abraham. I think you are going to be a big help to Miss Georgie and me. If you will help clear these bowls to the other table, we will start today by learning some letters."

As soon as the bowls were cleared away, Maria took chalk and one of the slates. She wrote a big "A" on it for all to see. Georgie did the same. "This letter is called a big 'A.' It is the first letter of our alphabet, children. The letters of an alphabet make up all the words you will learn to read and write. The letter 'A' starts Abraham's name," Maria said, placing her hand on the boy's shoulder.

Maria walked around, pointing to the letter for each child to see. Next she wrote Abraham on her slate. " 'A' is the letter we learn today." She clapped to the beat of the words. "Let me hear you say that rhyme after me. " 'A' is the letter we learn today."

"Very good, children," Georgie said, passing a slate and chalk to each child. "Now you can all practice making a big 'A' on your slates. Miss Maria and I will come around to help. We will all think of words that have an 'A' sound."

Maria's heart was as light as a feather. *This is the direction the Lord would have me take. Please continue to strengthen me, Lord. Use my life to share your love with these little ones. Especially bless the efforts of Abraham. The boy tugs at my heart.*

Georgie walked around the table reading rhymes containing "A" sounds from the Mother Goose book. The door at the top of the stairs creaked open and a tall, rail-thin colored man stood quietly, looking down. Georgiana stopped reading and raised her eyes from the book. The man's presence could not be ignored.

"I be here for Abraham and the chirun," the man called down in a deep voice.

Abraham jumped up from his chair and turned to Maria. "Would that be your father?" she asked.

"Yes'm. We best hurry." Abraham clapped his hands and the children's gazes flew to him. He bowed his head. "Thank you, Jesus, for our 'A's an' fo' Miz Maria, an' Miz Georgie." Abraham pointed at the children. They bowed their heads and did their best to repeat his thank-you.

Maria's eyes glistened as she and Georgie helped the children with their wraps and led them to the stairs. Abraham was the last to race up the stairway and step into the vestry behind the children.

The boy's father tipped his cap, flashing a heartwarming smile before he closed the door.

He must be proud of Abraham and oh, how Carolyn would be proud of me, Maria thought. *I can't wait to tell Henry all about this day.*

Chapter Twenty-Nine

"It's a treat to have you here for Sunday dinner, son. I expect Miss Maria thinks so too. Hmm, my dear?" Mr. Simms asked, smiling at her.

Maria sat at Mr. Simms's right, across the table from Henry. She blushed, giving a ready smile back to Edward Simms, and then to Henry. "Indeed I do, sir."

"Well, I'm thankful for this chance, believe me," Henry said. "I haven't had a good home-cooked meal like this in a month of Sundays. Thanks are also due you, Father, for speaking to Surgeon General Hammond about my commission. Now that I have it, it will make it much easier on me when I get back to New York."

"I hope that doesn't mean you will be taking Maria away soon," Virginia said. Maria sat very still, her brow knit in a frown.

Georgie's eyes darted from Maria to Henry. "What does the commission have to do with staying or going?" Georgie asked.

Henry stroked his side-whiskers, glancing at Maria. He had intended to tell her about this, but they'd had so little time alone. Neither had he anticipated these questions.

"The truth of it is, Hammond has secured cooperation from state governors with a new plan for surgeons. New York, like other states, has agreed to have a Reserve Surgeon's Corps. Not only will doctors with commissions be paid more for service, we will only have to serve the Medical Department on demand, with minimum days of service. For me, it means I'll be able to leave service here before the New Year, but I may be on call to come back, if needed."

There was an awkward silence. Something seemed amiss with Maria. She toyed with the scraps of food left on her plate. The smile was gone from her face, and she kept her eyes cast down when Mr. Simms responded to Henry's remarks about the Surgeon's Corps.

Georgie broke the silence. "Father, as long as Henry has a carriage today, do you suppose he could take Maria and me up to St. Aloysius after dinner?" she asked. "We've been wanting to show Henry our classroom, and we do have preparations to make for tomorrow's lesson."

Maria's head snapped up and her mouth opened, but she said nothing.

"I can't see any harm in that, Georgiana," Edward said, "although I think Henry will want to wait for Elizabeth to bring in his favorite dessert. It's cherry pie today, son."

"Wouldn't miss that for anything, Father," Henry said.

Georgie reached across Maria to tuck a lap robe over their knees.

"You are the best sister in the world," Henry said, pinching his sister's cheek. The three were squeezed together on the seat of a one-horse shay. Henry gave Maria's gloved hand a quick press before he snapped the reins.

Maria had been very quiet since they left the house, and she did not respond to Henry's touch. She guessed at Georgie's real intent for this trip to the church, but her mind was beset with questions and doubts about what Henry had revealed at dinner.

"From what you have told me about this class of yours, I'd

say you two are first-rate teachers. Georgie tells me that the children love you, Maria. That's not in the least surprising," Henry said. His eyes gleamed as he aimed a smile and a wink in her direction. "Who wouldn't?"

Still she did not respond.

"You must be proud of their progress, my dear," he said.

"Of course I am proud of their progress," Maria said with an edge to her words, "but more than that, it's their eagerness to learn that warms the heart." Her voice softened. "The children try so hard, and they have so little. It's very easy to please them."

"Teaching them to write their names was like giving them a shiny gold piece, Henry," Georgie said. "Tomorrow we are making paper bookmarks with a place for each one to print his or her name."

"Sounds like an ambitious project, but what in the world would they do with bookmarks? Most of them have probably never held a book in their hands."

"Well, that will soon change. Father has promised to get us books of rhymes to give to the children at Christmas. So that's the reason for the bookmarks. And that's what I'd like to work on when we get to the church. Bookmarks."

Maria gave Georgie an inquisitive look. "Did Pastor Wiggins give you a key for the vestry door?"

"No, but there's no need to go inside the church. People will be using the lower church rooms for choir practice starting this evening, so the lower church door should be open. We can just go around to the side and down the ramp."

Georgie twisted around Maria to look at her brother. "Maria hasn't seen much of the city, Henry. While I get our project started, perhaps you would like to drive her around a bit. There isn't much left of daylight, and she might enjoy seeing the square."

"However well intentioned, Georgie, I don't think that's the plan your father agreed to when you asked if Henry could bring us in the carriage," Maria said, pursing her lips and looking straight ahead.

Henry winked at his sister. "Well, mum's the word then, Miss Georgiana," he said, reining the horse around the side of the tall brick church.

Without hesitation, as soon as the buggy stopped, Georgiana hiked up her skirts with one hand, holding fast to the large carriage wheel with the other. Surprising them both, she stepped down onto the carriage block, and jumped to the ground.

Before either of them could react, she turned to wave them away. "Don't be too long," she called. "Twilight's upon us. It feels like snow."

There was a hint of snow in an oyster sky, and Maria shivered, watching Georgie walk down the ramp to the side entrance. The dappled mare snorted and stamped in the cold air.

Henry gathered the reins in one hand, and squeezed Maria's gloved hand again. "You probably think my sister is a schemer, I know, but she is really an answer to my prayers today. Although my father probably wouldn't object, I've been trying to find a time and place when we could be alone to talk, if only for a little while. I am thankful Georgie is so observant, and you should be, too."

Maria bit her lip. "I know your sister means well. I should not be taking my frustration out on her."

Henry hawed to the mare, trying to guide her on a steady course over the frozen ruts of North Capitol Street. Above the jingle of harness, he began to sing as the horse clomped along through the fading afternoon.

"That's a song the soldiers love to sing, Maria. It's called 'Lorena.' Do you like it?"

"I do love to hear you sing, Henry, but it's such a sad song and . . . and, I'm trying to keep a rein on my feelings right now."

"I think I know why. I meant to tell you that news about the Reserve Surgeon's Corps when we were alone. I know it's a bit of a shock to you, but it's really more of a blessing than you know."

"I don't see how it can be, Henry. Last month, when your letter came about leaving service by year's end, I thought we had at last put all the waiting and wondering behind."

"Well, we really have, Maria. I'm pretty sure I'll be allowed to leave soon after Christmas. If you are willing to leave your teaching duties, we can begin to plan our wedding."

Maria shook her head and straightened her shoulders. "When my father finds out you could be called back for service, I don't think he will listen to any wedding plans."

Henry reined the horse in under a copse of trees to the side of the square. A few people strolled in the square, bundled up in scarves and winter cloaks, but they were hardly visible from where the carriage stood. Barren though they were, the trees provided a little barrier from a cold wind that had begun to blow.

In a one-arm squeeze of her shoulder, Henry pulled her to him on the narrow seat. He cupped her chin in his hand, tilting her head to meet his gaze. "Maria, Maria," he sighed. "In the past, when I received your letters, I could rest your words in my heart, even though I couldn't hold you in my arms. Now that you are here in my embrace, have you no words of encouragement for me?"

Maria hung her head and knotted her gloved hands together tightly. "It's because I was counting on not waiting anymore, Henry. You said in your letter you wanted me in your life now."

"You know I meant that, dear heart. We *have* waited a long time, but weddings do take planning. If we set a date for spring or summer, that's only months away. I doubt that I will be called back into service in those months."

"I'm not sure Papa will see it that way. He will probably ask why we do not wait until the war's end?"

"And if he does, well, I'll just tell him that most of the officers I'm in contact with think that the war *will* end this year. I trust in God that it is not just our soldiers' yearnings for peace."

She leaned her head on his shoulder for a brief moment. "I hope you can convince my father of that."

"Maria, there is such longing in my heart for you, that I don't think *anyone* could dissuade me from this point on, your papa included. Trust me. We *are* going to set a date." He put both arms around her, drawing her close.

She rested her hands against his chest. "But, Henry, we are here in the middle of town and—"

"And I mean to kiss my lady love," he said.

Big lacy snowflakes were falling, unnoticed, all around them. As Henry bent to kiss her lips, star-shaped flakes blew into the carriage like thistledown on a sudden breeze. They settled on Maria's nose and hair.

"Oooh!" she cried, blinking in surprise.

Holding her tightly, Henry chuckled. He pressed his cheek to hers and rocked back and forth with her on the narrow seat. They watched the fast falling snow settle on the carriage.

"First snow of winter, dear heart. Looks like a phantom world of white out there already, and you are my phantom of delight. Remember?" Without waiting for an answer, he settled his lips very gently on hers.

When she opened her eyes, they widened with a sudden light, rendering them luminous as cat's eyes. "Just look at the snow on the trees, Henry. They've lit the gas lamps and it makes the branches look like they've been strung with tiny twinkling lights."

Henry nodded and reluctantly released her. "We should be getting back to the church. As certain as nightfall, if these gas lamps have come on, Georgie will see the snow. She will be worried about getting home."

Henry reined the horse about, letting it find its stride on the snow-covered street. The muffled jingle of harness over new snow sounded like a softly strummed harp to Maria's ears.

05 December 1863
Washington City
I should have had more faith in Henry today. Instead, I let my worries and foolish pride get the better of me. Dear Henry has been my strength and my hope for all that is right in this terrible war. I must remember to leave our love in God's hands. It is frightening, though, to think of going home and facing Papa. Jo's letters say that he speaks of me lately with kind words, but that remains to be seen. I pray that I will find something to do in New York as worthy as my teaching the children at St. Aloysius. I shall miss them, and only hope that I have made a little difference in their lives.
Maria O.

Chapter Thirty

Edward Simms unpacked a box of books he had ordered from McLaughlin Brothers in New York. He looked at the cover and flyleaf, *Mother Goose's Melodies.* "These should fill the bill, my dears. Nursery rhymes for the children's Christmas," he said, handing books to Maria and Georgie.

Georgie leafed through the illustrated pages. "They are just perfect. I was hoping you might come to the children's party and play Father Christmas."

"It will be my last day with the children," Maria added, "and it would make it very special, Mr. Simms, if you would give the gifts to the children."

"Now, now. These are *your* gifts to the children, as it should be. I am only happy to have been able to get them for you. You deserve all the 'fruits of your labor,' as the Good Book says. You've done wonders with the children.

"Furthermore, Father Higgins wrote a glowing description of your charitable work. He describes your talent and skills with children and the outstanding job you do at the church. I shall see that you get a copy. It may lead to more 'fruitful labor' in store for you, Maria, when you get back to New York."

"I'm thankful to the pastor for his kind words, but it is you, Mr. Simms, who have made it all possible. You have been more than gracious. First to the Grishams, and most especially to me. You have made me feel like part of your family."

Edward leaned forward to squeeze Maria's shoulder. "Well, God willing, my dear, you *will* be family soon. Henry has asked me to accompany the two of you to New York. He is hoping to get permission to leave Georgetown right after Christmas, but as you know, he's waiting on a date from the Surgeon General."

"That would be wonderful, if you would come. I know my father would be pleased to have you visit Evergreen Park."

"I'm sure Henry can convince your father about a wedding without me along, my dear, but my son seems to think he would have a stronger case with me by his side. I've agreed to go, as long as my girls can manage here for a week or so without me."

Washington City
23 December 1863
The party for the children at St. Aloysius will not be as joyous as I expected today, but it is going on as planned. Light snow followed by an ice storm last night almost canceled everything. The lamplighters cannot get around town, and the streets and rails are covered with ice.

The worse thing is that Georgie is down with a terrible grippe and won't be able to go with me. She feels so sad about missing it after all our preparations. I know the children will miss her too.

Henry's sisters knitted stockings for each child and we filled them with oranges, sweets and nuts. The church will provide cake and hot cocoa and, of course, the books are all wrapped and waiting. I will read the Nativity story and the children will sing carols.

After Carolyn died, I prayed that God would give me strength to depend on Him alone . . . that He would steady my heart and help me to move forward with love and hope.

He answered that prayer and opened the narrow gate to this new life for me. I may be alone at St. Aloysius today, but Carolyn's spirit will be with me.

Mr. Simms hired a buggy to bring me to the church himself, but he is unable to stay due to an appointment he must keep with the Surgeon General. A good result of that will be that Dr. Simms will come with the buggy at five to bring me home from the party.

Maria O.

"I'm so glad you could stay to help me clean up, Abraham. You're such a good helper during our classes. I would have expected nothing less from you today. Everything looks in order here now, thanks to you."

Abraham gathered his old Army coat. Maria asked, "How will you get back to your camp? The roads are a mess of ice, and it's much too cold for you to walk."

"Father Higgins got some chores for me to do upstairs in the vestry, Miz Maria. An' then I can lock up the church and go to the rectory. Father says he'll bring me home. He told my pappy he was mighty pleased with our singing about Baby Jesus today."

"You must have practiced with the children. I've not heard such beautiful singing of carols."

"That's 'cause Miz Georgie, she teached us good."

"She would have been proud today." Maria shook her head slowly. "She was so sad not to be here to see everyone open their books."

"Yes'm, I knows they all missed her too. I have somthin' for Miz Georgie and for you, too." Abraham fished in his coat pocket and brought forth two small parcels. He put one in each of his hands. "Christmas gifs," he said, holding them out.

"Oh my, Abraham. Shall I open mine?"

"Yes'm." His eyes brightened with a smile.

Maria slipped off the newspaper wrapping revealing a tiny carved wooden figure. The infant Jesus with arms out-stretched from a crude manger.

"Pappy taught me how to whittle. I hopes you like it."

"Like it? Why, it's beautiful. I love Him, and I know Miss Georgiana will too. Thank you, Abraham," she said, squeezing his shoulder. "God has certainly blessed you with many talents."

Maria carried the gifts to the oil lamp near the door to look closely at the carving. "I shall treasure this, and I have just the spot for it." She placed the gifts in her basket and glanced at her timepiece. "Almost time to go, Abraham. Would you mind checking outside for me to see if Dr. Simms's carriage is coming up the road?"

"Right away, Miz Maria," he said, scurrying to the big side door.

Maria took one last look around the room as the door clanged shut behind Abraham. Turning down the oil lamp, she fastened her cloak against the room's chill. *Seems all the warmth and joy left with the children.*

Heaving a sigh, she tied on her velvet bonnet and carried her basket to the door. She looked again at the time. *I wonder what's keeping Abraham? Surely he would come back inside if Doctor's carriage wasn't there.*

Holding the heavy door open Maria peered out into inky darkness. Her heart slammed against her chest. A weak stream of light from the room revealed a small dark form hud-dled on the snow a few feet up the ramp. "Abraham!" Letting go of the door, she lurched forward.

A hand clapped over her mouth, pulling her roughly from behind, jerking her back against a rough, bearded cheek. The basket flew from her arm. She twisted her head, struggling to scream, but the hand clamped tighter. She gagged from the foul odor of whiskey breath.

An arm snagged around her cloak, yanking her against his side, dragging her up the ramp with him. He jerked to a stop and prodded the still form on the ground with the toe of his boot. Abraham did not move.

The steel glint of a pistol shook in her face. "Don't fight me, little lady, or I'll finish this gutter snipe off here and now."

Terror gripped Maria's heart. She choked down her panic and tried to look down at Abraham. All she could see over the man's hand was ragged butternut pant legs ending in worn farmer's boots.

She felt the gun press against her side as the man stuck the pistol in his belt. Her mind began a frantic prayer. *God, have mercy . . . please, Lord, have mercy.*

Stumbling and slipping in her thin boots, she was pulled up the ramp and dragged into the frozen churchyard. The man's bearded face scraped against her cheek, locking her to him as he staggered over the crusted snow, dragging her with him.

When she twisted her head left, she could see that this person was no taller than herself. A slouch hat hid much of his face, but nothing masked the stench of stale sweat and unwashed flesh, nor the musty wool smell of his coat. Long hair brushed against her cape and neck. She tried to pull away and he yanked her closer, tipping his hat to hide his hand covering her mouth.

"Yer a plump li'l chick, missee, just right fer pluckin', I'd say. Yessiree," he grunted in her ear.

Maria shuddered, struggling for breath.

The jingle of harness sounded behind them and Maria struggled to turn around. His calloused hand clamped tighter. They had reached the front of the church. Her eyes searched wildly for someone—anyone.

A lone artillery wagon clattered by on the cobblestones, the mules making hard work of the ice. Soldiers on foot slipped and slid along behind it, singing loudly, paying no mind to anything but their drunken song.

Her captor staggered up the step to the church door, holding Maria to him like a vise. "We're goin' in here jes like good Christian folk. So you do jus like I say. Go in nice en quiet like, an' yer goin' to be my lookout while I get me some of them gold goblets the padre uses." The man pulled her roughly against him as he opened the door with one hand. "Yessiree." His foul breath rasped in her ear. "Gold will do me fine 'fer now."

Terror seized her. Every instinct told her to fight. She drew in a ragged breath and bit down hard on the fingers clamped over her mouth, drawing the bitter taste of blood.

The man bellowed a curse. He backed against the door, dug his fingers into her shoulder and shoved her inside the church. In one swift movement, he followed and pinned her against the door.

The vestibule was dark and empty, but she couldn't escape his wild eyes boring into hers, his mouth twisted in an ugly scowl.

"Why'd ya have to spoil it, huh?" Splaying his bloodied hand across her throat he squeezed with a death-like grip. "I oughter choke the life outta ya fer that."

Maria tried desperately to pry his fingers loose. She kicked at his legs until he released her throat, but in the next second he grabbed her by the shoulders, slamming her head against the door hard enough to rattle her teeth.

Pain blazed in her head and down her throat. Her eyes rolled back and she gave in to the comfort of darkness.

Chapter Thirty-One

The lantern light swayed, sending a short ripple of light over the churchyard. Henry reined in the gig at the carriage block, humming to himself as he jumped down and secured the reins.

A pale winter moon was starting its rise. He made his way carefully across the ice-crusted churchyard, blowing great puffs of breath into the frosty air. "It's going to be a cold one tonight," he said to himself, pulling his muffler tight around his neck. "Too cold to snow anymore."

He slipped and stumbled down the icy ramp leading to the side door, almost falling over something in his path. "What in tarnation—" Henry peered down at a huddled figure on the ramp. In the darkness it looked like a young soldier curled up in a big old Army coat. He bent and gently turned the shoulder. "Merciful Lord, it's a mere boy!" he whispered.

Blood oozed from a wide gash on the boy's head, staining the snow crimson. His dark eyes were fluttering open and a faint moan escaped the child's lips.

Henry removed his muffler, propped the boy up against his bent knee and wound the scarf around the boy's head. "Easy now, it's all right. You're going to be all right, boy. Hang onto my shoulder and let me get you inside."

"Mmm . . . Mmmiz Mm—Miz Maria . . ." the child stuttered, staring into Henry's eyes.

"Miss Maria! Good Lord, who are you? What about Miss Maria?"

"I'm Abraham," he said, struggling to stand. Dizziness overcame him and Henry pulled him close, propping him up against his side. The boy's eyes grew round. He stared ahead and pointed at the ground near the door. "That's Miz Maria's . . ." Abraham moaned, stumbling forward to pick up an overturned basket.

Henry grabbed his arm and quickly opened the door to ease the boy inside. An oil lamp burned low on the nearest table, but in the semi-darkness they could see that the room was empty.

Henry was beginning to panic. "What's happened here? Think, Abraham. Where could she be?"

Henry looked at the stairs leading to the vestry. Abraham tried to shake his head, winced and held the scarf to his ear. "Miss Maria wouldn't be upstairs in the church—she sent me outside lookin' for a carriage. I no sooner stepped out and somethin' hit my head real hard."

Suddenly he cast frightened eyes at Henry. "The basket! She musta come outside lookin' for me . . ." He started back to the door.

Henry got there first. He lifted the boy off his feet and set him on the nearest chair. "Now you best sit right here, Abraham. You can't be roving around with your head bleeding. I'll check the front of the church and I'll be right back."

Before Abraham could object, Henry was out the door and up the ramp. His eyes searched across the empty churchyard. Where could she be? The rising moon suddenly broke through clouds over the bell tower, shedding pale light on the icy snow. Footprints were visible, breaking a wobbly, winding path over the crusty snow alongside the church.

Henry's feet fairly flew. Slipping and sliding, he tracked the footprints to the front walk. In two long strides he was up the step, flinging open the door under the bell tower.

The vestibule was dark. He stepped up to an arched doorway. Sanctuary candles threw a spiritual finger of light up the main aisle. The light stopped at a velvet bonnet on the floor near Henry's feet.

Eyes blazing, he tried to swallow a lump of fear rising in his throat. As he stooped to pick up the bonnet he caught the sound of movement in the west wing of the nave. A soft thud. His eyes shot left. Moonlight filtered through stained-glass windows along the far aisle.

Starting toward it in a rush, he slowed his steps at the sight of a dark figure. A man in a slouch hat was bent over the rear pew in the last aisle.

Henry's eye caught the glint of movement farther down the same aisle. A scarf-wound head that barely reached above the pews was bobbing silently toward the figure.

The man in the pew straightened, pulled off his hat and wiped his brow with his sleeve. Henry inched closer. There was no mistaking the tattered Rebel coat. Nor could he miss Maria's cloak and thin boots sticking out from the end of the pew.

Henry charged forward, his face a taut mask of fury. Reaching over the back of the pew he grabbed the soldier's coat front in his fist. In a voice trembling with rage, he shouted, "Back away from her. Now!" He yanked the soldier sideways out of the pew.

Stumbling into the aisle, the Rebel let fly a string of oaths. Henry vaulted around the pew to face him.

Cowered in the shadow behind the soldier, Abraham watched in horror as the soldier whipped out a pistol. "No!" the boy shouted, leaping forward. Both arms locked around the man's waist, Abraham pushed with all his might. The soldier stood fast, then twisted around and kicked at Abraham, sending him backward. Gunshot splintered the wooden pew and echoed off the walls.

Henry shot forward, landing a vicious blow to the soldier's head, knocking him off his feet. The gun clattered to the floor.

Chapter Thirty-Two

Tears streamed from Georgie's eyes at the pitiful sight of Abraham being carried on a stretcher by two soldiers. Henry's blood-soaked scarf was wound around the boy's head. Someone had removed his boot, cut his pants leg away and wrapped his leg in bandages.

"Lucky thing Father Higgins sent for the Capitol Police, Miss," one of the soldiers said. "They commandeered our ambulance. Your Dr. Simms couldn't have made it here alone with two patients in that small buggy."

"We're thankful to you, and to Father Higgins. I'm sure Dr. Simms will manage just fine now. Please follow me into the kitchen," she said, leading the way down the hall of the Simms residence.

It wouldn't do for Abraham to see her tears. She dashed them away and tried to put on a brave smile as the soldiers lifted the boy from a stretcher to a makeshift pallet near the stove.

"If it hadn't been for Dr. Simms, we wouldn't have known what to do with this little darkie," the soldier said, tipping his kepi hat. "We'll see ourselves out, Miss."

After the soldiers left, Georgie leaned down to pat Abraham's shoulder. "Dr. Simms told us how brave you were," she said. "If I didn't have this nasty grippe I'd be tending to you myself. It wouldn't be wise for me to get too close, but you are in good hands here with Elizabeth. She'll take care of you until your father gets here."

A puzzled look flickered across the boy's face. "They sent for my pappy?"

"Yes, I believe Father Higgins did. Henry—Dr. Simms is my brother, Abraham. He says a bullet grazed your leg, but the wound is not serious. It will heal, and you're going to be just fine."

"Miz Maria? She gonna be awright?"

"Dr. Simms is seeing to that. He's upstairs with her now. We shall put our faith in the good Lord. I'm sure that's what you did today at the church, and He kept you from serious harm. Rest easy now, Abraham, and let Elizabeth clean you up."

Upstairs in Edwina's room, Virginia and Edwina stood on one side of the bed, Henry on the other. Ginny had removed Maria's cloak and boots, and loosened her shirtwaist. Eddie had placed a warm flannel brick at her feet, covering her with a patchwork quilt.

Her eyes were closed. Henry searched her face while he swabbed the bruises on her neck and cheek with ointment. His hands trembled at the little moans she made, but she did not stir. He put the ointment on the bedside table and stood back staring at her. It was hard to watch the torment in her face.

He could not hide his anguish over the unthinkably vicious attack. Every horrible moment in the church flashed before his eyes. The thud of Maria's bruised body dumped unconscious in a pew, the soldier's face like a dread specter pointing his gun, the boy bleeding on the church floor.

Henry was pulled out of his dark reverie with a start at his father's voice. "Would you feel better if I sent for Dr. May, son?" Edward Simms hovered near the bedroom door.

Henry shook his head, crossed the room and took his father's arm. They walked out into the hall and Henry closed the bedroom door.

"No, Father. Maria's most serious injury had to be to the back of her head. She was fighting her way back to consciousness when I put her on the litter in the ambulance." He pulled at his mustache. "She took such fright to see a soldier that she . . . she slipped away again. I've seen this happen with shock victims."

Something like dread flickered in his eyes. A muscle twitched in his jaw. "Maria may not remember much but . . ." He swept his hand across his side-whiskers and looked into his father's eyes. "I think I got there before he . . . he . . ." His words drifted off, unable to give voice to the ugliness.

Edward grasped Henry's shoulder. "This war has made beasts of men."

"And perhaps, even of me. When I picked up the soldier's gun I wanted to use it on him. If the pastor hadn't come into the church at that moment, I might have."

"The drunken soldier was no doubt ablaze with greed and lust. He deserves justice for that vicious attack, but he deserves mercy as well. God asks us to pray for those who persecute us. We must leave the business of judgment to the Lord. Go back to Maria, son. Be there for her in prayer."

Despite questioning looks from them, Henry sent his sisters downstairs to help Georgie. He pulled a chair up close to the bed.

Staring intently at Maria, loving her with his eyes, he reached for her hand. But for the purplish bruises on her chin and neck, her face was pale as the pillow. He had always seen her hair wrapped in a twist at the back of her neck. He marveled now at long russet waves spilling over the cover. Very gently, he brushed a strand away from her cheek.

The thought of her anguish wrenched his heart. He held her hand.

"Help her, Lord . . . Give her strength . . ."

Maria was dreaming. In a whirl of soft music, Henry's strong arms guided her around a ballroom. He stood in the glade, holding her hands as a storm brewed over the lacy treetops at Evergreen Park. "My love for you, Maria, is a deep abiding love. It is so strong that wherever I go, I carry you forever in my mind and in my heart." Gentle fingers stroked her cheek ever so softly. "I want you in my life, now."

Her fingers suddenly curled in Henry's hand and slowly her eyes fluttered open.

"Henry?" she whispered.

"I'm here, my love."

She turned toward him. "Henry," she said softly, again.

He stood, brushed his lips across her fingers. "Yes, dear heart."

She searched his face, his shadowed green eyes. Raising a faltering hand, she traced trembling fingers over his cheek.

He smiled into her eyes. "I'll be with you always, my love."

Maria sat by the window, watching the wind-driven snow swirling around the street below. The storm had raged all day, but she felt safe inside this house, warm and protected.

The pain in her head and throat had eased, but she stayed on in Edwina's room the next day. She was fearful of going downstairs and seeing the wounded soldiers in the house . . . fearful that the horrifying images of the Rebel soldier would come back.

Virginia and then Georgie sat with her while Mr. Simms took the rest of the family to midnight mass on Christmas Eve.

"I've little right to feel so fearful. Everyone has been so kind and I'm not hurt nearly as bad as poor little Abraham. I'm sorry, Georgie, to be spoiling your Christmas."

"Nonsense. You showed much more courage than I could have mustered. Your head will mend, Maria."

"Maybe my head, but what about my mind? I don't know if I can forget it."

"It will take time. When I was little and scared to go to sleep in the dark, my mother used to tell me to think happy thoughts. 'Bad thoughts make the angels weep, think happy and angels will lull you to sleep,' she'd say. Think about all the happiness and joy you brought to the children. That is what Christmas is all about. Joy to the world, a Savior is born."

Christmas day dawned little different than the previous two days. Henry had to make rounds at the hospitals, holy day or not, and the unusual winter storm made getting around very difficult.

"I have good news, Maria," Georgie said, as she carried a breakfast tray into Edwina's room. "It's bound to bring a smile to your face." She set the tray on a small table by the window. A bud vase on the tray held a beautiful red rose.

"Oh, Georgie. A rose in winter? However did you—"

"Not I, Maria. You must know this is Henry's doing. He asked that you have a rose this morning, and Father was lucky to find a flower shop open last night."

Georgie poured tea for Maria and helped herself to a cup. "The good news I was talking about was not on this tea tray. It's about Abraham.

"Father Higgins has given Abraham's father a permanent job helping to build a hospital for wounded soldiers just north of the church. And best of all, he's found a little house near it for Abraham and his father to live in."

Maria clasped her hands together in front of her lips. "Oh, thank heavens. I prayed so hard for Abraham. To think he risked his life for Henry and for me." She shook her head. "He deserves so much better than he's ever had."

"Yes, he does. Truth is, I've never known a child like him."

Maria nodded at Abraham's carved figure on the bedside table. "When I couldn't go to church with the family last night, it was as though the Christ child was here with me. He's answered my prayers."

"All of our prayers. Abraham told Father Higgins that he was 'sho enuf goin' to miss Miz Maria.' We will all miss you," Georgie said, gripping Maria's hand, "especially me. Abraham has promised to be my assistant after you leave . . . as soon as his leg mends, that is."

"I don't like to think about leaving, Georgie. Henry says he's not even convinced that I'm ready for the trip north. I suspect he's hesitating for other reasons."

"I'm not sure what you mean." Georgie paused, looking hesitatingly at Maria. "Since Father learned that the soldier—the renegade who attacked you—has been brought to justice, I think Henry has come to terms with it." She closed both hands over Maria's. "I hope you have."

"I've prayed over it, and your father did help me to put it in God's hands. He is such an understanding, faith-filled person."

"I'm sure he inspired Henry to do the same, so you can rest easy about that." Georgie raised an eyebrow and smiled. "You want to know what I think? I think your doctor just wants to be sure you are strong enough, *and* he's wanting more time to be close to you. Give him a few more days."

★ ★ ★ ★ ★

Snow continued to fall the next day. Rooftops and rutted streets were covered with a white blanket, relieving the city of ugliness. Henry hitched a ride on a medical supply wagon going to the Capitol building. It was tough going for the driver trying to get the horse through deep snow. Henry hopped off at Third Street and slogged through knee-deep snow to his house.

Stamping his boots at the back door, he surprised Elizabeth in the kitchen. "Miss Maria still upstairs?" he asked.

"Yes, sir, she is. I've just fixed a supper tray for her. Miss Virginia can't seem to coax her downstairs yet."

"I'll take that up to her, Elizabeth. I have some strong persuasive powers up my sleeve to fix this situation." He left his coat and hat on a kitchen chair and took the tray upstairs.

"Aha, ladies," he said at the bedroom door. "Supper time for some, work time for others." He gave a nod and a wink to Virginia.

Virginia gathered up her sewing. "If she put you on kitchen duty, Henry, I'm sure Elizabeth must need my help." Giving Maria a parting smile, she left the room.

Henry put Maria's tray down. "Not one bite of food, Miss, until you hear my news. It's what we've waited for. I've finally gotten word, Maria. This is my last week in government service."

Maria pressed her hands together in front of her mouth. She tried to smile but fear clouded her eyes, and words stuck in her throat.

"Father's promised to try and secure tickets for us to leave for New York right after the first of the year. Now, dear heart, you must follow Elizabeth's orders. You are to eat all of the chicken pie," he said, motioning to the supper tray.

Maria's eyes finally brightened with a smile. She looked at

her tray, picked up a fork, then put it back down, her brow furrowed. Henry grasped her hand. "Don't tell me you are unhappy about leaving?"

"Not about leaving. I am happy, Henry." She tried to find words to express her fears. "It's only that Virginia was just telling me the trains have had great delays because of this snow. There are so many troop trains trying to get into the city, and if the storm keeps up, maybe the trains won't run at all. Maybe waiting a bit longer . . ."

Henry tilted her chin up with one finger. "No waiting, love, and no sense worrying about the train until trouble throws its shadow."

Henry pulled a small box tied with red ribbon from his jacket pocket and placed it in her hands. "My Christmas gift to you, dear heart."

She slipped the ribbon off the box and caught her breath. Diamond earbobs glittered in a velvet-lined case.

"Ooh, they are so beautiful, Henry."

"Remember our first carriage ride in the snow?"

"The one Georgie suggested, yes."

"When I saw these they reminded me of the sparkly snow-flakes that graced your face the night of that carriage ride. You are still my phantom of delight, and I have a glorious plan for you and me, alone. On New Year's Day we are going to celebrate! I've hired a cutter for the afternoon. I plan to give you a final tour of the city, a sleigh ride in style."

"But what would your father say about us going off alone?"

"Why, he'd smile his approval, dear heart. It was his idea!"

Chapter Thirty-Three

Winter sun glistened on the snow-blanketed city. The sun held little warmth, but it brought hearty citizens and children out with shovels, sleds and cutters. The jingle of sleigh bells and shouts of glee could be heard up and down the streets.

A smart-stepping pair of matched bays pulled a fancy red cutter up to the Simms house. Henry tethered the animals to the ring on a hitching post, barely visible above a snow bank. "Thank goodness Father had Massie shovel a path," he said to himself, "or I'd be hard put getting to the door."

Henry lost no time looking in the downstairs rooms for Maria. He rushed up the stairs, pausing at Edwina's room for a second before knocking softly and entering.

"Is someone here waiting for a sleigh ride?" he asked, raising an eyebrow and extending his hand in a slight bow. "Your driver awaits."

Georgie was rummaging through Eddie's trunk at the foot of the bed. "Just one minute," she called over her shoulder, pulling out a bright red scarf. "You'll need this," she said, winding the scarf around Maria's neck. "It's pretty nippy out there."

"But—"

"No buts," she said, putting a finger to Maria's lips. She turned to Henry. "She's been watching at the window for you, and sure as the sun rose this morning, she needs to get out in it," Georgie said, brooking no argument.

Henry laughed as he followed his sister, who was tugging Maria out of the room and down the stairs, Georgie talking all the way.

"Abraham will want to know that you're feeling fit and able to take the air. It will put some color in your cheeks." Georgie opened the front door. "Why, just look! We haven't had this much snow in a dog's age. All Washington's sins are covered in pure white today."

Georgie stepped back to let Henry take Maria's arm. "Go with God's blessings, as Father Higgins says. I'll want to hear all about it. Now off with the two of you, and have fun."

"A report you shall have, Miss Georgiana," Henry called over his shoulder as he guided Maria down the path to the cutter. His strong arms lifted her up to the bench seat. He took the reins and climbed up beside her.

Sleigh bells jingled as the cutter turned down Third Street to Pennsylvania Avenue, gliding smoothly over the snow.

Huge blocks of snow-topped marble lay scattered like giant squares of frosted cake in front of the domeless Capitol building. Children were sledding down a wide expanse of lawn, their shouts of glee mingled with the scrape of metal as soldiers shoveled the rise of steps.

"This was to be our first stop, but I'm afraid there's not much to see at the Capitol today, dear heart. I think we'll backtrack down Pennsylvania to the president's house."

Henry had to make a wide circle to turn the sleigh around a horse and troop wagon off to the side of the avenue, stuck in the ditch.

Soldiers were trying to push the wagon out of the deep snow, swearing at the panicked horse. The frantic mare rose up on her hooves, whinnying fiercely as a soldier cracked a whip.

Maria tensed, burrowing her head against Henry's

shoulder. She could hear the echo of her assailant's angry oaths in the back of her mind. Her stomach knotted and she squeezed her eyes shut.

Henry pulled on the reins. He looked down at her hunched shoulders and lifted her chin to meet his gaze. Her eyes opened wide, shadows of fear flickering in their depths. "It's all right, Maria. Nothing is going to hurt you again, my love. Trust me to see to that, will you?"

She nodded hesitantly. Having harbored the burden of fear for so many days closed up in Edwina's room, it was hard to drive the thoughts away. She settled back on the seat, staring straight ahead at the sleek horses nickering and straining to pull the cutter.

Henry snapped the reins and they pressed forward up the wide avenue, harness and bells jangling. When Henry smiled down at her and began to hum a tune, Maria knew that he was trying to lighten her mood. She fixed her thoughts on the melody. "That sounds like the tune that you sang to me on our carriage ride. Is it called 'Lorena'?"

"Right you are. I remember that you thought 'Lorena' to be a sad love song then, but just listen to this verse, and maybe you will change your mind." He sang soft and low and she strained to hear.

The snow is on the grass again.
The sun's low down the sky, Lorena,
The frost gleams where the flowers have been.
But the heart throbs on as warmly now,
As when the summer days were nigh.

He bent to her ear, speaking softly. "That's how I feel whenever you are near. You make my heart throb."

Maria began to relax with the rhythm of the horses and the

231

hiss of sleigh runners moving swiftly over the snow. "It feels like we're gliding on a cloud, Henry."

"We are gliding right up to Lafayette Square, matter of fact. You should be able to see a good likeness of Andrew Jackson—that is, if the general is not buried in snow.

"Uh-oh." He reined in the horse. "You can see from here that General Jackson is wearing a heavy new coat of white. It would be foolhardy to tramp through the snow to see him up close. Just so, we can sit here for a moment."

He reached one arm around her shoulder. "Let's savor this moment in time, dear heart, for we shall be leaving this troubled city soon . . . leaving what's best forgotten *and* also what we hold dear." He pulled her close and she felt his warm breath on her cheek.

"Always remember, no matter what happens from here on out, be it Washington City or Evergreen Park . . . remember that I love you beyond all telling."

He pressed a gentle kiss on her lips. Maria's burden of fear dropped away. She laid her head on his chest, her heart filled with hope.

Chapter Thirty-Four

05 January 1864

Evergreen Park

I cannot describe my mixed feelings as Papa welcomed us home yesterday. I was sad to leave the Simmses' house, but overjoyed to see my sisters, and they, me. Papa embraced me rather stiffly, I thought. He has always been formal with us older girls since Mama died, but yesterday, he seemed almost timid. I am caught between wishes and regret. Regret that I was not always the model daughter in the past, and wishes that Papa will be happy for Henry and me.

Sarah and Jo practically dragged me up the stairs to our room. I hardly had time to wash the dirt from the train off my face and hands before they asked to hear all about the classes for the colored children. I told them about Abraham (except for the brave thing he did to save us). When the time is right, God will help me talk about that terrible incident. With Henry's strength, and Mr. Simms's assurances, I have conquered my fears and put it behind me. I showed the girls my gift from Abraham. It is sitting in front of me on my writing table, my perfectly carved Baby Jesus.

It was hard to leave Henry's sisters, but good to be home with mine. Jo wanted to know if Dr. Simms was in New York to stay, and if he was going to ask Papa for a blessing. I told them about our hopes and dreams.

> *Mr. Simms, Henry, and I were exhausted from the trip,*
> *so everyone retired early tonight.*
> *Maria O.*

"Annie told me about New Year's Day, Sarah. She said she counted fourteen callers. Were you impressed with anyone in particular?"

"They were just the usual friends, but Jo saw to it that everyone enjoyed the food," Sarah said.

Jo poured hot cocoa into Maria's breakfast cup. "It was such a cold and sleety day that Father allowed mulled cider. I'd say we had a festive New Year's, all in all. How about Washington City? Did Henry's sisters have many New Year's callers?" Jo asked.

"No, sad to say, most of the young men they know have gone into the Army. Of course, the Simms residence is like a small hospital, not very conducive for social calls. Besides that, the city was in the grips of a terrible snowstorm, and it was hard to get around."

Jo's eyes twinkled and she raised her eyebrows. "Speaking of New Year festivities, Bridget is preparing a belated New Year's dinner for tomorrow. She says it is for Mr. Simms, because he has to leave soon for New York City."

"That will be a nice tribute for Henry's father.. He's such a wonderful man. I knew his plan was to take a few days for sightseeing here before leaving to spend some time with his daughter, Sienna, in New York. No dates were firmed up as far as I know."

"Bridget always knows more about what's going on around here than anyone," Sarah said. "She's one step ahead of Father most of the time, but then, Papa has been very quiet lately, not saying much to anyone."

"I think he's brooding about Andrew's request to join the

Navy when he finishes school," Jo said, shaking her head sadly. "Poor Andrew. Heaven knows what Papa said to him about that. He's dead set on Andrew studying law."

"Mr. Simms is worried about his youngest son too," Maria said. "Fortunately, a letter came from Philip just before we took the train for New York. The letter told of his safe arrival in America, and the weeks he was spending with Mr. Simms's cousin in New Orleans. Henry's cousin gave Philip firsthand information about factoring, but he also advised him to return home and seek reconciliation with his father."

Sarah started to clear away the breakfast things. "I'm sure everything will turn out all right, Maria, for Andrew and for Philip Simms, and especially for you and Henry. Just wait and see."

"I hope you are right. Henry is waiting for the right opportunity to speak to Papa, and I've got my fingers crossed for this afternoon. Papa planned a carriage tour up the shore to Sands Point so Mr. Simms can see the lighthouse."

Maria settled close to Henry as Martin started the horses for the drive to Sands Point.

"This is a typical January thaw for our area, Edward. Freezing cold one day, and mild winter sunshine the next," Horatio said.

"It almost feels like spring today. I'm guessing the snow is all melted in Washington by now," Maria said.

Henry squeezed her hand. "Look out the carriage window, Father. Just see how the sun glints on the water of Long Island Sound. Doesn't look much like the Potomac, does it?" Henry asked.

Edward looked out at white sails scooping the wind in the choppy, gray-blue water. "No, I'd say not. I can also see how it would be an attraction to live hereabouts; have your medical practice here, too. Mighty beautiful country-side, it is."

Horatio turned his eyes to Henry. "I'm glad your father's here, seeing something of our island, but does this trip mean you are back to New York for good, Henry? Have you been given leave of your duty to the government?"

"I have, sir, and in a way, I'm back to stay. I've also gained a commission with my father's help, and that puts me in good stead for the Surgeon's Reserve Corps."

Maria looked askance at her father. She fidgeted fretfully, poking through her reticule for a handkerchief.

"I'm not sure I understand the details of this Reserve Corps you mention. I read about it in the press when Governor Seymour announced it, but it was a rather sketchy report."

"A very wise plan though," Edward commented. "I'm sure that's why New York and the other states joined efforts to make it work. With so many states sharing the burden, doctors like Henry will only be on call when and if they are needed."

Henry reached for Maria's hand. "There is not much like-lihood of my being called back in the near future, sir."

Horatio looked at each of them in turn before he spoke directly to Maria. "Your sisters have been dropping hints for days about making things for your hope chest, my dear. I did not acknowledge their allusions, nor do I make judgments lightly, as you well know, Maria."

He harrumphed and turned his eyes to Henry. "But I suppose, now that there is no immediate threat of your being called back to service, my blessings for a wedding are in order."

Henry's jaw dropped open but no words came.

236

"My sentiments exactly, sir," Edward Simms said, pumping Horatio's hand.

Henry turned to Maria with a glowing smile. He thrust his hand out to Horatio. "Thank you, sir, you've made us very happy," he said.

Maria watched a sudden sadness fill her father's eyes. She reached to grasp his hand in hers. "Oh, Papa . . ." Whatever she was going to say next was lost in the unspoken communion that settled between Maria and her father as he bent to kiss her cheek.

Horatio spoke to Henry's father as they gathered at the dining table for Edward's farewell dinner. "I want you to know how grateful I am for the hospitality and kindness shown to Maria in all these past weeks. I agonized over it, but I knew she was where she wanted to be."

"It was our pleasure to have her at home with us, but now that I am a guest in your home, I would really like to offer thanks to the Lord for this wonderful dinner with your family. May I?"

Horatio nodded and smiled. "Of course."

Edward blessed himself with the sign of the cross, bowed his head and clasped his hands together.

"Thank you, Father, for your many gifts this day. We ask your blessings on Maria and Henry, and for their loved ones gathered at this bounteous table." Edward paused a moment as a fleeting frown passed his brow. "And for those who are unable to be with us. Bless us, oh Lord, for these, Thy gifts, which we are about to receive from Thy bounty, and if it be Thy will, we ask for the grace of peace in the New Year, eighteen sixty-four, through Christ our Lord, Amen."

Dinner was enjoyed in relative quiet as everyone passed

the dishes family-style: duckling with plum sauce, mashed potatoes, winter squash and a variety of the girls' preserved fruits.

"If you take many more meals like this, Henry, you will be plump as this duck we've enjoyed," Edward said.

Horatio cleared his throat. "Well, I hope you all have room for dessert. Bridget will serve a figgie pudding. She made the puddings for the holidays, for we all hoped Maria would be at home with us." The wistful sound of his voice was not lost on Maria.

Annie helped Bridget clear the dinner plates. As she took Henry's plate, she bent to his ear. "Maria has been telling us what a grand singing voice you have, Dr. Simms. Would you sing for us after dinner, if Sarah accompanies you?"

"Annie!" Maria said, surprised by Annie's boldness.

Henry shushed Maria, turning to her sister. "I'd be happy to, Miss Anna, if you will agree to sing a song with your sister Jo. I've heard Jo's sweet voice in Washington City, but I've not heard yours."

Annie beamed. "Oh, yes," she said. "Right after the pudding."

Both fathers gathered at the piano. Each seemed to be deep in thought.

"Mine eyes have seen the glory of the coming of the Lord—" Henry sang the camp meeting song he had heard the Union soldiers sing. Sarah's fingers knew the melody of the popular song by heart.

Edward closed his eyes, listening. He was thinking of Philip, tormented by Philip's absence and the nature of his work. It might have marred the joy of this special trip to New York if Georgiana had not received the letter announcing Philip's plan to come home.

Henry's rich baritone rang out.

He hath sounded forth the trumpet that shall never call retreat;
He is sifting out the hearts of men before His judgment seat;
Oh, be swift my soul to answer Him, be jubilant, my feet;
Our God is marching on.
Glory! Glory! Hallelujah! Glory! Glory! Hallelujah!
Glory! Glory! Hallelujah! His truth is marching on.

Maria looked at her father as the song ended. *Such sad eyes,* she thought.

"Sarah," she called out, "play 'Dixie's Land.' Annie knows that tune."

"Yes, yes," Annie shouted, pulling Jo close to her side. Jo started the song, and everyone smiled, hearing their lively duet.

After the chorus, Henry came to Maria's side. As their eyes held a moment, he caught a glimmer of a tear on her cheek. He took her arm and drew her toward the door to the veranda. They stepped out into the weak winter sunshine.

Maria shivered, pulling her shawl close. Henry put his arm around her waist, stroked her hair and wiped the tears from her face with his thumb.

"My dear, whatever could be wrong on such a happy day?"

"It's Papa. He hasn't seemed himself since we arrived home. At first I thought his dour spirit was because I stayed on in Washington without his consent after Carolyn died. But he's been in a somber mood since we took the carriage ride. He did agree for us to set a wedding date, and he seemed to favor our plan. Wouldn't you think he could find joy in his heart today for our sake?"

Henry looked thoughtfully at Maria for a long moment.

"I think, dear heart, that your father is sad because he is losing you. You *are* the first to marry in your family. Your father sees you as a grown woman now, with your own goals and convictions. Why, he even told my father that he hoped we would never be separated again."

Her eyes widened, and she instinctively moved back and braced herself against one of the tall, wide columns of the porch. "I wish he had told me that. All he said in private to me was that my mother would have been happy for my choice, and he was sure that you would be a fine husband."

Henry smiled. "And I intend to be, dear heart. Soft words may not come easily to your father, but he will miss you. I'm sure that is what he is sad about."

"It's not as easy to read my father's feelings as it is your father's. Mr. Simms is so open with everyone, and he was so sweet to include us in the dinner blessing."

Henry took both her hands in his. "Remember the line from the song I just sang?" Henry sang the words softly, pressing his cheek to hers. " 'He is sifting out the hearts of men before His judgment seat.'

"God knows the hearts of our men. When I sang those words, I looked at my father because I know he's been worried about Philip. I'm sure Philip will make the right decision about his future when the time comes, just as your father did about us."

Maria suddenly closed the distance between them and reached up to clasp his face in her hands. "In the darkest moments, you always make things bright for me."

She kissed him on the lips with all the love and tenderness she possessed, the way she'd dreamed of doing so many times.

When she pulled away, she saw the surprise in his eyes. The moment suddenly filled with promise. Henry gathered her into his arms. He kissed her brow and her eyelids, the point of her chin and the corners of her mouth, finally settling his lips with care upon hers.

"My dear, dear heart. Nothing will separate us ever again. I promise."

Epilogue

In August 1864, the Simmses and Onderdonks gathered together at Evergreen Park.

Maria's younger sister, Annie, captured the happiness and
the sadness of the occasion in her diary.

> *Sunday, August 24*
> *This is the last Sabbath before Maria will be a bride. And a*
> *sad thought it is. Maria is packing up this p.m., and has been*
> *putting up things some time past. Jo and I trimmed the parlors*
> *with evergreens above the arch over the doors, très jolie.*
> *Annie O.*

> *Tuesday morning, August 26*
> *Jo, Libby and I are finishing the decorations for the parlor.*
> *They will look very pretty. Doctor brought Maria a present*
> *consisting of a pin, bracelet and pair of earbobs. He and*
> *Father will go down tomorrow morning and not return till*
> *Thursday evening. Maria will go down Thursday morning*
> *and dine at the St. Nicholas with Doctor, Mr. Edward*
> *Simms, his two daughters, Judge Smith and lady, and per-*
> *haps some others. In the afternoon they will leave the city*
> *for Manhasset. Father has engaged an extra coach for the*
> *stage, and will come up himself with the music, table, fix-*
> *tures, and waiters.*
> *Annie O.*

Wednesday, August 27
Tomorrow it will be Dr. and Mrs. H. C. Simms. This is the last evening that Maria is Maria Onderdonk.
Annie O.

Thursday, August 28
Today was the festive day. All busy making preparations for the evening. Jo arranged the flowers, bouquets, etc. Libby made a rather burnt blancmange and I made the lemonade. Sarah rode to Flushing. The afternoon was not very pleasant but none of the guests thought of that. At about seven o'clock the bride and groom arrived, also the Misses Simms and groomsman. Then came Mr. Edward Simms, Mr. Philip Simms, etc., and then a load of baggage. Father, the musicians, the waiters and the table came afterward. A harp and a violin were the instruments employed for the occasion. At eight o'clock and a few minutes, the bride and groom made their appearance escorted by three bridesmaids and three groomsmen. Sarah, Jo and Eddie Simms were bridesmaids. Mr. Phil Simms was one of the groomsmen. Reverend Mr. Demarest pronounced the ceremony, which by the way was very, very long according to the common opinion of the evening. It was performed with a ring as a pledge and was much admired. The bride was said to look beautifully exquisite. As were also the maids. After the wedding dancing was the order of the evening. The first was a bridal quadrille. The groom danced with all the sisters and several other ladies. I danced but little, once with Dr. Simms, the quadrille, with Mr. Augustus Bogart, another, and the polka. The rest with sister, Jo. Libby danced with George Lock. The bride and groom received congratulations from all. Most celebrated Lawyer Allen and Cousin Andrew. About 150 present, great

242

crowd. The bridal party all stayed till Saturday morning.
Annie O.

Eight months later two letters were sent to Dr. Simms in
quick succession:

Washington City
05 April 1865
Dear Henry and Maria,
My sisters and I were so happy to receive the news that we
will soon be aunts! Virginia and Edwina are busy sewing little
things, and I have started knitting a carriage robe. Father is
hoping for a boy.

When Father brought the news, it was like a double cele-
bration. The State Department recommended an illumination
on the same day in honor of the victory at Richmond. We were
hardly prepared for such a grand display by all the public
buildings, each outshining the other in unbelievable splendor.

Many private residences were decorated and Father or-
dered the store and bank festooned with bunting. All up and
down the Avenue, the hotels, restaurants and offices glittered
like stars.

Father rented a carriage at Pumphrey's Stable and took us
to watch the illuminations along 17th Street. Men stood ready
with matches at the windows of the Treasury Department of-
fices. They gleamed instantaneously as a trumpet blast gave
the signal and a band played the 'Star Spangled Banner.'

Mottoes, ensigns and flags are displayed everywhere. The
lights in the Capitol building are so brilliant we can see them
from our home. From Father's store on the Avenue we can
read the words of a huge gas-lit transparency over the pediment
of the Capitol: "This is the Lord's doing; it is marvelous in our
eyes."

Yesterday, Palm Sunday, the congregation at St. Matthew's prayed in thanksgiving that we are at the end of this dreadful war. Many parishioners were weeping openly.

This morning we were shaken in our beds by the percussion of guns fired from the battery on Massachusetts Avenue. The morning paper brought the news of the surrender of Lee's Army at Appomattox. It is over! At long last, it is over. I need not tell you how strengthened and joyful we all are. This year, Easter will surely be a time of fervent rejoicing that our nation is at last at peace.

Your loving sister,
Georgiana

Washington City

April 19, 1865
Dear son,
Our lives have been grievously affected by the terrible events of Good Friday. Bells that tolled during the weeklong rejoicing in our city, tolled on Saturday in terrible mourning for our slain President.

Throngs of stunned citizens crowded the streets and there were guards on all the roads leading out of the city. The government departments, banks and business houses closed. Gala decorations disappeared behind lengths of black shroud.

After leading our nation through this long and terrible war, President Lincoln spoke only words of reconciliation and healing at war's end. I'm afraid reconciliation with the South will be a long time coming.

Thousands have come to Washington to pay their respects. Some waited almost six hours to view the catafalque in the East Room. Our Militia Society was ushered in for a special

viewing at 5:30. We marched to the Marine Band in his fu-
neral procession with all city bells tolling.

I predict President Lincoln will be looked upon as a mar-
tyred hero for years to come. I hope you will have the opportu-
nity to see the funeral train that is scheduled to stop in New
York en route to Illinois.

My heart is full, but I am comforted by the scripture of
Daniel: "And those who lead the many to justice, shall be like
stars for all eternity."

In prayer, I remain your loving father,
· Edward Simms

After President Lincoln's assassination, most public reaction in the South went strongly against the assassin, John
Wilkes Booth. Many in Washington City felt the disgrace of
the crime and hastened to disown it. By a cruel twist of fate,
shame added to Edward Simms's sorrow over Lincoln's
death, and he couldn't truly disown the crime.

Shortly after Booth had been captured and killed, Edward
learned that his second cousin, Dr. Samuel Mudd, was one of
those arrested for conspiracy to kill the president. Although
there had been little contact with Edward's mother's family
over the years, the accused, Dr. Mudd, was one of her kin.
Dr. Mudd's grandfather, Alexius, was Edward's maternal
uncle.

Author's Note

Members of the Simms and Onderdonk families actually lived in the era of *Four Summers Waiting*. I have taken the novelist's liberty to fictionalize their lives and alter the dates when events occurred to facilitate the flow of the story. Some minor characters and certain incidents are creations of my imagination. In such cases, I disclaim any responsibility for their resemblance to real people or events.

Certain diary excerpts and letters included in the story are authentic. For permission to use diary excerpts, I extend thanks to the Bryant Library Local History Collection, Roslyn, New York.

I am proud to relate the story told in dialogue in Chapter Nine, about a youthful Edward Simms meeting President Thomas Jefferson. It is based on a true incident.

Many thanks are due my son, Philip Simms, for researching his ancestors, the Simms and Onderdonk families. Without Philip's help and the encouragement and support of my husband, Tom, the story would not have been told.

About the Author

As a child, Mary Fremont Schoenecker drew inspiration to write poems and stories about American history from her early years growing up in the Revolutionary War village of Schuylerville—*Old Saratoga*—New York. Dr. Schoenecker was Associate Professor of Education at SUNY College, Oneonta, for the last sixteen years of her career as a teacher. Presently, she lives with her husband, Tom, in Cape Haze, Florida. When not writing or reading, she enjoys golf and the beaches of the Gulf of Mexico.